PRAISE FOR THE NATIONAL BESTSELLING ITALIAN KITCHEN MYSTERIES

The Wedding Soup Murder

"A tightly plotted whodunit that will have readers guessing right to the end, the book blends mystery with comedy, romance, family drama, a vivid and affectionate portrayal of the Jersey shore, and . . . oh, yes, cooking."
—*New Jersey Monthly*

"I love the characters and the atmosphere."
—*Suspense Magazine*

"Genova has served up another tasty read. . . . This story is well crafted, and I found myself turning those pages so I could find out whodunit."   —MyShelf.com

"The characters continue to grow. The friendship between Vic and Sofie is spot-on. Interfering but loving family, again, right on the money . . . a great read."
—Kings River Life Magazine

"Genova's books are filled with tasty Italian treats and plenty of family drama to balance out each whodunit. Readers who are looking for a mystery that will tantalize the palate, as well as energize the mind, will love this one!"
—Debbie's Book Bag

"*So* good. A well-written, enjoyable cozy mystery that had me hungry for more."   —Brooke Blogs

"I'm happy to be back on the boardwalk. In addition to a solid mystery, Rosie Genova has given us another fun look into the Rienzi family and their relationships with each other as well as their restaurant, the Casa Lido."
—Cozy Up with Kathy

continued . . .

Also by Rosie Genova

The Italian Kitchen Mystery series

A Dish Best Served Cold

◇◇◇◇◇◇◇◇◇◇◇◇◇◇◇◇◇◇◇◇◇◇◇◇

An Italian Kitchen Mystery

◇◇◇◇◇◇◇◇◇◇◇◇◇◇◇◇◇◇◇◇◇◇◇◇

Rosie Genova

AN OBSIDIAN MYSTERY

OBSIDIAN
Published by New American Library,
an imprint of Penguin Random House LLC
375 Hudson Street, New York, New York 10014

This book is an original publication of New American Library.

First Printing, August 2015

For more information about Penguin Random House, visit penguinrandomhouse.com.

ISBN 978-0-451-41516-5

Printed in the United States of America
10 9 8 7 6 5 4 3 2 1

Penguin
Random
House

To John, the last to sail away—with love and pride

Acknowledgments

Many thanks are due my editor, Sandra Harding, and my agent, Kim Lionetti, for their support and understanding when it was most needed. Couldn't have done it without you, ladies!

I am also indebted to:

Retired Fanwood Police Sergeant Brian L. Bantz, for once again sharing his knowledge of police procedure.

My brother-in-law, Kenneth Harms, for answering my questions about golf and providing details about the Atlantic City Country Club.

My coadviser, Nicole Scimone, and our journalism students at Westfield High School, for their continued support and inspiration, particularly for the scenes at Vic's old school. I will miss you all dearly!

My valued friends and critique partners, Loretta Marion and Sarah Pinneo, for reading pages and providing encouragement and laughs along the way.

Lori Caswell and the Great Escapes bloggers, for receiving my work with such enthusiasm and support.

My guys: Anthony Paul, Adam, and John—you make it all worthwhile.

My husband, Anthony, whose endless patience, skills with the grill, and heroic rescue of my computer truly made this book possible.

And finally, to all those in my home state who offered food, clothing, charging stations, and other means of support to residents affected by Hurricane Sandy—this story is for you.

Chapter One

A mingled blast of garlic and alcohol hit me as soon as I opened the back door. The reek was emanating from Pietro Petrocelli, known colloquially as "Stinky Pete." Naturally, I never called him that to his face (or in front of my grandmother, whose family knew him from the old country). Pete listed to one side, then the other, blinking his bloodshot eyes and grinning at me with his nearly toothless mouth. Recoiling from the stench of unwashed skin and lack of dental hygiene, I took two steps back into the restaurant kitchen.

"Uh, hi, Pete. Nonna's not here at the moment." I started to close the door, but Pete, who was pretty quick for a drunk, held it fast.

"It's *La Signorina Scrittrice,*" he slurred. "The lady writer. How you do, *signorina*?" He stuck his unshaven face inside the door opening, treating me to another whiff of garlic breath. "Is your papa here?"

"No," I said firmly. My dad, Frank, who had a soft spot for Pete, would sometimes give him a glass of homemade wine, but only when my grandmother wasn't around.

Nonna would feed Pete if he was hungry, but she drew the line at liquor.

"Hokay," he said with a sigh. "So maybe, Lady Writer, could you do an old man a favor?"

"Not if it involves wine." I gripped the side of the door, trying unsuccessfully to push it closed.

"C'mon, *signorina*. I am parched in the heat." He pressed his free hand against his chest. "I have a great thirst."

"I'll bet you do," I said. "You can have some water. And if you're hungry, I'll give you a panini. But that's it. And then you have to go."

He finally let go of the door and shook his head. "It is not for water that I have the thirst. But I will take, how you say, a 'suh-nack.'"

"One 'suh-nack' coming up. But you have to wait there, okay?" I said, closing the door. I grabbed a roll, threw on some salami and cheese, and wrapped the sandwich in a paper towel.

When I handed it to him, Pete stuck the sandwich into the pocket of his tattered shirt and winked at me with one droopy eye. "For later," he whispered. Taking advantage of the open door, he pushed his head inside again; I tried very hard not to inhale as he spoke. "If you give me *il vino*, I can tell you stories. For your books." He raised his hand in a scribbling motion to illustrate.

"I can't, Pete. It's not good for you. Nonna won't let me."

"Oh, your grandmother, she is a saint," he said, clapping his palms together as though in prayer.

"Uh-huh." *She's a saint, all right.* "You need to go, Pete." I shoved harder against the door.

He tapped the side of his head. "Me, I know t'ings. Many t'ings I could tell you for your murder books."

"I'm sure you could, but you really have to go now."

Pete nodded, pulled his head back from the doorway, and patted his breast pocket. "Thank you, *signorina*. And remember what I said," he called as he stumbled off. "I have stories to tell."

Stories involving the grape, no doubt, but probably little I could use for my "murder books." I bolted the door behind me, still wrinkling my nose as Pete's smell lingered in the air. I grabbed the bowl of fresh tomatoes that sat on the counter; just picked from our garden, they were a perfect, ripe red. I scrubbed my hands and found Nonna's best knife, chopping the tomatoes quickly to release their sweet, earthy scent. Then I grabbed a handful of basil from the refrigerator, stuck my nose in it, and sniffed deeply.

"Victoria," my grandmother called out sharply, "what are you doing to that basil?"

She stood in the doorway to the kitchen, her hands on her hips and a frown on her face—her usual pose when greeting me.

"I'm starting the bruschetta. But I'm also clearing my nasal passages. Pete was here."

"That's Mr. Petrocelli to you. Have some respect."

"Ugh, Nonna, he's disgusting. He came around hoping Daddy was here to give him wine."

She shook her head and made a tsking sound. "A terrible affliction. Pietro was once a cabinetmaker, a craftsman. And a man like that turns to drink. Such a shame."

"Why are you nice to him? Why do you even let him come around?" I asked, giving the basil a quick rinse at the sink.

"Back in Naples, he knew your grandfather." At the mention of her late husband, Nonna crossed herself and looked at me expectantly.

"May God rest his soul," I said quickly.

She nodded her approval and resumed her story. "Pietro's older brother, Alfonso, was also close to your grandpa's *fratello*, your great-uncle, Zio Roberto. But such troublemakers, those two." She shook her head again. "Got in with criminals. Your grandfather's family never talked about Roberto. Now leave that basil and start on the vegetables."

I put the basil away and gave my grandmother my full attention. A long-lost great-uncle who "got in with criminals" and was a forbidden subject in the Rienzi family? This was rich material for my novel—not the murder mysteries from which I made my living, but the new historical I was writing based on my family. I grabbed my waitress pad and a pen from the pocket of my apron; they would have to do in lieu of my computer.

"What happened to him?" I casually set the pad down on the counter, trying to keep it out of her sight. If she thought I was writing instead of prepping vegetables for lunch, I'd be in for it. I set the bin of carrots on the counter for effect.

"He died in the old country. No one was sure how." Nonna, who'd been scrubbing vigorously at the sink, dried her hands on a towel and tied an apron around her waist. "Have you chopped the onions and garlic?" she called over her shoulder.

"Uh-huh." I scribbled away in secret on the other side of the carrot bin. "So, did he just disappear? I mean, did they have a funeral for him? Is there a death certificate?"

She pinched her fingers and shook her hand in the classic Italian gesture. For as often as I'd seen it, I was surprised her hands weren't frozen in that position. "What are you, the police?" she asked. "Why all these questions?"

"I want to know about our history."

"Well, I want to know about the vegetables. Bring me that onion and garlic so I can start the sauce."

I brought her the open containers from the refrigerator, my eyes tearing up at the smell. I was still learning about cooking, but I knew the garlic and onion had to be kept in separate containers. You have to start with the onions, as they take longer to cook; garlic burns if you're not careful, so that gets added later. A perfectly sautéed onion and garlic mixture formed the basis of most of the Casa Lido's celebrated sauces. "Would you tell me more about Zio Roberto?" I asked.

"I will if you put that pen away and clean those carrots like you're supposed to."

I sighed and took a vegetable scraper from the drawer. As my brother, Danny, once observed about our nonna: *She don't miss a trick.* "Yes, Nonna," I said.

I watched her pour a generous helping of extra-virgin olive oil in the bottom of our biggest stock pot, heard the sizzle as the onions hit the hot oil. She talked while she stirred. "Your grandpa Francesco's mother was married very young and had Roberto right away. But then for many years she had trouble having babies," Nonna explained. "Your grandfather was what we used to call a 'late life' baby. His mama must have been forty when she had him."

"So Grandpa and Zio Roberto had a big gap between them?"

"*Sì.* Maybe fourteen, fifteen years. Your grandfather barely remembered him. All he knew was that Roberto got involved with the wrong people and died back in Italy. End of story." She stopped stirring long enough to scrutinize the chopped garlic. "Did you take out all the sprouts?"

My grandmother was obsessive about garlic preparation. "Yes," I said, holding up my hands. "And I have the smelly fingers to prove it."

"Part of the job," she said shortly. "Use lemon juice."

"Speaking of garlic," I said, "Stink . . . uh, Mr. Petrocelli said that he 'knows things' that I could use in my books. Do you think he might have meant information about his brother and Zio Roberto?"

"Who knows?" She lifted one broad shoulder in a shrug. "He's an old man and old men like to talk and make themselves important. He probably just repeats the same stories to anyone who will listen." She paused. "I suppose they could be about Alfonso. But he turned out bad, and may God forgive me, so did your zio Roberto."

"Yeah, you said that." *But bad in what way?* Could they have been Mafiosi back in Italy? I imagined the two young men in Naples, dressed in suspenders and flat caps, looking like extras from *Godfather: Part II.* Though my book wasn't a *Godfather*-type story, I couldn't help being curious. "So Grandpa's brother died young. What happened to Alfonso?"

"Last I heard he had emigrated here. But that was many years ago." She shook her wooden spoon at me. "I thought you wanted to know about your great-uncle Roberto."

"I do." I lifted a carrot high in my right hand while my left crawled across the counter toward my pen and pad. But before I could grab either, my grandmother's words assailed my ears.

"You pick up that pen, missy, and I shut my mouth."

I let out a loud huff, prompting my grandmother to

shoot me a look that froze my blood. "Okay," I said, resigned to the inevitable. "No pen. So I'm supposed to just remember it all," I muttered.

"You're *supposed* to be working. Come to think of it, I have more important things to talk to you about than dead relatives. We have the anniversary celebration to think about."

I stifled a sigh. Nonna was obsessed with the Casa Lido's upcoming anniversary; it was clear I'd get no more family history out of her today. I briefly considered talking to Stinky Pete to find out what he actually knew about my grandfather's mysterious brother. Grimacing at the thought of a one-on-one with the odiferous Signor Petrocelli, I told myself I didn't have much time for writing anyway.

It was August, and we were coming to the end of a busy season, one that would be capped off by a celebration of the Casa Lido's seventieth anniversary and the last rush of Labor Day weekend. They were likely to be the restaurant's most profitable events of the year, and we were counting on that revenue to make up for our slow start in the spring. (A dead body in the tomato garden tends to keep the customers away.) As I thought about the events of the last weeks, it struck me that I'd been back in New Jersey for nearly three months—almost a whole summer season. In that time I'd gotten myself involved with two men *and* two murders. That was some crazy arithmetic, even for me.

My thoughts were interrupted by a loud rapping noise and I jumped a mile. "I'm talking to you, Victoria," my grandmother said, banging her wooden spoon on the countertop. "Stop daydreaming. Hurry and finish those carrots; then bring me four jars of tomatoes from the pantry. And when you've finished that, you can write down the menu for the party as I dictate. It will be summer dishes—antipasto and bruschetta, cold salads, and maybe some shrimp . . ."

She was off and running. And in all the bustle of preparation for the dinner service and the plans for the Casa Lido's big day, Zio Roberto, his friend Alfonso, and Stinky Pete were quickly forgotten. Which turned out to be a mistake, because Stinky Pete was right: He *did* have a story to tell—one with more twists and turns than any mystery I'd ever written.

The last week in August would mark seventy years that the Casa Lido had been serving homemade Italian food to tourists and townies alike. Our plan was to have an outdoor celebration, and on the morning before the party, the restaurant garden was abuzz with busy servers, short-tempered chefs, and harassed-looking party-store employees. (My grandmother was directing them as they set up the tables. It wasn't pretty.)

Behind all the bustle, though, was a hint of unease. The delivery guys glanced at the cloudy sky as they unloaded; our servers moved double time setting up, as though something was chasing them. Something was—a hurricane making its way up the coast from the Carolinas; there had been storm warnings all week. Originally, it was supposed to have moved out to sea, but the latest predictions had it heading inland. Nonna, however, who saw herself as a fair match for Mother Nature, denied all weather reports and plowed ahead with plans for an outdoor gathering. I checked the weather app on my phone, which hadn't changed from the last time I'd looked, roughly two minutes ago. I stared at the tiny map of New Jersey on my screen and the swirling red image that represented the storm: *Yup, still heading our way*.

I searched out my mom in the swarm of figures; she wasn't hard to find. My mom was sixty, but looked at least a decade younger. And let's just say that her fashion choices were memorable, to say the least. She still wore her curly hair long, and last month's purplish auburn had lightened to more of a strawberry red—a color that was just as unnatural but a lot less jarring. Today she was sporting a yellow sundress in a vintage floral pattern that was visible from one end of the garden to the other. The halter top only emphasized her already generous curves. I waved her over, and she tottered toward me on four-inch platform wedges. "Hey, Mom," I asked, "are you at all worried about the weather?"

She pushed a stray curl off her face and sighed. "Of course I am. But Nonna and your dad won't hear of moving the party inside."

"Do we at least have a backup plan?"

She nodded briskly. My mom had lived for too long with Frank Rienzi, bettor of long odds, not to have backup. "Yes," she said. "Lori and Florence will have the whole dining room set up and ready to go—linens, silver, everything. We've got some extra servers lined up so we can clear the outside at the first raindrop or gust of wind. If we have to hurry inside, we'll have diners carry their own plates, we'll gather linens in bags, and the staff can store the rented tables in the shed. Last year we had hurricane screens installed for the big windows in front, so we'll be safe inside. And as we speak, your father is getting the generator ready in case the power goes out."

"Nicolina Rienzi, you never fail to amaze me."

My mother patted my cheek. "Thank you, darling."

She looked over at the old grape arbor, now draped with white linen and decorated with tiny lights. "Thank goodness your grandmother didn't want a tent—imagine us trying to take *that* down in a storm."

"I shudder to think." Scanning the group, I saw our head waitress and my old friend, Lori Jamison, who was carefully decorating the slate board that would feature tomorrow night's menu. A number of our summer hires were out here, too, as well as Florence DeCarlo, a career waitress who called everyone *hon* or *babe*. Flo was a favorite among the five o'clock crowd, the group we privately called the Hungry Silverhairs. She gave us a cheery wave from across the garden, which I returned, but my mother did not.

"What was that about?"

My mom gave a small sniff. "Nothing. I don't particularly like Florence."

"I know why," I said grinning, "because she's always showing her cleavage." Florence wasn't particularly well endowed, but made a habit of leaning over the male diners in a manner that probably brought her good tips in her younger days. "And she's always talking to Daddy," I added.

"Oh, stop it. Daddy is a very sociable man, hon. If I had to worry about every woman who—"

"Nicolina! Victoria! You have nothing to do but stand out here and talk?" The voice of She Who Appeared When Least Expected made us both jump. But before we could answer, my attention was drawn to a male figure in the parking lot.

Walking toward us was Father Tom Figaro, pastor of St. Rose's Church, family friend, and occasional member of my father's Rat Pack poker games. I'd known Father Tom for most of my life, ever since he'd arrived in Oceanside as a young priest. He'd confirmed me and coached Danny in the church basketball league. He was a man of contradictions — a Golden Gloves boxer in his youth in north Jersey, he exuded a tough guy air. But he was also an opera buff, one of the most well-read people I knew, and a connoisseur of all things Italian. He was a regular patron of the restaurant, and from time to time Tim Trouvare, our sous-chef (and my ex-boyfriend), slipped him extra food for needy families in our parish.

I turned back to my mom. "What's Father Tom doing here?"

My mother's eyes darted toward the blue garden shed and then to my grandmother, who crossed her arms and tightened her lips. I looked back at Father Tom, who was carrying a mallet-shaped object I'd rarely seen outside Mass. "And why does he have that . . . that holy water thing he uses in church?"

My grandmother's nostrils flared; my mother just looked nervous. "It's called an aspergillum, Victoria," my mom said. "It's for—"

"You never mind what it's for," Nonna snapped.

My mother took a deep breath, her bosom heaving like that of a middle-aged romance heroine. "You see, darling, Nonna thinks that we should bless the garden."

"I don't get it." I gestured to the rows of ripe vegetables and bushy herbs. "The garden's doing fine." I pointed to the chipped stone statue of Mary that stood forlornly in the corner of the field. "And you've already got the Holy Mother looking after it, right?" I said, smiling.

My grandmother did not smile back. Still participating in her own version of *omerta*, she remained silent. Mom tilted her head ever so slightly back to the blue shed, her curls bobbing. The garden shed. Of course. The place I'd found the body of the dead television producer. And then the light dawned like sunrise over the ocean.

"Hang on a minute: Are you telling me you want Father Tom to *exorcise* the garden?"

"*Zitte!*" Nonna put a finger to her lips. "Don't say such things!"

"Oh, honey, no," my mother said with an artificial laugh. "We're just . . . *cleansing* it."

I frowned. "It's not like that weird thing you guys do with the hair and olive oil for the evil eye, is it?"

"Again!" my grandmother said, making the sign of the horns with both hands. "Why must you tempt the Fates by mentioning such a thing?"

"Sorry," I said, and with no other option before me, I made a hasty sign of the cross. I could never quite understand the Italian inclination to conflate religion and superstition, but conflate it they did. Father Tom's "blessing" of the garden was just the Catholic version of keeping evil spirits away. But as I glanced at the blue garden shed, I couldn't help suppressing a shiver. The discovery of a dead body in one of my books was only a pale imitation of the real experience. And I'd been nowhere near as brave as my fictional detective, Bernardo Vitali, who'd solved eight mysteries with confidence and aplomb. My real-life experience had left me decidedly jumpy, so a few prayers and some holy water certainly couldn't hurt. And if they brought some comfort to my eighty-year-old grandmother, who was I to judge?

"Gather round, everyone," Nonna called out, and clapped her hands loudly for attention. Servers, chefs, and anyone else in the garden froze in place; then one by one made their reluctant way to where my grandmother and Father Tom waited, hands clasped behind his back.

"What's she doing?" I hissed to my mother.

"She's calling everyone together, hon. For the blessing," she added helpfully.

"Wait—are you telling me I have to participate in this weird ritual?"

"You won't be alone." She gestured to the back door of the restaurant, where Tim, our line cook, Nando Ortiz, and our head chef, Massimo Fabri, were filing slowly out the back door, looking like a group of errant schoolboys about to face the principal. The three men took their places at the back of the crowd—Nando respectful, Chef Massi annoyed, and Tim cranky. (I knew Tim's cranky face very well; it was one he wore in the kitchen most of the time.)

Father Tom bowed his head and we all followed suit. "Dear Lord," he said, "please bless this place of bounty and labor. Bless those whose hands till its soil and harvest its gifts. Protect it—and us—from the forces of darkness that gather around the unwary."

Forces of darkness? Sheesh, Father Tom. Laying it on a little thick, no?

"Lord," he continued, "remember us in this undertaking, as we prepare to feed the multitudes."

My grandmother was nodding, whether in agreement with the blessing or in hopes of "multitudes" showing up tomorrow, I wasn't sure. As Father Tom concluded his prayer, he shook the holy water over our heads, and I blinked as the water hit my face. I couldn't help thinking that this tiny shower was a harbinger of a much larger one to come.

"Maybe he should have added some prayers to hold off that storm," I said quietly to my mother. But Nonna's sharp ears picked up every word.

"There is *not* going to be any storm, Victoria. Those weather people are never right. My whole life I've lived on this coast. That hurricane will blow out to sea, you mark my words."

Oh, I marked them, all right. For all the good it did me.

Chapter Two

*T*he next day dawned bright and sunny, and I began to think that Nonna had taken Mother Nature in the first round. I stood outside admiring the handiwork of our staff—the grape arbor forming the centerpiece for ten circular tables set with white linens and jars of fresh flowers. A long table covered in a red-checked tablecloth was set up as a bar—my dad's domain. I smiled as he lined up the stem glasses and turned every wine bottle so that the labels faced the same way. When he saw me, he smiled and waved me over.

"Hey, Vic, did you see my latest wine labels?" He held out a bottle for me to inspect.

"Frank's Thursday Chianti," I read aloud.

My dad pointed to the label. "You know it's the old joke about homemade wine, right? *When was it bottled? Thursday!* Get it?"

"I get it, Dad. It's funny. And the printer did a nice job on these. I like the gold lettering and the little grapevine. Very classy."

"Thanks, hon." He looked back at the bar. "You know what? I think we need a few more whites."

"Don't let me keep you," I said, and patted his arm. "I have to finish setting."

As I placed votive candles down on each table, I tried to ignore the insistent breeze that lifted the corners of the tablecloths and sent the tomato plants swaying. I was deliberating about looking at my weather app again when a familiar number appeared on my phone.

"Hey, stranger," I said. Cal Lockhart was renovating our antique wooden bar, and we'd been casually dating for the last month or so. But he'd been away on one of his mysterious errands for the last week, which tended to get in the way of our relationship. "What's cookin'?" I asked.

But he didn't respond with a joke or his usual *How are you this fine mornin', Victoria?* In fact, his voice was tense. "Is your family still plannin' to go ahead with the party tonight?"

"Of course. You know Nonna."

"You've seen the weather report, right?" he asked, his voice growing louder with each word. "That hurricane's heading this way, *cher*. It's on a straight course; there's no avoidin' it. Tell them to cancel. Or at the very least, bring it inside."

The man on the other end of the line sounded nothing like the laconic, soft-spoken guy I knew. But I understood the reason for the panicky edge in his tone. "Listen to me, okay?" I lowered my voice in the hopes that he would do the same. "It's already been downgraded from a category three to a two—"

"Even a category two can wreak all kinds of havoc," he interrupted. "Dangerous winds. Flooding. I don't have to tell you that, do I? You grew up on a coast."

"And you lived through Katrina," I said. "And that's your point of reference. I can't even imagine how terrible and terrifying that must have been, but this storm is nothing like that. By the time it hits us it'll just be a good old-fashioned summer thunderstorm," I added, sounding more confident than I felt.

"You don't know that, Victoria. And I sure hope you don't have to find it out the hard way." There was a momentary silence and then I heard him sigh. "Will they at least have it in the restaurant?"

"At the first raindrop or gust of wind, we'll move indoors—I promise. In fact, they're setting up the dining room right now, just in case."

"Okay. I'm heading back in a little bit."

Cal was off on one of his mysterious errands, and while it was a little early in the relationship to press for details of his comings and goings, that didn't stop me from wondering. "You're still my date for tonight, right?" I asked.

"You bet," he said, sounding more like his old self. "But I'm not sure how much of a date it's gonna be. If I know Giulietta, she'll be putting you to work, girl."

Cal was the only person I knew who got away with calling my grandmother by her first name. Perhaps she'd fallen for his Southern charm, but more likely it was that her granddaughter was involved with someone *other* than Tim. "You're right about that," I said. "And speaking of work, I've got to get back to it. I'll see you later. And try not to worry, okay?"

"Easier said than done, *cher*," he said.

I finished up some of the other details outside and took a last look around the garden and then up the sky. The first clouds were rolling in.

Back inside the Casa Lido, all hands were on deck in the kitchen, including mine. I was at my usual place, the veg-

etable and salad station, where I was chopping fresh arugula by hand. Heaven forfend I should use the food
processor and bruise the precious produce. Nando was
carefully slicing pancetta, and Tim was at work on his
specialty, homemade pasta. And all the while Chef Massimo bellowed orders at us in a confusing mixture of Italian, Spanish, and English.

I looked up to find Tim at my elbow, and he pointed
out the window that overlooked the garden. "It doesn't
look good out there," he said, shaking his head. "And by
four it will only get worse. Having this party today is a
bad idea, Vic."

"You sound like Cal."

He made a face. "You mean there's something Lockhart and I agree on?"

"Besides me, you mean? Apparently."

"Funny. I still say we should have postponed it."

"Who's 'we,' Trouvare? The Rienzis own this place.
You just work here, remember?" I said it with a smile,
but sometimes my ex needed reminding that he was still
a sous-chef, and that he'd only been hired back last year
because of my parents' forgiving natures. As I watched
Tim work, head bent, a loose curl over his forehead and
wearing that work frown I knew so well, eight years
seemed to roll away. It didn't seem that long ago that we
were young and in love, making plans for a life together
that included taking over the restaurant someday. But
Tim broke my heart and lost his job at the restaurant. So
I took myself, most of my belongings, and my unused
business degree and ran away to the big city, where to my
shock and surprise, I ended up writing mysteries.

"Ah, lass," he said in his favorite Irish brogue, "I remember it all."

So do I, I thought but didn't say. "Regarding the weather, though," I said, "I think we're stuck going through with this. We can just bring everything inside at the first sign of the storm."

He jerked a thumb back at the window. "The first signs are already out there."

It was clearly time for a change of subject. "What are you working on, by the way?"

"The *bagna cauda.*" He added a bunch of peeled garlic cloves (courtesy of me) to the food processor, then one by one, some drained anchovies. It was the base for a spicy dipping sauce that literally means "cold bath." He lifted the top of the processor, about to stick his finger into the pungent mixture.

"Uh, uh, uh. I wouldn't do that if I were you."

"What are you talking about? I can't make it without tasting it."

"Well, you do what you have to do, but do you really want to breathe all over Lacey after tasting raw garlic and anchovies? She's coming tonight, right?" Of course she was—she'd been glued to his side for about a month now.

Tim's expression softened and he grinned in a way that used to (okay, maybe still did) reduce me to the consistency of cannoli cream. *Note to self: Remind Lacey of the dangers of Irish-Italian men.*

"Yeah, she is," he said. "She's really looking forward to it."

"Will she stay for the whole thing?" I asked innocently. "I mean, isn't ten past her bedtime?"

He shot me a look of disgust. "She's not that young, Vic. She's twenty-eight, for Chrissakes—"

"Tim," Chef Massi interrupted, "the seafood delivery

is here. We need to get it on ice as quickly as possible."
He clapped his hands. "*Subito*, Chef!"

Ugh. Much as I loved shrimp, I had a pretty good idea
who would be cleaning it and deveining it. I'd come back
to the Casa Lido to learn how to cook and do research for
a new book, but thus far my training had only extended
to the dirty work. Literally. I glanced at the kitchen clock;
it was already nearing eleven. Five hours seemed like
very little time to finish the prepping and cooking. I
squinted at the menu, written in Chef Massi's typically
European hand, full of loops and flourishes:

Scallops with pancetta
Proscuitto and cantaloupe
Antipasto alla Casa Lido
Bagna cauda with celery for dipping
Shrimp cocktail
Fusilli with fresh chopped tomato sauce
Beef carpaccio
Grilled watermelon with salata ricotta cheese
Assorted pastries and seasonal fruit

I was so lost in thought I didn't hear the kitchen door
open and didn't see our busboy until he was right at my
side. Jason Connors, one of our summer hires, was a local
kid who'd just graduated from Oceanside High. A dark,
silent boy with an acne-scarred face, he barely spoke to
the rest of the staff, though he sometimes exchanged a
word or two in Spanish with Nando. But we kept him
around for a simple reason: He worked hard. He stood
silently next to me, holding a black bin against one hip.

"Oh . . . Jason, hi. I didn't see you there."
He blinked, looked at a spot somewhere above my

head, and gave me the universal greeting of teenagers everywhere. "Hey."

"Um, hey. Do you need something?"

"Yeah." His face was impassive, difficult to read, and I wondered how his parents dealt with him. "Your grandmother told me to get the silverware from the dishwasher and wipe it down."

I gestured to the dishwasher door. "Help yourself."

The only sound in the kitchen was the crash of silver in the bin. As always, when there was an awkward silence, I felt compelled to fill it.

"So Jason," I said in a hearty tone, "where're you headed in the fall?"

"County," he said without looking up, continuing to throw forks, knives, and spoons into the bin.

He probably meant county college, and not jail, but with this kid, who could be sure? "It's good to get those required courses out of the way," I said. "You do a good two-year program and you can pretty much go wherever you want."

"I guess." He straightened up, shifted the bin to both hands, and eyed the door. "D'ya have a towel?"

"Oh, for the silver, sure. Here you go."

Were all teenagers this hard to read? I thought as he left the kitchen. Or just our silent busboy?

By three thirty there was a steady wind blowing in from the ocean, with the sun hidden behind masses of gray clouds that looked like tufts of unappetizing cotton candy. Nonna was still adamant about having the party outside, so I decided to appeal to my dad. I found him out near the Dumpsters, frowning down at an ancient generator.

"Hey, Daddio," I said brightly, then decided to plunge

right in. "Listen, I'm here to plead my case for moving this party inside."

My dad tugged nervously at his straw fedora and shook his head, whether at me or the metal monstrosity at his feet, I couldn't tell. I waved my hand in front of his eyes. "Hello, Frank Rienzi? Come in, Frank."

"Sorry, baby," he said with a sigh. "I can't seem to get this thing going. I already tried the choke twice. And if the weather gets bad—"

"Our power might go out. That settles it, Dad. We need to move the party into the dining room. I'll stand out in the garden greeting people and then usher them inside. Then we don't have to worry."

"Oh yes, we do, baby." He pushed his hat back on his head and grinned, looking a whole lot like my brother, Danny; they had the same tanned, square features and hazel eyes. "I'd rather take my chances with a hurricane than cross your nonna," he said.

I sighed. How could one old woman instill such fear in those around her? "But you've seen the weather reports, right?"

His face brightened. "Yeah, I did. In fact, now they're saying there's a twenty percent chance it'll head out to sea."

Ah, Frank, I thought, *it's just like you to back the long shot.* "If you say so, Dad." But his attention was back to the paint-chipped cylinder at his feet. He fiddled with a lever, hesitated, and then gave the generator a swift kick. When he pressed the button, the thing suddenly roared into life. "See that?" my dad yelled over the noise. "We're good to go!"

"I hope so!" I yelled back. I glanced at my watch—3:37—almost time to get my derriere moving. The first brave guests would be arriving soon.

I ducked into the restroom for quick once-over in front of the mirror. In lieu of our usual white blouses and black slacks, we were all wearing stylish black shirtdresses. I'd turned up the collar on mine and pushed the sleeves to my elbows, added a string of pearls, a silver belt, and a pair of black pumps. And in an attempt to channel my inner Audrey Hepburn, I wore my hair up. If I had to work, at least I'd do it in style. But whether that style would hold in the wind that was whipping up was another matter entirely.

As I approached the three waitresses outside, it struck me that despite the similar outfits, each woman had dressed in a way that revealed her personality. Our head waitress and my oldest friend, Lori Jamison, was wearing her dress in typical Lori fashion—which is to say, no fashion at all. It was buttoned up to the neck and accessorized with a pair of black kitchen clogs. Flo, on the other hand, had a few too many buttons undone and had hiked her dress above her skinny knees; her dyed black hair was styled in a beehive that was so out of date it was fashionable. Alyssa Madison, our newest hire, looked like a sorority girl on a job interview. Her blond ponytail was immaculate, her dress starched and crisp, her black ballet flats polished to a high shine.

"You look great, Vic," Lori said. "I like your hair that way." She scrutinized my dark blond hair more closely. "Did you get highlights?"

"Maybe. Okay, yes. My mother strong-armed me."

She raised an eyebrow, a knowing look on her round, freckled face. "I don't suppose it has anything to do with your new boyfriend?"

At that, a look and a smile passed between Flo and Alyssa. *The perils of dating within the workplace,* I thought.

Everybody knows about it. "No," I said. "And yes, before you ask, he's coming." I pointed to the busboys putting the finishing touches on the setup. "I can't believe how quick these guys are working." In their black shirts and slacks, they swarmed the tables like a colony of oversized ants. Only one of them stood alone, and he happened to catch Flo's eye.

Hands on hips and frowning, she called out to him in a harsh tone, "Hey, Jason! Did you light those candles like I asked you to? Is every one of those silver setups neat and straight? Those tables better be perfect, mister!" Jason, his expression blank, merely nodded and went back to his work.

"Go easy on him, Flo," I said. "I know he's not the most personable of kids, but he does his best."

"Yeah, well, his best isn't good enough," she muttered.

"So, what do we think, chickadees?" Lori asked, gesturing to the gray sky. "We gonna stay ahead of this storm?"

But before we could answer, the first guests appeared around the corner of the building.

"We'll find out soon enough, girls," I said. "Ready or not—it's showtime."

Chapter Three

*A*long with the heavy canapé trays, I carried the fervent wish that my feet would hold out in heels. As I circulated a bit unsteadily among the guests, I came face-to-face with our redoubtable mayor, Anne McCrae.

"Why, hello, Victoria," she said, wearing her best politician's smile, a Hillary Clinton pantsuit, and a year-round leathery tan from too many hours on the beach, the tennis court, or her garden. (All three were places where she spent more time than town hall, that was for darn sure.) She'd lived in Oceanside Park her whole life; single and in her mid-forties, she was obsessive about bringing more tourism (read "dollars") to our town. Anne barely tolerated my family, as we always seemed to be on opposite sides of town issues. And not long ago, when the Casa Lido found itself in some trouble, she swiftly lined up a buyer for the restaurant—one who planned to turn the space into a Starbucks.

But I flashed her my brightest smile and held out the tray of canapés. "Would you like a scallop wrapped in pancetta? Perhaps some prosciutto and melon?"

Her pale gray eyes held a hint of slyness. Was she up

to something? "Yes, thank you," she said, putting two of each on her plate. At least the woman knew good food. "How are you, Victoria? Isn't the new Vick Reed book releasing soon?"

Darn the woman, she had an elephantine memory. Not long ago, I had made a hasty promise to speak to her book club this fall. But I kept smiling. "Yes, it is, Anne. *Murder Della Casa* comes out the first week in September."

"Cute title," she said through a mouthful of melon. "And very appropriate. It means 'murder in the house,' right?" She tilted her head in the direction of the blue shed. As if I needed reminding that a corpse had ended up in the Casa Lido garden. "And that timing works nicely with our book club meeting," she added.

I ignored the jab and went with the lesser of the two evils Anne was setting before me. "I haven't forgotten," I said. "I'll be happy to speak to your club." It was time to escape, but before I could make a move, Anne put a hand on my arm.

"Before you go, dear—a word to the wise. Would you let your father and grandmother know that I don't appreciate their rabble-rousing at town meetings?"

"I'm sorry?" I shifted the tray to my other hand, attempting to remain balanced in my heels. "I'm not sure what you're talking about."

She gave a short, barking laugh. "Then you're the only one in town who doesn't. We're planning to sell the carousel, and apparently the Rienzi family does not approve."

"The carousel? But . . . but you can't be serious," I sputtered. "It's a nineteenth-century carousel. It was made in Italy. All those horses are hand-carved. It's a work of art. And you're talking about selling it off?"

"Well, we're hoping of course that we get a buyer who will keep it intact. But it's too difficult to maintain and doesn't bring in the revenue it used to." She ate her last canapé in one bite and swallowed quickly, just the way a snake eats its prey. "Now if you'll excuse me, Victoria, Richard Barone is over there. And his foundation has *very* deep pockets. Who knows?" she said with a wink. "He may even be in the market for an antique carousel."

I steadied the tray, taking a deep breath. The Oceanside Park Carousel was something of a historical landmark in our town. We'd ridden it every summer of our lives from the time we could sit on the horses. I'd loved riding in the beautifully decorated chariots; when I waved to my mom and dad in the crowd, I'd felt like a princess in a magical carriage. *Every kid should have that experience,* I thought. *Who is Anne McCrae to take that away?*

But I would have to save my righteous indignation for another time. I had a job to do, so I headed for friendlier territory, the corner of the grape arbor where my brother and sister-in-law stood talking, heads bent close together and blissfully unaware of anyone around them. It was good to see them close again; their marriage had had its ups and downs, partially because of Sofia's involvement in my sleuthing adventures. But now she was newly pregnant, giving off a glow that rivaled the lights on the boardwalk. And my brother was over the moon at the thought of being a dad.

"Hey, guys. I'd kiss you both, but this tray is cramping my style. Anybody hungry?"

Danny's answer was to put four canapés on his plate. "I'll take a piece of melon," my sister-in-law said, "but no meat." She carefully unwrapped the ham and placed it lovingly in Danny's mouth.

"You two are kind of disgusting, you know that?"

"But in a good way, right, sis?" My brother grinned. "We got a good turnout. Ma and Pop must be happy."

I pointed over at the bar, where our parents were providing the guests with generous pours of house wine. "They're in their element, that's for sure." I glanced at the darkening sky. "I just hope we can move this thing along before that storm comes."

"By the way, Vic," Sofia said, "where's your mysterious date? Looks like Mr. Down on the Bayou is nowhere to be found."

"He'll be here, don't worry."

"Was he away again last week?" my brother asked. "Where does he go when he's off on these jaunts of his?"

Good question, big brother. I spread my palms out. "Who knows? He's a very private guy."

My brother rubbed his chin, a sure sign that his detective wheels were turning. I held up my hand. "Danny, I hope you're not thinking of running a check on him."

He grinned. "Did it already. No priors."

"That's comforting. Listen, he and I aren't serious and I'm not in high school. You don't have to vet all my boyfriends."

Sofia unwrapped another piece of melon. "You say that like there are so many."

"Moving away from my love life," I said, "do you believe that Anne's trying to get rid of the carousel?"

"I know," Danny said. "There's a big movement to save it. Petitions, even a Facebook page." He glanced over to where Anne was still deep in conversation with Richard Barone. "I don't know how much luck they'll have, though."

"I can't believe I didn't hear about it," I said.

"You've been holed up in your cottage," Sofia said. "Working on your *magnum opus*. How's it going, by the way?"

I sighed. I'd come back to the shore to take a break from my mysteries to write a historical novel based on my family. But so far, I hadn't produced very much. (Mostly because corpses tend to interrupt one's work.) "Slow. I told my agent I'd have a draft for him to look at in eight or nine months."

Sofia patted her barely visible bump. "Let's hope we both deliver on time."

"Ha!" I said, but my laughter died on my lips when I realized my grandmother had spotted us. Nonna threw up her arms in welcome, kissing my brother on both cheeks. I rarely got even one. *"Daniele!"* My grandmother always called my brother by the Italian version of his name, yet another sign of her favoritism. "Sofia, how are you feeling, *cara*? Are you hungry?" She pointed to my tray. "If you don't like the appetizers, Victoria will be happy to go into the kitchen and get you something else."

"Of course she will," I muttered.

"Now, you two have a good time." Nonna pointed a gnarled finger at me and frowned. "You, miss, start bringing guests to the tables. The boys will be bringing out the *bagna cauda* and the antipasto platters soon."

"Yes, ma'am," I said through my teeth. "Later, guys."

After depositing my tray, I made my next round through the garden, attempting to usher people to tables. I was arrested by the sight of a brunette standing with Richard Barone. Both tall and dark, they made an attractive couple. The woman turned and began waving wildly. I blinked. *It can't be.*

"Iris? Iris Harrington?" I moved toward her as fast as

my heels allowed and gave her a hug, taking in her familiar patchouli scent. But her perfume was the only thing that hadn't changed about Iris. I stared at her curly cropped hair and her cocktail dress, patterned with purple irises. "What have you done to yourself, lady? You look amazing. And that's a statement dress if I've ever seen one."

As the proprietress of the Seaside Apothecary, our natural pharmacy, Iris was a well-known figure in town. But that figure was transformed. Gone was her long graying hair; gone were the hippie clothes and Birkenstock sandals. For years Sofia had threatened to give Iris a makeover, but somebody else had gotten to her first. And he was wearing an expensive designer suit.

"It was time for a change," she said, her face pink. "Victoria, do you know Richard Barone?"

I reached out a hand. "No, but I know that your foundation does wonderful work in the community."

"You're very kind, Victoria," he said. "It's so nice to meet you at last." He clasped my hand. "Iris talks so much about you and about your work as Vick Reed. And I confess I wasn't a mystery fan until Iris gave me a copy of your latest. Well done." He smiled, his teeth a flash of white against his dark beard and mustache. My hand was growing warm in his, and I could feel my cheeks follow suit. Barone exhibited a smoothness and charm particular to certain Italian men—Tim had it, and so did my dad. And so, certainly, did Richard Barone. It was easy to see why Iris was smitten and why she'd gotten that dramatic makeover.

"Thank you," I said. "Listen, I'm supposed to be reminding you that the antipasto course is being served."

"We'll go find our seats," Iris said, taking Richard's hand.

"Hey, who's the hottie?" Flo asked from behind me.

"Richard Barone," I said, "head of the Barone Foundation."

"Nice," she said, nodding. "Bet he's got a buck or two."

"Yup." *But he's a heartbreaker,* I thought. A category of men with which I was a bit too familiar.

As the guests finished their antipasto, Lori, Florence, and I stood near the kitchen door waiting to start the dinner service. "Hey, Lori," I said. "Are we about ready to serve?"

"If we're not, we oughtta be," she said. "That wind is coming in stronger every minute."

"But your grandmother don't wanna rush nobody, never mind the weather," Florence said. "Hey, Bright Eyes," she barked into the open kitchen window. "That pasta course plated yet?"

Chef Tim, aka "Bright Eyes," answered with uncharacteristic good humor, "Just about, beautiful. Give us another two minutes, okay?"

"You got it, Chef," she answered.

Tapping my foot nervously, I wondered where Cal was. Maybe the impending hurricane had kept him away. *Or maybe you're being stood up?* But I broke into a smile when I saw a man walking across the parking lot. Was my date here at last? I squinted to get a better look at our visitor.

"Oh no," I said, pointing to the stumbling figure. "And I thought the storm was the worst thing we'd contend with tonight."

Lori put her hands on her hips and frowned. "You've *got* to be kidding me."

Alyssa joined us, her arms full of dirty plates. "Oh my goodness," she said, her blue eyes wide.

For there, in all his tattered glory, was Stinky Pete himself, heading straight for us. *"La festa! La festa!"* he shouted, raising both arms in a celebratory (though shaky) gesture, repeating the phrase until he reached the garden. "Are we all having fun?" he asked no one in particular. As he stumbled among the tables, the guests smiled in a frozen manner or pretended not to see him. And more than one nose wrinkled at his pungent presence.

"Dov'è il vino?" Pete called out. "Where is the wine? A man must celebrate at *la festa*, no?"

It was only a matter of time before Pete spotted the bar table. I hurried to where my father and grandmother were chatting with guests. My grandmother frowned at the interruption, until I tilted a head in Pete's direction.

Nonna clasped her hands together. "Oh *Dio*," she said. "Not tonight, of all nights."

"Daddy, you have to get rid of him," I said.

"No." My grandmother put a restraining hand on his arm. "He sees Frank and he thinks he's getting some wine. I will speak with him. He'll listen to me."

"Are you sure, Ma?" my dad asked.

She nodded. "Poor soul."

I watched in wonder as my normally harsh and forbidding grandmother suddenly morphed into the Nonna I'd never known. She greeted Pete with a kiss on each cheek and took his hands in hers, speaking quietly to him in Italian. She drew him away from the guests, who'd begun to studiously avoid him, and their relief was palpable. As Nonna talked, she led him out to the parking lot; she disappeared inside the restaurant briefly and returned with a container of food and a bottle of water. He dipped his head, said something to her, and then turned to go. My heart contracted a little as I watched him lurch away. *I hope he has somewhere to sleep tonight.* But he had a meal, at least, and no wine. His shambling figure grew smaller and smaller until he rounded the corner of the restaurant and finally disappeared.

Chapter Four

For the next hour or so, dinner service went off without a hitch, and we were beginning to think we might just pull it off. I was also beginning to think that I was indeed being stood up, until my date finally appeared. My face broke into a smile and I waved as he walked toward me. A transplant from New Orleans, Cal had a laconic charm that was one part Southern Accent and two parts Hot Cowboy.

"Hey, you," I said.

"Hey, yourself." He took both my hands and held out my arms as though we were about to dance. "Well, would ya look at you? Very nice, *cher*."

As I looked at Cal's face, it struck me that eyes said a lot about a person. Tim's, for instance, were a changeable, stormy gray that pretty much summed up his personality. Cal's, one the other hand, were a peaceful, woodsy green. I looked into them and was immediately comforted.

"Wow," I said. "You're quite a surprise tonight."

"Why? Did you think I wasn't gonna show up?"

"Oh no, it's just that I'm not used to seeing you out of your work clothes—" *Victoria, you did not just say that.*

One lift of an eyebrow from Cal was enough to set my cheeks burning. "I mean . . . well, you know what I mean."

He pressed a kiss to my forehead. "Sadly, I do. You mean I clean up nice, right?"

"You know you do. And I've seen you in dress clothes before. It's just that tonight you look especially—" *Tasty* was the word that came to mind. But I was still enough of a lady not to say it out loud. "—nice."

"I could say the same to you." He stood close to me, putting his lips to my ear. "I like when you wear your hair up. 'Cause then I get to fantasize about takin' it down."

Despite dropping temperatures and a gusty wind, I was suddenly feeling very hot. But my mother's voice provided the cold shower I needed.

"Hello, Cal," she said coolly. "Thank you for coming."

"Don't you look lovely, tonight, Ms. Rienzi," Cal said.

My mother nodded in a queenly manner, but didn't answer. In my mother's mind, Cal was a distant second in the Who's Right for Victoria Sweepstakes. Tim would always be the front-runner. "Victoria, dear," she said, "don't you have some work to do?"

"You sound like Nonna," I grumbled. "Let me just get Cal a seat, okay?"

"Don't worry about me. I'll catch you later." He nodded to us. "Ladies."

I watched him walk away, admiring the set of his shoulders in that suit. Next to me, my mother was about to let loose on the wisdom of getting involved with Cal. "Not. One. Word," I warned.

"You know my feelings on the subject."

"Indeed I do, Mother. Need I remind you that Tim is dating Lacey Harrison?"

She sighed. "No. Is she coming tonight?"

"Supposedly. But thus far there's been no sign of her—" I was interrupted by a sound in the distance, a soft rumbling that boded no good.

My mother's eyes grew wide. "Was that—?"

Before I could answer, the air reverberated with another soft *boom*. My mother grabbed my hand. "C'mon. We need to get everybody inside."

In a matter of seconds, the sky darkened and the first fat drops of rain splashed around us. We went from table to table to gather our guests, smiling to mask our nervousness as the wind blew harder. As I watched the empty chairs overturning and the linens on the grape arbor flapping like sails, I was seized with a sudden fear. The wind whipped the trees; the creak of branches presaged the first sharp flash of lightning, followed by a thunder crack that set my heart pounding. The statue of Mary seemed to shiver in the wind, but her serene, sorrowful face betrayed no fear.

Old habits die hard, and as I grabbed chafing dishes and silver, I found myself reciting my own version of the childhood prayer: *Hail Mary, full of grace, please don't let me be struck by lightning or hit with a branch. Help us get everyone inside safely. Don't let the restaurant flood. And while you're at it, make sure the dunes hold.* My little beach cottage would be vulnerable if there were storm surges.

The men heaved tables and stacked chairs; one of our temporary hires, a guy I didn't recognize, his hair shaved close to his head, was folding tables at double speed. He carried two under each arm, his forearms straining.

"They go in the shed," I called over the wind.

"Got it," he said, without looking up. As he passed me, I noticed colorful tattoos on both arms, bright images of animals and leafy vines. *Hmm,* I thought, *bet those sleeves were rolled down and buttoned when he was hired or he wouldn't have gotten past Nonna.*

I followed Lori, Florence, and Alyssa, each carrying stacks of plates, and helped guide diners through the restaurant doors. After insisting that Nonna wait inside, my parents and brother directed it all calmly. There was an almost festive atmosphere as the guests pitched in, scurrying behind the waitresses and laughing as their napkins sailed in the wind.

In all the movement, only one figure was still: Cal. He stood under a tree, staring upward, his arms nailed to his sides as the rain fell on his face. In the next flash of lightning I caught a look at his stricken face; even in profile, I could see the fear.

"Cal!" I yelled over the wind. "Get away from that tree!"

He shook himself out of his daze and pointed toward the restaurant. "Get inside, okay? I'll meet you there in a minute," he called.

I kept watching as he joined Jason and a few of the other servers in shifting tables into the shed. What had happened to him under that tree? But my brother was at my elbow. "Inside, sis. Now!"

Once inside, Detective Daniel Rienzi took over, bringing the noisy, confused group to attention with two words. "Excuse me," he said, and the room quieted. "First of all, thanks for helping us move this party inside, which is the safest place to be right now. We'll keep you updated on the storm."

I was surprised at the number of diners who'd opted to stay and ride out the storm with us. But shore people are used to bad weather, and we don't like to let it get in the way of our fun. I waved across the room to Iris, where she and Richard Barone were sitting with Gale Spaulding, the town librarian. Anne McCrae was also still with us, shaking hands and chatting as though she owned the place.

After putting on a pair of flats, I helped Lori get people settled at tables while Flo and Alyssa started the coffee service; in the meantime, my dad went from table to table pouring anisette and amaretto, making sure the conversational buzz wasn't the only kind in the room. Apparently, however, I wasn't moving fast enough, because Nonna gave me the evil eye from the corner of the dining room; it was one of the more charming ways she summoned me.

"Yes, darling Grandmother?" I asked her.

"Don't be smart, Victoria. Go see what's taking so long to get the dessert out."

"We only got people inside five minutes ago—" But she gave me a look that was known to wither tomatoes on the vine. "Okay," I said. "I'll go move things along."

I headed down the hallway to the kitchen, but hesitated when I heard voices at the other end. Tim and Lacey. She must have come in through the kitchen. Her light cotton dress was soaked through, providing me with a clear view of her toned, slender body. Tim was leaning over her with a white kitchen towel, smiling, gently drying her hair in so intimate a gesture my breath caught in my throat. But I couldn't look away.

Tim and I had been apart for a long time. But you can't undo your history. And standing there watching them, I felt just as I had the night that Tim confessed he loved someone else. As though I'd lost him only a minute ago and not eight years before.

"Hey, guys," I said, my voice unnatural, my heart

thumping. "Uh, sorry to interrupt, but they sent me to see if the desserts have been plated."

"They're good to go," Tim said without looking up.

But Lacey turned around and gave me a warm smile. "Hey, Victoria. Bet they're keeping you busy tonight. You look great, by the way. That dress is adorable."

As much I wanted to hate Lacey Harrison, I couldn't. She was gracious, smart, and frankly, a good catch for any man. When she'd first met Tim, she confessed to me that she'd had a broken engagement, and I found myself worrying about *her* feelings instead of Tim's.

"Thanks, Lacey. And I am busy—in fact, I'd better get back out there."

"C'mon, babe," Tim said, putting his arm around her waist. "I saved you a plate in the kitchen. I know how you love my homemade pasta . . ." His voice trailed off. *In the kitchen,* he said. Tim never invited anyone into the kitchen, and he always made me feel as though I was in the way. As they walked away, I felt a sense of loss so deep that my very bones ached. *Stop it, Vic. Do not do this to yourself. And there's a very nice man waiting for you out in that dining room.*

That man was sitting quietly by himself at the bar. After making the rounds with a coffeepot, I found him sipping a whiskey.

"What's up, handsome?" I kissed Cal's cheek, still damp from the rain. "You okay? You looked kind of strange out there under the tree." I was about to ask if he'd been having flashbacks to his experience in New Orleans, but his shuttered face told me enough.

"I'm fine," he answered. "Just having a quiet drink here—can you join me?"

"Would that I could. We're about to serve dessert."

He briefly rested his hand over mine. "I'll find you in a few minutes, then."

I left the bar, and still pondering the mysterious ways of men, I caught sight of Father Tom coming through the restaurant doors.

"Is it bad out there?" I said, taking his wet raincoat and umbrella.

He brushed his hands over his cropped salt-and-pepper hair. "Bad enough," he said, "but probably not the worst the Lord has thrown at us."

"Have you had dinner, Father? We're starting dessert service, but I can get you something from the kitchen."

"Coffee and dessert is fine, Victoria." He glanced around the dining room. "Is your brother here? I need to speak with him for a minute."

"He's at the corner table with Sofia. Is everything okay?"

"I hope so," he said with a smile, but I noticed he took my brother aside to speak to him privately. If I knew my sister-in-law, she was burning up with curiosity. Well, we'd find out what was happening one way or the other.

While our guests happily tucked into cannolis, Napoleans, and our special shell-shaped *sfogliatelli*, Chef Massimo circulated among them. Resplendent in his high toque and crisp white chef coat, he shook hands and accepted compliments as though they were his due. Then my dad started the music going with the Other Frank who held a special place at the Casa Lido—Mr. Sinatra. While I hummed along to "Summer Wind," its namesake was howling outside, accompanied by a driving rain that lashed the windows and beat a tattoo on the roof. I scanned each table to make sure the candles were lit, just to be sure.

"Hey, Vic," Lori called from the coffee station. "Have you seen Alyssa?"

I shook my head, but Florence answered, "Last I saw her she was helping Jason with busing. Which is *not* her job, by the way," she said, backing out of the kitchen with a tray of fruit. "I have no idea where they are now. That damn kid is never where he's supposed to be, anyway." She shook her head in annoyance. I frowned as I watched her serve the fruit. Why the antipathy for poor Jason? What did she have against him?

The subject of my thoughts emerged from the hallway, wiping his hands on his dark slacks. He'd probably had to use the bathroom. *You better have used soap, kid,* I thought. "Hey, Jason, have you seen Alyssa?"

He looked up and blinked, as though he hadn't expected to see me. "Naw," he said. "Dunno where she is."

"Um, you can probably finish clearing the dessert dishes now."

"Okay," he said, and shambled over to pick up a clean tray. I shook my head and jumped at a tap on my shoulder.

"Looking for me?" Alyssa said, smiling, not a blond hair out of place.

"Actually, Lori was."

"Oh, good. I wanted to ask her how we were splitting tips tonight, because I want to be sure the boys get something. Some of the temps are going home early."

"That's sweet of you, Alyssa. You know I don't get a cut, so maybe share that among the guys. But talk to Lori first."

"Will do!" she called, her ponytail whipping around behind her. *We sure have an interesting group of summer hires,* I thought. An aging coquette, a sorority girl, and a sullen, silent adolescent. I found myself wishing for September.

*   *   *

By about eight thirty, when the guests were lingering over after-dinner drinks, I saw Danny making the rounds among the crowd. Well-brought-up Italian children are trained to never leave a place without, as my mother put it, "making your good-byes." Depending on the size of the party or the number of relatives, this process can take anywhere from ten minutes to an hour.

"Did you get a call, Dan?" I asked.

He nodded shortly. "Yeah, we gotta clear the beach." He shook his head. "God preserve me from storm-watchers. These idiots think it's fun to stand outside in a hurricane."

"Please. You used to do it yourself. I remember you and Tim bringing your surfboards down there. Drove Mom crazy."

"I didn't know any better." He glanced at his watch. "In a little while, people are gonna be hot to get out of here; it might be better for them to wait for the eye of the storm, when there's a lull."

"We can't stop them if they want to go, Dan. But it's raining pretty hard out there. And right now no one seems too concerned." I gestured to the crowd, many of whom were now dancing to Rosemary Clooney's infectious version of "Mambo Italiano." It appeared that while music played and wine flowed, our guests were content to wait out the storm in our cozy dining room.

"Until the lights go out," he said grimly. "I gotta hit it. Listen, if I don't get back here, would you and Cal get Sofia home?"

I promised him I would. "Hey," I called. "What was all that about with Father Tom?"

He turned, arms crossed in his familiar Tough Cop

stance. "Nothing *you* need to worry about." He turned abruptly and strode out the door without looking back.

"Okay, I think I hate all the men in my life tonight," I said under my breath.

"But not your dear old dad, right, baby?"

"Where'd you come from? And you are exempted from my list, yes. And maybe Father Tom," I added.

I linked my arm through his and tightened my hold as Florence came toward us. "Hey, boss," she said with a wink. "You got that generator good to go in case the lights go out?" She dropped her voice on the last three words in a pitiful attempt at flirtation, which thankfully was lost on my father.

"It's out back," he said. "And I got plenty of extension cords."

"You think of everything, Frank," Florence said as she sashayed away, her skinny hips swinging. I shook my head at such desperation, until the voice of my conscience issued a reminder: *That could be you in ten years. Show a little mercy.*

"So it worked out okay tonight, Dad."

"Told you it would, honey. That rain's letting up and I think the eye is about to pass over and everybody will get home safe." You had to love my father's optimism. "Yup," he added, "I'm betting we won't even need that generator."

A bright flash illuminated our faces, followed by a crack of thunder that shook me to my toes. And then everything went black.

Chapter Five

*T*he gasps and shrieks that came from our guests as the lights went out had a fun-house quality, the kind that says, *I'm scared, but it's kinda fun.* One by one, phones glowed as people fumbled for their possessions and chattered excitedly before making a dash for the door. Only one voice could be heard above the din.

"Please, everyone," Mayor McCrae called out, clapping her hands for attention. "Let's do this in an orderly way to get everyone out safely. If you have a phone, please use that to find your way to the main doors of the restaurant. If not, I'm sure the Rienzis won't mind if you use the candles from the table."

A guttural grumble from somewhere behind me said that Nonna would, in fact, mind very much. As my eyes got accustomed to the darkness, I saw my dad materialize at the mayor's side.

"For those who would like to stay out of the rain a bit longer," he said, "I'm about to get my generator going, and we should have lights soon. But whether you stay or go, I'd like to thank you all, on behalf of my family and me, for helping us celebrate our seventy years in business here in Oceanside Park. *Buon notte*, and come back to the Casa Lido soon."

There was a smattering of applause. *Way to take the floor back, Dad. Bravo*. Grabbing a votive from a nearby table, I joined my mom at the door to help usher people out. Holding candles and phones, they made a weird procession as they walked out into the darkness. Tim and Nando stood in the parking lot with flashlights and helped to direct traffic out. Once the lot had emptied, I stood outside with an umbrella, staring at the dark and deserted boardwalk. On impulse, I crossed the street and scurried up the ramp, holding my candle out in front of me. Standing in the center of the boardwalk, I looked down toward the rides pier, but without the lights of the Ferris wheel and the carousel house, it was only a shapeless gray mass in the darkness. On the other side of me, the ocean was roiling, the waves frothing and breaking high on the beach. When a gust of wind nearly took my umbrella from my hands, I came to my senses and turned to go, colliding with a man holding a flashlight. It was Cal, with more thunder in his face than the storm.

"What the hell are you doin' out here?" he rasped, gripping my wrist and half dragging me down the ramp. "What is wrong with you?"

"Cal, take it easy! I just wanted to see how far down the power was out. You can let go of me now, okay?"

"Not till I get you back inside. You think this storm is over? It ain't over yet. Once that eye passes, that wind's gonna kick up again, and worse than before. What were you thinking?"

We crossed the deserted street; still in Cal's death grip, I struggled to hold the umbrella and the candle. My mother and Sofia, both looking worried, greeted us at the door.

"Victoria, what were you doing outside?" my mom said. "You know better than that, young lady."

Great. Now I'm twelve. "What is everybody making such a big deal about?" I exploded. "I just wanted to see how much of the boardwalk was out. I wasn't out there for more than a couple of minutes, and I didn't go anywhere near the beach. Sheesh."

"It's just so out of character for you, Vic," Sofia said dryly. She raised an eyebrow. "Doing anything risky, I mean."

"Ha-ha, Sofe. And thanks for that."

"Listen," Cal said. "I'm gonna head back to see if your dad needs some help with that generator, and then I'll take you both home, okay?" He sounded calmer, and even grinned at Sofia. "That work for you, Miss Firecracker?" he asked, using his pet name for her.

"You bet," she said. "But I think Vic's on cleanup detail for a little while."

"I am," I said. "But it will be a challenge in the dark."

My mother put an arm around her daughter-in-law. "Well, Sofia is going to sit and have a nice cup of tea while you finish up, hon." I exchanged a look with my sister-in-law and we both grinned. When she and Danny had been having trouble, she and my mom were not the best of friends. But a baby on the way had changed everything.

While Sofia basked in the attentions of my mother and grandmother, the girls and I worked cleanup using flashlights and candles. I had an armful of dirty linens when the lights suddenly blazed on, and we all gave a cheer. Once we finished, the waitstaff, Chef Massi, and Nando all left, among my mother's repeated admonitions to be careful. Tim and Lacey were the last to leave, arms clutched around each other's waists. I was relieved to see them go.

Besides my family, the only guests who had stayed were Cal and Father Tom. We all sat at the family table sipping coffee and anisette while the storm howled outside.

"I hope everyone gets home safely," my mom said.

"They will, baby," my dad said. "Anyway, the storm's been downgraded again."

"That don't matter," Cal muttered. "Ya can't assume it's not dangerous."

"Listen to Calvino," Nonna said, patting Cal's hand. "He has been through this."

I opened my mouth to speak and snapped it shut again. But here was what I wanted to say: *You were the one who insisted we hold a party in a hurricane, and now you're calling for caution?*

I caught Father Tom's eye, and I could swear he winked at me. But his expression grew serious when he spoke. "I will continue to pray for everyone's safety."

Before he was done speaking, the door burst open and my brother stepped inside, his black slicker dripping with rain. He pushed back his hood, and his expression said it all. "It might be too late for that, Father," Danny said. He looked at my grandmother with a sympathetic glance. "I'm sorry to have to tell you guys this, but there's already been a casualty of the storm. They found Pete Petrocelli's body down in the carousel house."

Chapter Six

"Oh no!" my mother gasped, and put a hand over her mouth.

"What a shame," my dad said, and followed Father Tom's lead, as both men dropped their heads in prayer. For a moment, there was silence at the table. In our worries about the party, the loss of power, and the safety of our guests, we'd forgotten about poor Pete, a drunken, elderly man who'd been out alone in a storm. I stared down at my coffee cup, a little ashamed. But it wasn't long before my curiosity began its gentle tugging on my brain.

"Dan, what do they think happened?" I asked. "Did he fall and hurt himself?"

"We won't know for a while. But the carousel house was flooded, and he was facedown in the water. It's possible he drowned."

Father Tom looked over at me. "That's why I came to see your brother. I saw Pete up on the boardwalk earlier tonight. He was stumbling, very unsteady. It looked like he was carrying something, but I couldn't tell what."

The dinner my grandmother had given him, or something else? Like a wine bottle maybe? Sofia shot me a questioning glance that I pretended not to see.

I looked back at my brother, who ran a hand down over his face. Our eyes met, and I saw the guilt in his. "I didn't go out after him," he said. "When I called in, I told the dispatcher, but we had other stuff on our plate tonight. Lightning hit one of the transformers. That's why part of the town is out."

"Oh," I said, "that must have been that big flash right before the lights went out. I wonder if Pete was already out there."

My mother shook her head. "The poor soul, out there all alone. *Dying* alone." She shuddered, and my dad put an arm around her and kissed her temple.

I glanced at my grandmother, who'd been silent the whole time. Without thinking, I reached across the table and squeezed her hand, which she acknowledged with a brief nod.

Danny took Sofia's hand and helped her to her feet. "We gotta go, hon. I've only got a little time and I want to get you home." He took off his slicker and wrapped it around Sofia's shoulders. "I don't want you to worry," he said to her. "We've still got power, the windows are covered, and both sump pumps are going."

She wound an arm around his neck and kissed him. "I'll be fine till you get home."

Cal stood up, too. "Victoria, I think we better get you outta here, too."

After some hasty good-nights (and lots of *yes, Mom, we'll be careful*s) the four of us headed out the back way, my brother stopping us in the kitchen.

"Listen, Vic, there are reports of flooding on some of

the beach blocks. I don't think you should stay at the cottage tonight, but I didn't want to say anything in front of Ma."

My cottage—strictly speaking, Sofia's cottage, because I was renting it from her—was the last house on a beach block. "This is why I love you, brother. You knew she'd be hustling me off to stay with her and Daddy tonight."

"You could always come back to our house," Sofia said, and then broke into a grin. "Unless you'd like to check on your basement for me. It always gets water in a hard rain."

It always gets water in a hard rain. I strained to keep my voice normal. "Thanks, but I'd rather be home."

"If you're sure," my brother said, but his eyes were on Cal.

"I'll make sure she's taken care of, Dan," Cal said, reaching for the back door handle. "Okay, it's now or never, folks." He heaved the door open and the wind took it from him, banging it against the restaurant's outer wall. Together we got it shut, and I heard the lock click into place.

"G'night!" Danny yelled, practically carrying Sofia to his car. "Be careful!"

Cal grabbed my hand and we sprinted for his truck. "Can we hurry, please?" I called over the wind. At that, Cal gripped my waist and lifted me from the ground with one arm. With his free hand, he opened the passenger door of his truck and shoved me inside.

He slid behind the wheel and shook out his wet hair. "Where's the fire, *cher*?" he asked, a little breathless from heaving my hundred and thirty pounds into his truck.

"No fire," I said, "but maybe a flood. And I left my computer in the basement."

*   *   *

As Cal drove me down Ocean Avenue, he gripped the wheel, his face grim as he navigated the dark street. "Victoria," he said, "do you know what an *eyewall* is?"

"Should I?"

He shook his head with impatience. "In the eyewall are the highest winds that come after the eye passes over. We're in 'em now. This is also when you're likely to get ocean surges. You realize this is maybe the worst time you could pick for rescuin' your computer, right?"

I dropped my head. "I know. And I'm grateful to you for taking me. And for not lecturing me about backing up my work."

"I don't have to tell you to back up your work, do I? Storm did that for ya. But why'd you leave it in the basement?"

"I was working down there. It gets really hot in my bedroom sometimes." *And not in a good way,* I thought, glancing at Cal's profile. Would that change any time soon? And did I want it to?

To his credit, Cal kept a straight face. But dodging tree branches and flying debris in a hurricane did not exactly inspire flirtatious banter. Cal's mood was serious, almost businesslike. And behind that was something else, a fine thread of fear, whether for himself or for me, I couldn't tell. But this storm had him spooked.

As we rounded my corner, the flicker of flashlights and candles was visible in my neighbors' windows. But the houses were shut tight; a few were completely dark with no cars in their driveways. "Looks like some people evacuated," I said.

"They're smart. C'mon," he said. "You got your key ready? We're gonna run for it the minute I open the door of this truck. You keep your head down and listen to me, hear? There's already been one fatality tonight."

"That's reassuring." The thought of Pete dying alone in that carousel house made me shiver. Had he gone there for shelter? Had he gotten there before or after the power went out? How frightened he must have been on his own out there. But was he on his own? We'd all assumed he was but that didn't mean—

Cal's voice jolted me from my thoughts. "Victoria, if you're waitin' for the weather to improve to leave this truck, you're gonna be sitting here all night."

"Oh, sorry. My mind was wandering." I put my hand on the door handle. "Ready when you are."

The truck doors burst open and we spilled out into the rain. Clutching my keys in chilled fingers, I hurried across the small lawn to my porch with Cal right behind me. Inside, I felt along the wall for the light switch in my living room. "No power."

"Well, we figured as much. Are all your windows shut tight?" he asked, leading the way with a flashlight he'd taken from the truck.

"I'm pretty sure I closed everything up before I left for the restaurant." But a quick check of the first-floor rooms revealed an open kitchen window with a nice puddle forming on the floor. "I don't mind dealing with rainwater," I said as I mopped it up. "But seawater is something else again. When you live at the shore, salt is *not* your friend."

"Heck no. Salt's corrosive. And it gets into everything: electrical wires, pipes, even concrete. Salt sits in concrete long enough, it breaks it right down."

"Wow—really? You're a font of storm information, you know that? But I guess that comes from experience."

But getting Cal to talk about that experience was apparently fruitless, as his only response was to ask where the basement door was. And the minute we opened it, we heard the trickling sound. And when Cal shone the light downward, I could see the glimmer of water.

"Crap."

"Crap, indeed," Cal said. "Ya got maybe two inches down here." He knelt, sweeping the light along the concrete floor. "But I think this is coming up through the foundation. The ground's soaked from the rain and it's seeping up this way."

"That's good, right?" I asked, looking over his shoulder at the growing puddle.

He stood up with a grunt. "Well, it's good in that you got no ocean water in here. But Sofia's gonna have to do something about a drainage system." He handed me the flashlight. "Time to get what we came for, Victoria. Then I'm gettin' you out of here."

I gathered my computer, cord, and some notes from my writing table. "Listen, Cal," I said as we walked back up the stairs. "I can probably stay here tonight."

"No way," he said, shaking his head. "For one thing, you got no power. Yours is the first house between the ocean and the street. I think those dunes will hold, but why take a chance? You saw how far up the beach those waves were breakin'. Not only that, but your windows aren't covered; it's not safe, Victoria—plain and simple."

While I wasn't worried about some water in my basement, the thought of shattered windows was enough to give me pause. I let out a breath. "I really don't want to go back to my parents' house."

"You don't have to," he said. "You can come home with me."

"Uhhh . . . thank you, but I don't think . . ."

"I meant as my guest, *cher*." He smiled and kissed the top of my forehead. "As in, you'll take the guest room."

"Oh. Okay." *Hmm, a little disappointed, are we, Vic?* "Sure. Just let me go pack a bag."

Up in my bedroom, I threw some things in an overnight bag, changed from my dress to a T-shirt and jeans, and traded my wet leather flats for flip-flops. Looked around the room and figured the water would never get this high in a category-1 storm. On the way out, I glanced at my poster of Bruce Springsteen. "Well, Boss," I said, "wish me luck."

But for what? No hurricane damage? Or for the prospect of spending the night at Cal's?

Cal was right about the weather on the other side of the eye. The wind shrieked in my ears, and I got soaked just darting from my front door to his truck. Nervous at the thought of shaking tree branches, I struggled with the heavy door of the truck. Cal shoved me inside and closed the door behind me.

He shook his wet hair as he slid into the driver's seat. "'Baby, it's bad out there,'" he sang in a low, soft tenor, and my head jerked up at the sound. The man could carry a tune. He stopped when he caught me frowning.

"What? Don't you like that song?"

"No, it's not that. You can *sing*. That gives me one more thing to add to my meager collection of facts about you."

He trained his eyes on the dark street ahead. "Ain't that mysterious, *cher*."

Oh yes, you are. "What's that?" I pointed to a grocery bag on the seat between us.

"Stuff from your fridge and freezer that might spoil. Though how you make a meal from designer ice cream and margarita mix is beyond me."

"Those are two all-important food groups. Hope you got the container of frozen marinara sauce—it's my one claim to fame."

He grinned. "I got it. I'll take it as payment for my hospitality."

"It's yours. Seriously, though, you thought of everything tonight."

"Right. Learned it the hard way from a sassy gal named Katrina. Right before she run me out of town." But he didn't elaborate.

I noticed lights emerging along the highway in places where the power was still on. "Hey, we're heading west," I said. "I thought you told me you lived in Seaside?"

"Nope. Moved from that place. I'm in Riverton now, 'bout ten miles inland, which is safer than staying at your place or at your parents."

A half hour later, we pulled into a new-looking apartment complex. Though the wind had died down a bit, it was still raining, and we made one last sprint to his front door.

"It ain't much," he said as he opened it, "but it's home."

But there was very little about the spotlessly clean and spartan apartment that said *home*. The living room held a couch, a table, and a standing lamp of good quality but nondescript style. Maybe the guy was a minimalist, but there wasn't a photograph or a framed print on the walls, and none of the small, personal details that tell the story of a person's life. Every room appeared to be painted white, and the same beige carpet ran throughout the apartment. *In some way,* I thought, *Cal is hiding himself in all this bareness.*

"So, how about a drink to warm them bones?" Cal took off his wet jacket and rolled up his shirtsleeves, and my eyes strayed to his tanned forearms.

"I wouldn't say no." Still holding my bag, I followed him to the kitchen, where he motioned me to sit. I plopped down on one of the kitchen chairs with a groan. "What time is it, anyway?"

"It's after midnight." He set down a tumbler in front of me partially filled with a clear brown liquid.

"Isn't that an Eric Clapton song?" I sniffed the glass and took an experimental sip. Almonds. He'd wisely poured me amaretto instead of whiskey—one taste of whiskey and I'd be under his kitchen table.

He swirled his drink, an amused look on his face. "What do you know about Eric Clapton?"

"Please," I said, waving my hand at such ignorance. "I listened to 'Layla' at my mother's knee."

He raised his eyebrows and grinned. "Wouldn'ta pegged your mom for a Clapton fan."

"Ah, she's full of surprises."

"She don't like me much." He took a sip of his drink, his face thoughtful.

"That's not so. You're a very likable guy."

"Maybe." He looked down and swirled the whiskey in his glass. "But I'm not Tim."

"No, you're not. And for that I am grateful." I took another sip of the sweet drink. "Now, my nonna, on the other hand, is Team Cal all the way."

He smiled. "She's a pistol, that one."

"She sure is. I just wish she didn't—ahem, *go off* all the time—around me."

He laughed and shook his head, and I had the satisfaction of knowing I was involved with a guy who laughed at my jokes.

"S'cuse me a second," he said, pulling his phone from his pocket. "I just wanna check the weather." He swept his finger across the phone and held it up for me to see. That angry red swirl that had been hovering over the coast was heading out to sea.

"Thank God," I said. "I think we're through the worst of it. And up north all they'll get is a thunderstorm."

"You still can't be too careful with hurricanes," he said quietly.

I stared down at my glass and took another sip for courage. "Was it terrible?" I rested my hand on top of his.

He turned up his palm, linked his fingers in mine. "*Was it terrible?* you're asking me. *Terrible* don't begin to describe it, *cher*." He shook his head slowly, back and forth twice, as though he still couldn't believe what he had seen. "The panic. The smells. People dyin' in their own homes. All those 'X's painted on houses to show where there were bodies." He stared down at his glass. "And me, I lost everything. My woodworkin' business, my house, and then my wife and—yet I'm one of the lucky ones. 'Cause I got outta there alive. And what y'all saw up here on the news? That wasn't the half of it."

I tightened my grip on his hand. "Tonight in our garden, when you were under that tree—was that like a flashback of some kind?"

"Guess you could say that, yeah."

"But here we are, safe and sound. Back in Occanside the most we'll have to deal with is some water in basements and spoiled food."

Cal stood up and pushed in his chair. "A man's dead, Victoria. We didn't escape unscathed."

"No, I guess we didn't. Thanks for talking with me. And thanks for rescuing me and my computer from the storm." I stepped into his arms and rested my cheek against his chest. "It's been a long night," I said through a yawn.

He hugged me a little closer and kissed the top of my head. "It sure has. And you need to get some sleep." He lifted my chin and pressed a light, quick kiss on my mouth that ended any wondering I might have had about how the evening would play out.

I followed him down a short hallway (also painted white) where two bedrooms sat across from each other. He gestured to the smaller of the two.

"You'll be in here. Just give me a minute to tidy it, okay?" He slipped inside, leaving the door open a crack and giving me a glimpse of yellow walls. *So not everything in the place is white.* I glanced across the hall at the closed door of his room. What would Cal's room be like? *You can find out,* a little voice said. *One quick turn of the knob before he comes back. Go ahead, take a peek,* it urged. I took three baby steps across the hall, close enough to reach the door, but just as I reached out my hand, Cal swung open the door of the smaller bedroom.

"Oh, hey," I said, my heart pounding, "you all done?"

"Yup." His smile looked strained; he had a bag tucked under one arm and seemed in a hurry to take it across the hall. "You go ahead and put your things in there. Let me just get this stuff out of the way."

The room was small but cozy, its yellow walls trimmed in white. A patchwork quilt done in bright primary colors covered the narrow bed. There was even a white throw pillow propped against the wooden headboard.

Then a thought pricked itself under my skin and lodged there like a splinter: *This room looks feminine.* Just how many guests did Cal entertain here?

"Bathroom's at the end of the hall, by the way. I left towels for you." Cal stood in the doorway but made no move to come into the room. The mood between us had shifted from a friendly warmth to a polite coolness. "So, y'all set?" he asked.

"Yes, thanks. And I appreciate this, Cal."

"Not at all. Good night, Victoria." He backed out, closing the door with a soft click.

"Good night," I said to the closed door. "And what was that about?"

After washing up and brushing my teeth, I crept back down the hallway, stopping at Cal's door. A sliver of light shone from underneath it; he was still awake. I lifted my hand to knock and then let it fall. What would I say? *Why do you have a yellow guest room tricked out with a homey quilt and curtains in the middle of this white refrigerator you call an apartment?* We didn't know each other well enough for that.

Back in "my" room, I settled under the covers and grabbed a paperback I kept in my bag for emergencies—my favorite Agatha Christie, *Sleeping Murder.* But I had trouble concentrating on the plight of the heroine, as my eyes were drawn to that closet door. I threw off the blanket and tiptoed across the room. I turned the knob as slowly as I could and pulled open the door to reveal . . . an empty closet with a deep shelf that was bare. *Turn off your writer's imagination, Vic, and go to sleep.* I looked around again. There was no dresser; there was no anything. Certainly no evidence of someone using this room on a permanent basis.

But there *was* one more place to look. I dropped to my knees to peek under the bed and spied a small, shadowy mass. Flat on my belly, I reached out my hand, straining to reach the object. My fingertips brushed something soft; I pinched the fabric with two fingers and pulled out a stuffed animal, a replica of the Velveteen Rabbit. I sat up and stroked its tiny head and stared into its button eyes.

"I wonder who it is you belong to," I said softly. "You look well used." *Real*, as the horse in the story explained.

I dropped the toy back under the bed, leaned back against the small white pillow, took in the yellow walls and white curtains. Despite its bare walls and empty closet, Cal hadn't succeeded in wiping every trace from this room. And this was not a room decorated for a woman, but for a little girl.

There was really only one logical conclusion: Cal Lockhart had a child.

Chapter Seven

Cal and I were both quiet on the ride back to Oceanside Park the next morning. Did he regret inviting me to his home? The yellow room rose in my memory—a nearly empty yellow room with little in it but a child's toy. From the corner of my eye, I glimpsed his serious expression. His hair was still wet from the shower, tucked behind his ears. He wore it a little long, giving him a youthful air, in pleasing contrast to the lines around his eyes. What could I learn from his face that I couldn't from Cal? There was humor there, and warmth. Loyalty to those he cared about. A trace of loss and sadness. But something else, too. A wariness that said *don't get too close*. Unthinking, I shook my head.

"What?" Cal asked.

"Oh," I said. "Just going over everything I have to do today. Wondering if I've got power in the cottage. Hoping my dad's generator holds out."

"You expected at the restaurant?"

"What do you think? I'm on lunch service, though, so maybe I can get some writing in later today."

"How's the new book comin'?"

"Well, I've gotten Isabella to America. She's looking for work at the moment. But she hasn't met Tomasso yet."

"Who's Tomasso?"

"*Who's Tomasso?* you ask! Only the love of her life. A blue-eyed boy that she'll fall in love with at first sight."

"Sounds romantic," he said wryly. "But I'm not sure about those things in real life."

"What, love at first sight? Italians even have a name for it: *un culpo de fulmine*. The lightning strike. One look and boom, it's all over."

"*Un culpo de fulmine*, huh? I kinda like that."

"Hey, your accent's not bad."

"You forget my mama's half Italian."

At this opening, I decided to plunge in. "Are your parents still living?"

"My mom's still in Louisiana. My father died when I was in high school."

"Oh, sorry. That's a tough age to lose somebody."

He shrugged. "He wasn't the best guy. Mama and I did all right on our own." He turned his attention to the road, and it was clear I wouldn't learn anything else.

But my questions nagged at me: *How did you meet your wife? Why did you break up? Why do you live like a monk, without a picture or a knickknack? Do you have any children? And if not, who belongs to the Velveteen Rabbit?*

But we were turning onto Ocean Avenue, and even if I'd gotten the courage to ask, I was nearly home. We were just past the restaurant when I had a thought.

"Hey, Cal? Do you mind dropping me on the next corner—right there at the boardwalk ramp? I'd like to check out the damage and see what's going on."

He frowned. "You sure? It's a long walk to your cottage from here."

"I'm used to it. I can walk off all that pancetta I ate last night." He pulled over and I gathered my things. Maybe Cal *was* holding himself back from me, but despite his own fear and misgivings, the guy had driven in a hurricane to save my computer and put me up for the night. I kissed him on the cheek and thanked him again.

"My pleasure, *cher*," he said. "Any time you need rescuin' you give me a call."

"You got it." I slung the bag over my shoulder and closed the truck door. "You're not coming in to the restaurant to work today, are you?"

"Nope," he called through the window. "Saturday's my day off."

And what do you do on your days off, Mr. Lockhart? I thought as he drove away. Just one more question to which I didn't have an answer.

Out on Ocean Avenue, the public works guys were already picking up branches and debris from the storm. I strolled the nearly empty boardwalk, noting a few brave souls out on the beach. The water was likely to be rough, and probably cold, but that wouldn't deter a weekender who was determined to squeeze out some vacation time, storm or no storm. It was, in fact, a perfect beach day: The sun was shining and there were only the gentlest of breezes blowing across the sand.

But once those beachgoers wanted to eat lunch or take their kids on a boardwalk ride, that was where their fun would end. The entire eastern end of Oceanside Park was still without power, including the rides pier. Those with food stands were already packing up or throwing away their perishable stock. The T-shirt stores and souvenir shops had their metal gates down. The arcade was dark;

inside, people milled about sweeping debris and wiping down the machines. Two men wearing green sanitation uniforms and matching caps stood outside, leaning on their brooms and talking. The taller of the two said something in the shorter man's ear, who threw back his head and laughed so hard his gold tooth glinted in the sunlight.

"I'm glad they're amused," I muttered to myself. "God knows what there is to laugh about today."

I kept heading east, toward my cottage and the rides pier. At one point, the red beach trolley chugged past me, and I waved to the driver. The trolley up and running was a good sign, even if there weren't any passengers at the moment. In the distance I could see the roof of the carousel house and the top of the Ferris wheel, unmoving.

As I got closer, I saw the yellow police tape around the carousel house, an elaborate nineteenth-century structure, its copper roof now an oxidized green. The building's circular form was decorated with small windows framed in neoclassical designs of vines and leaves. Over each window was a mythical face, whose stark expressions frightened me as a child. It was jarring to see that tape. The carousel house wasn't a place for death; it was a place of magic and history. And it struck me that Mayor McCrae would now have a perfect excuse to sell the carousel. Who would bring their children to a place where a man had died?

I walked over to where my brother and a few other cops were milling around. He stepped away from them, his face grim. Possibly he wasn't thrilled that I was here.

I pointed to the tape. "Does that mean it's a crime scene?"

"No, it means nosy people should keep out."

"C'mon, Danny—spill. Do they think Pete's death is suspicious or not?"

"You know the answer to that, sis. We won't know anything until—"

"The autopsy results come in," I said. "Right. I know the drill. But that doesn't mean that you boys in blue might not have some theories."

"Vic, he was a drunk. He was elderly and unsteady on his feet even when he was sober. There's nothing to suggest that his death was anything but an accident."

"So, what do *you* think happened to him, Detective?"

"I think he drank too much and passed out, and either hit his head or drowned in shallow water. Hey, he might have had a heart attack, for all we know."

"But what was he doing here in the first place?"

"Probably for shelter. Somewhere to get out of the storm." He crossed his arms and narrowed his eyes at me. "Don't you have a book to write or something?"

I held up my hands in surrender. "I'm going. I need to check on the cottage anyway. I had some water in the basement. Hey, is Sofia in the studio today?"

Danny pushed his cap back and stuck his face close to mine. "Why? What do you need Sofia for?"

"Geez, can't a girl visit her sister-in-law without inviting suspicion? I want to let her know about the water in the basement of the cottage."

Danny smirked in a way that had annoyed me since I was eight and he was eleven. "Right," he said. "And Pop's horse is gonna come in at Monmouth later today."

"Stranger things have happened, brother," I called over my shoulder. I took a last look at the carousel house. Too bad I couldn't get in there to look around. But what would I expect to find that the police hadn't? Any evidence was already bagged, noted, and safely stowed away at the station. *Stop spinning tales, Vic,* I told myself. *Or at least save them for your books*. Poor Stinky Pete shouldn't have been out in that storm, period, and his death was likely an accident.

In another ten minutes I was at my cottage, where the first thing I did was throw open the windows for some sea air. While I never minded the musty smell of the shore, it was on the strong side this morning, and there were still a couple of inches of water in my basement. But sitting in a dry corner was a shiny new sump pump; taped to its side was a note in my dad's handwriting: *Who loves ya, baby?* I smiled at the thought of my ever-optimistic dad buying me a sump pump I couldn't use without electricity. But I guess it was the thought that counted.

Luckily, my stove and hot water were fueled by gas. I'd have warm showers and I could heat restaurant leftovers, assuming that old generator would hold out and the restaurant could still serve food. If I charged my laptop at the Casa Lido, I'd have a couple of hours of writing time when I came home. *I can deal with this,* I thought, *as long as I can blow-dry my hair somewhere.*

After a quick shower (thank you, natural gas) I hopped on the beat-up Schwinn I used to get around town. I wasn't the best of bike riders anyway, and the weight of my laptop in the basket made it hard to balance. Making my wobbly way down Ocean Avenue, I waved to store owners as they cleaned up their sidewalks. I stopped at the Seaside Apothecary, where Iris had put a WE'RE STILL OPEN sign in her window. The old-fashioned bell over the door tinkled when I pushed it open.

Iris, in skinny jeans and a white T-shirt, stepped out from behind the counter with a smile. "Hey, Victoria."

"Hi, Iris." I motioned to the dry floor and neatly stacked

shelves. "Looks like you did okay in the storm. The store looks perfect."

She nodded. "I was lucky. The basement's a little damp, and that's it. Of course, without power I don't have my register, but I can still do cash transactions." She held up an old cigar box with a grin.

"I hope you get customers. This whole end of the street is without power, and we need to get it back before next weekend."

"I can't believe Labor Day is around the corner," she said. "But you're right. A lot of us do our best business Labor Day weekend." She pointed out the window. "It's the boardwalk stands who will be hurt the most, I think. But at least the Casa Lido managed to celebrate its anniversary."

"Nonna wouldn't have it any other way, storm or no storm. And thanks for coming last night, and for sticking around in all the craziness." I looked her up and down. "Gosh, you look great. I'm still getting used to this new look of yours."

She dipped her head modestly. "Thanks. And we had a lovely time. The food was amazing, as always. Richard was very impressed." With the mention of Richard Barone, Iris's face glowed.

"He's quite the dish, by the way," I said. "That Italian charm will get you every time."

"I do like him," she said in a tone that gave it all away. It was clear she had it bad, and I hoped that Richard felt the same way about her.

"How long have you been seeing him?"

"Just a couple of months. His divorce is fairly recent, so we're taking it slow."

He is, at least. "That's good," I said. "I imagine his foundation takes a lot of his time."

"Yes, unfortunately. But his family's been in the shore area for generations, and he really cares about the communities down here. In fact, he's in the office today, generating help for storm cleanup and putting the pressure on the power company to get us back online."

I held up both hands with crossed fingers. "May he be successful. Well, my friend, I have to hit it. I want to stop at Sofia's before I go down to the restaurant. And I'll tell everybody you're still open."

"Wait, before you go," she said, "you heard about poor Stinky Pete, right?"

"I did. Danny stopped back at the restaurant to tell us. Nonna was friendly with him."

Iris shook her head. "It's such a shame. I felt so sorry for him when he came into the party. But your grandmother took care of things nicely."

"She's good at taking care of things," I said as I turned to go. "Bye, Iris."

"Bye, Victoria! See you soon."

It wasn't until I was pedaling away that I had the sinking realization that yet again, someone had left the Casa Lido and ended up dead.

Sofia's dance studio was another business along Ocean Avenue that seemed to be prospering despite the lack of power. There was a class going on when I got there, and it was a pleasure to watch Sofia, ever graceful despite her baby bump, execute *pliés* and *pas de chat*. Afterward we sat in her office, which twice now had served as our base of sleuthing operations.

"So, are you here to report, SIL?" she asked, using our personal abbreviation for *sister-in-law*.

Had she spoken to Danny? Did she know I'd already been up to the boardwalk? "About . . . ?" I asked.

"Your night with Mr. Down on the Bayou, of course. Tell me everything." She dropped her voice suggestively. "And I do mean *everything*."

"There's not much to tell. Well, actually there is." I gave her a description of Cal's place, right down to the yellow "guest room" and what I found there.

Sofia sat straight up in her desk chair. "Wow. You think he's got a kid?"

"Quite possibly. But I suppose the bunny could belong to a niece or nephew, though he's never mentioned any siblings."

"Or it could belong to the child of somebody he dated," she said with a knowing look.

I winced a little at that one. "I hadn't thought of that," I said. "But I can tell you this, Sofe. Until I know more about Cal and his past, I don't plan to get any more deeply involved with him."

One side of her mouth lifted in a grin. "And by *getting more deeply involved*, you mean . . ."

"You know exactly what I mean, lady."

"I guess I do. But I also know you have trouble resisting his charms. But enough talk about pleasure—we need to move on to business. What do you think about Stinky Pete?"

"What about him?" I toyed with the paper clips on Sofia's desk, organizing them in little piles by color.

She swept the clips into a container and held out her palm for the one I was holding. "Give it here. Now answer my question."

I sighed. "Well, God rest his soul, as Nonna would say. But what I think is immaterial. Your husband is convinced it's an accident, and it probably is."

"I think that's the consensus," she said. "Have you seen this?" She turned her computer screen for me to see.

Nina LaGuardia, my favorite local news anchor, appeared on the screen as blond, bland, and perfectly coiffed as always. "Thus far there's only been one known fatality from the storm," she was saying into a huge mike, carefully angled so as not to block her face. "Mr. Peter Petrocelli of Oceanside Park was found in the carousel house behind me, dead of an apparent drowning. His death is currently under investigation. In other storm news, power is still out in a number of towns along the shore . . ."

Sofia hit PAUSE and leaned across the desk, her dark eyes gleaming. "What was Pete doing out there? Seriously: the carousel house? For what possible reason?"

"Shelter, I guess. That's what Danny thinks."

She shook her head. "Think about it. Homeless people have places they normally shelter in bad weather. Why wouldn't he have gone to one of those?"

"We don't even know what his usual places were. What if the carousel house was somewhere he normally went?"

"During the season, that rides pier is open until eleven every night. If Pete had tried to flop in any of those places, he would have been kicked out. And after it closes, that carousel house is locked up tight." She grinned. "I know this because we tried to sneak in there once in high school."

"Of course you did, you scamp. So you think someone asked Pete to meet him or her there?"

"I think it's possible. It's a long walk from the restaurant to that rides pier, and there must have been places along the way he could have taken shelter." She looked up at me, and it was clear that we had the same thought. "Field trip!" she called, and scrambled up from her chair.

We stood outside her studio on the sidewalk, taking turns looking up and down the block. We knew the center of town by heart, and it wasn't hard to name some of the places Pete might have stopped. Sofia pointed west. "Okay, the restaurant is about six blocks that way. But we can assume he didn't try to duck in anywhere near the restaurant, right?"

"We shouldn't rule anything out, but it's not likely. Our awnings were closed and the hurricane screens were pulled down. There's an overhang over the kitchen door out back, but we would have seen him there and shooed him away. And if he'd gotten inside, someone would have seen him."

"Do you know what time he left?"

A good question. What time had Pete made his appearance at the party and how long had he stayed? "We were still out in the garden when he showed up," I said, frowning from the bright sun and the effort to concentrate. "I remember we were clearing the antipasto plates. We started a little after four, served cocktails and canapés until about five. We took our time with the antipasto, so it was probably after six when he showed up. He was out there only a couple of minutes before Nonna whisked him away. It took her a few minutes to get some food for him, so maybe it was six thirty or so when he left. I watched him round the corner of the building before I went back to work."

"Dang," Sofia said. "We should've brought paper to start a timeline. Assuming he left the restaurant at six thirty, he would have gone somewhere to eat the dinner Nonna gave him."

"It wasn't raining yet, but it was windy. I don't think he would have gone up to the beach," I said. "But he could have plopped down anywhere to eat. One of the benches along the sidewalk or even one of the side streets. I guess it would be too convenient to find one of our specially marked food containers right where Pete left it, huh?"

"No such luck." Sofia pointed to the busy, sweeping figures all around us. "If he left anything to show where he'd been, it's cleaned up by now." She shook her head. "Wish we knew the time of death."

"Well, we can at least estimate the time of discovery of the body. The party was scheduled from four to nine. Do you remember when Danny got his call to go out?"

"I think it was about eight thirty or eight forty."

"That sounds right. I remember he was worried about the lights going out, and my dad had been fiddling with the generator. I think the lights went out close to nine."

"That's easy to check," Sofia said. "It's public record. At least we have that to go on. I think Danny came back to tell us about Pete sometime between nine thirty and ten. I can check that with him."

"Must you? He's already lectured me once about minding my own business."

"When?"

"Um, today, down at the carousel house. I stopped on the way to my cottage and the police were there, milling around."

She curled her lip in disgust. "And you tried to play this off like you think it was an accident. Your first free minute you're up on the boards snooping around."

"Okay, you got me. But back to the matter at hand—assuming Pete's body was found at nine thirty or so, what were his movements in those three hours? Did he speak to anybody?"

"Wait, Vic—I just had a thought. If the power went out around nine, that means the carousel house would have cleared out immediately. It would have to. Imagine the craziness if that merry-go-round was in motion and everything goes dark? There'd be a panic to get your kids and get out of there, right?"

"Hang on—that actually happened once during a bad storm in Seaside when my mom was growing up. The power went out in one of the arcades and kids were on the merry-go-round. It was this really famous story. Now I remember. After that, Oceanside Park put restrictions in place. At the first sign of a storm, the pier shuts down. You wouldn't want a bunch of people on the Ferris wheel with no way to get them down, would you? Again, Danny would know if they shut the pier down last night and when. But you've got me thinking: What if Pete was already in there when they closed up?"

"It's possible. But then why he was down there in the first place? And if someone killed him, how did the person get into the carousel house if it was locked? And there's another question we need to consider, Vic: Who would want him dead?"

"And why?" I added. "Why would anybody want to kill an elderly, homeless alcoholic?"

It wasn't until I was pedaling back to the restaurant that the answer to that question arrived in the form of Stinky Pete's own words to me not so long ago: *I have stories to tell.*

Chapter Eight

Saturdays during the summer season kept us running: figuratively, as in business is brisk, but also literally, as in sore feet and no time to breathe. And on this particular Saturday, there were already people lined up on the sidewalk outside, some of them carrying computers. I slipped in through the back, where I found my mom and dad going over the lunch menu.

"Hey, guys, what's with that line outside?"

"Oh, hi, honey," my mom said without looking up. "There are lots of people without power and some of them had to throw food away, so I think we'll have a busier day than usual."

"Yeah," my dad added, "and since we got power, I let people know they can charge their phones and computers here."

"Too bad we can't run an extension cord down to my cottage so I can pump that water out of the basement," I said.

My dad looked up with a grin. "So you got my present?"

"I did, thank you. Maybe one of these days I can use it."

"That power will be back on before you know it," my dad said.

"I hope so. In the meantime, I could use a working outlet." I hefted my computer from my bag. "Okay if I put this in your office, Mom?"

"Sure, hon. And then would you go help Nando finish prepping? We're doing a limited cold menu for lunch." She glanced at her watch. "We'll be opening our doors in less than a half hour."

And once those doors opened, I had very little time to contemplate whether Stinky Pete had been murdered or not. I was far too busy shuttling between the kitchen and tables of hungry customers, some of them working on laptops between bites. As long as my dad's generator was humming, our dining room would be full.

Between my late night and today's hectic lunch service, I was hazy and tired by the end of my shift. The minute I was done, I poured myself a double espresso. Grabbing a biscotti from Nonna's secret stash, I backed in through the kitchen doors to find a quiet spot to eat it. Nando had gone, and Tim was just arriving to start the sauces for dinner. I took a seat well out of his way but one that gave me a view of his work. (Not to mention his broad shoulders and well-muscled arms.)

"Hey," he said, buttoning his chef coat, "how'd lunch go?"

"Busy. People are kind of congregating here, which is nice, but I'm shot. This is the first I'm sitting down all day," I said with a yawn, and took a fortifying sip of my coffee. "You'll be hopping tonight, I think. And Chef Massi's not coming in, is he?"

At that, Tim stood taller, lifted his nose in the air, and tossed his head in imitation of our temperamental head chef. "I find I no longer wish to work on the week*ends*," he said with an Italian accent.

"Ha! Don't let him hear you imitating him—he'll have your head."

Tim grinned at me over his shoulder. "Or some other vital parts."

"True. Listen, I've got the onion and garlic prepped for you in the bins. They're in the walk-in fridge." I dunked my biscotti once—one must not oversoak them—and savored the coffee flavor.

"Thanks," Tim said as he readied two stock pots. "So I guess your dad's generator is keeping us going. Hey, did you have any water in your cottage last night?"

"Some, but Frankie left me a sump pump as a gift. Not that I can use it without power."

Tim appeared to be studying the pots as he asked me the next question. "Did you stay there last night?"

"I did not, as it happened. Not that it—"

"Is any of my business. I know." He strode past me to the refrigerator and came back bearing the onions and garlic I had so lovingly prepped. He held them up to me. "Good job, by the way. Your knife skills are getting there."

"Thanks," I said, feeling a rush of warmth that had little to do with the hot coffee or the August afternoon. "When are you going to teach me to make fresh pasta?"

"All in good time, lass. All in good time."

"So let me ask you, Tim—does Lacey find that Irish brogue of yours charming?"

"Lacey finds everything of mine charming."

"I guess I set myself up for that one. Did she have a nice time last night?" As I asked the question, I flashed on the image of Tim toweling her hair. *Do not go there,* my subconscious warned me.

"She did. We didn't have much time to spend together,

though." He shook his head. "My hours here are long. I gotta say, it's kind of an issue with us."

I tried to ignore the tiny lift of my heart at the mention of even the merest hint of conflict between Tim and Lacey. But I tried to be gracious. "It's always hard in the beginning of relationships. But she's a wedding planner; she must work her share of nights, too."

"Not as many as I do. I mean, you know what it's like, restaurant work. You grew up here." His expression softened and he smiled. "Geez, I remember you in a ponytail following me around when I bused tables."

"Must I remind you of the rules, Tim? There Shall Be No Reminiscing." But I couldn't help smiling at the memory of my thirteen-year-old self, crushing on a gangly, curly-haired busboy.

"I remember the rules, Vic. Believe me. But we can't unwrite our history." His words were an echo of my own thoughts. He set the flame going under both pots, and we were both quiet as he waited for them to heat up.

"Now, that's a surprisingly elegant turn of phrase there, mister," I finally said.

He turned to me with a grin. "And you think you're the only writer around here."

"Speaking of which," I said as I stood up. "I've got to grab my computer and get home and do some work. I've got a ton of research I need to do." I cleared the crumbs from the worktable and set my cup in the dishwasher.

Tim laid a hand on my arm. "Research for your book, right? Not any *other* kind."

"Yes, for my book." I gently removed his hand. "Why would you think otherwise?"

"C'mon. Tell me your wheels haven't been spinning since we found out about Stinky Pete."

"Maybe a little. I mean, I can't figure out what he would have been doing in the carousel house, though. And why would anybody want to kill him? Then again—"

"Enough!" Tim held up both palms. "The guy was drunk and probably fell facedown onto a flooded floor. Please, we've been through this twice. Do you really want to put yourself in danger *again*?"

"I'm not in any danger! I'm just curious. And what do you care anyway?" I shoved in the chair a bit more forcefully than necessary.

"I'll always care about what happens to you, Vic."

My anger dissipating, I rested my hand on his shoulder and gave him a quick kiss on the cheek. "Same here, Tim."

I *would* always care about Tim. But was that a good or a bad thing? I honestly didn't know.

By the time I sat down at my desk (I was back upstairs now, taking no chances), I was nearly convinced that Tim and Danny were right about Pete's death. That his *I have stories to tell* was nothing more than the ramblings of an old man. Sofia was always too quick to jump on the Murder Bandwagon, and I was too ready to climb right up there beside her. *Nope,* I thought, *it's time to get to work and forget about Pete's death.*

I opened the folder containing my handwritten notes for my historical novel. Set in the nineteenth century, it featured a character named Isabella Rossi, loosely based on my great-grandmother. Isabella was an Italian immigrant who had landed in New York City as a young woman, but that was about as far as I'd gotten her. Eventually, she'd get down to the Jersey shore and into the food business—hence my work at the restaurant—but both my heroine and I had a long way to go. As I sifted through the papers, I came across some scribbled pages from my waitress pad. On them were the notes from my conversation with Nonna about my mysterious great-uncle, Roberto Rienzi:

- *14–15 years older than Grandpa*
- *died in Italy/no information about death? Documentation?*
- *friends with Alfonso Petrocelli, brother of Stinky Pete*
- *"got in with criminals" in Naples*
- *Did Pete mean that his "stories" were about his brother and Roberto?*

Here was Pete again, just when I thought I'd dismissed him from my mind. What might he have told me about my great-uncle? And I wasn't sure I'd get much more from my grandmother. I drummed my fingers on my desktop and stared at the blinking cursor on my computer screen. Maybe Nonna wouldn't talk, but Google was a font of information; I typed in "Roberto Rienzi."

Judging by the number of hits for his name, I had more Rienzi relatives than I'd anticipated. Facebook alone listed a number of (presumably alive) guys named Roberto Rienzi. But if Zio Roberto had died in Italy, it didn't make sense to search for him within the United States. I added "Naples" and "deceased" to the search, but after several minutes of scrolling through references in Italian, I gave up. I leafed through my notes again and spied the fictional family tree I'd created for my character of Isabella.

"Yes!" I said aloud. "That's it." I logged on to the first ancestry site that offered a free trial and typed in the registration info impatiently, my mind whirling with names and dates. I would concentrate on the Rienzi side, with my focus on Zio Roberto. Judging from what Nonna had said, my grandfather had only one sibling. That would make things easier. Or maybe not. I knew for a fact that my grandfather had immigrated here, so I would probably find him on this site. But if his older brother had died in Italy, shouldn't I be searching an Italian database? *Before I deal with translating pages,* I thought, *let me at least try*.

My grandfather Francesco Rienzi was well documented. I found census documents, voting records, his draft card, and an address in Oceanside Park, where he attended high school and met my grandmother in the fifties. But his brother, Roberto, was another story—one about which I was growing ever more curious. There were a number of men named Roberto Rienzi who'd lived in Naples, but few fit my uncle's profile; census documents that listed the people in my grandfather's family didn't show an older brother. I let out a loud sigh. This was turning into a waste of writing time. I gathered my notes in front of me, looking again at my bulleted questions, my eye drawn to one of the names: Stinky Pete's brother, my uncle's friend Alfonso Petrocelli. I made the birth year 1915, which was likely Roberto's as well, added Naples as a place he might have lived, and typed in *Pietro Petrocelli* as a family member.

There was a 1932 ship's manifest from Naples with an "Alfonso Petrocelli" among the passengers. I scanned the "R"s, just in case, squinting at the cramped handwritten lists: Raimondi, Reese, Reo, Rinaldi. No Rienzi.

Well, I would follow Alfonso's trail and see where it led. *Okay, Alfonso, you're about seventeen, probably on*

*your own in America. You pick a heck of a time to show
up, in the middle of the Great Depression. Jobs are scarce,
so how do you make your way?*

As I searched more and more documents for Alfonso's
name, my grandmother's words echoed: *"They got in with
criminals."* Might Alfonso have continued his life of petty
crime here? And that was when a 1940 census document
from Atlantic City popped up on the screen. Atlantic City
was home to all sorts of vices and all sorts of criminals,
especially in that era. *Okay, now we're cookin'.*

I clicked it open, my enthusiasm dampened by my conscience. *Why are you doing this, Vic? Is it research for your
book or for something else entirely?* Ignoring the questions, I read on. The list appeared to come from an apartment building, and the names were grouped by households.
By 1940, Alfonso would have been in his mid-twenties,
and there he was, along with another Alfonso, an older
man, and a Pietro, who was younger—Stinky Pete. At
some point, Alfonso must have brought his father and
younger brother to America. But there was one more
name attached to the Petrocelli household: Robert Riese.

Riese? Hang on a minute. I clicked back on the ship's
manifest, my excitement growing. An "R. Reese" had
traveled from Naples on the same ship as Alfonso. And
eight years later, there was a "Robert Riese" living with
them. My gut was telling me that *Robert Riese* was an
anglicized version of my great-uncle's name, and the same
"R. Reese" on that ship's manifest. The difference in the
two vowels could easily be a spelling or handwriting error.

If my gut was right, Roberto Rienzi didn't die back in
Naples, but in fact, ended up in America. And that raised
a looming question: What happened to him?

Chapter Nine

*B*ut Robert Riese was elusive. There was little besides the Atlantic City census information that pointed to a Robert Riese whose profile fit that of Roberto Rienzi. If that Riese was indeed our missing great-uncle, I had a whole raft of questions: Why did he change his name? Did he know that his younger brother had also immigrated here? Did he remain in Atlantic City? If so, that would have put him within forty or so miles of his only sibling, a brother who believed that Roberto was dead. Did Roberto fake his death in Italy to come here? Had Stinky Pete's brother, Alfonso, helped in that deception and how much had Pete known about it? And more to the point—was that information dangerous to somebody?

I let out a breath and stared at my computer screen. *You're getting way ahead of yourself, Vic,* I told myself. *You don't even know that Robert Riese is the person you're looking for.* Worse, I was getting distracted from my writing. Ostensibly, I was researching our long-lost Zio Roberto for that purpose, but his connection to Pete was dangling before my eyes like a bright shiny object, and I just couldn't look away. But with less than thirty minutes of power left on my laptop, I wouldn't get very far in my searches.

"Well," I said as I shut down my computer, "it's time to do this the old-fashioned way." I got back on my bike, and in less than fifteen minutes I'd arrived at my destination—the Oceanside Park Public Library.

When I got there, the place was humming. On the west side of town, the library still had power; every computer was occupied, with patrons lined up to wait their turns. One of the tables had been set up as a charging station for phones, laptops, and devices. On another, coffee and water was set out with a sign that said HELP YOURSELF. Library volunteers circulated to help and politely nudge people along. On the children's side, parents were leaving with arms full of books, perhaps to read by flashlight later on. Gale Spaulding, the library's director and our recent party guest, waved to me from behind the reference desk.

"I've never seen this place so busy," I said.

"Isn't it great?" she said, beaming.

"If you like chaos, I suppose. And I notice that every computer is taken."

"Sorry," Gale said. "But sign in, and we'll get you on when we can."

"Actually, Gale, can you point me to some books on Jersey shore history? I'm particularly interested in Atlantic City history, between the thirties and the fifties."

Her eyes grew bright behind her wire-framed glasses. "Is this for your book? For the new one, right, not the mysteries?"

"Yes, it's for the historical. And a little family research as well."

"Come right this way," Gale said. "We've actually got a display over here." She led me to a shelf of books and handed me a thick hardcover. "This one's fun. It's about famous murders along the shore."

On the cover was a mug shot of a smirking but dead-eyed killer, a lock of greasy hair across his forehead. "Well, isn't he attractive?" I said. "But he does look like he's from the period I'm interested in. Gale, is it okay if I grab a few of these and find a quiet place to read them?"

"Help yourself. If you'll excuse me, I have to get back to the desk."

Besides the book about murders, I took another about the history of Atlantic City and a third that focused on immigrant groups at the shore. I doubted I'd find Robert Riese in any of the indexes, but I could at least get a feel for the period. Since the only unoccupied place I could find was in the children's room, I squeezed into a small chair, feeling like an overgrown Goldilocks. But I forgot my discomfort quickly enough.

Apparently, the Jersey shore had been a hotbed of crime in its day, and the loathsome guy on the hard cover was only one example of some pretty heinous types. Thankfully, Robert Riese wasn't among them. Setting the murderers aside for a moment, I focused on the book about Atlantic City. Having only my grandmother's word on it, I was operating under the assumption that Alfonso and Robert/Roberto had carried their nefarious ways into their new country, but if they were small-time criminals, it wasn't likely their names would end up in the history books. Still, I turned to a chapter on mob activities with hope in my heart.

By the time of the 1940 census in which Alfonso and Robert Riese appeared, "America's Favorite Playground" was nearing the end of its glory days. Prohibition had ended in 1933, so the lucrative bootlegging that went on in the days of Nucky Johnson were long over. But depending upon when they arrived in Atlantic City, that didn't mean the two men might not have been involved in the tail end of it or in two of the city's other favorite pastimes—gambling and prostitution.

Johnson, of course, had been the big crime boss and was still famous enough to be the subject of a cable drama. But the pages devoted to Johnson had no mention of either men, and by 1941, Johnson was in prison. It was more likely that Alfonso and Roberto occupied the fringes of the Atlantic City underworld, making them that much more difficult to find. I sighed and looked at the wall clock; the library would be closing in less than a half hour. Flipping to the center section of the book, I leafed through pages of chronologically arranged photographs, stopping at those taken in the 1940s. Face after face looked the same—menacing, dark-haired, dark-eyed men wearing low-brimmed hats and blank expressions. I was about to give up when my eye was caught by a caption under a group shot:

Leo Barone, a small-time bootlegger who coexisted uneasily with Enoch "Nucky" Johnson, extended his influence to other criminal activities, notably gambling, after Prohibition ended. While not having the high profile of Johnson or later Atlantic City mobsters such as Skinny D'Amato, Barone wielded much influence in the Italian neighborhood of Ducktown in the late forties and early fifties. Shown here are Barone, Alfonse "Alfie" Petrocelli, and three other unidentified men. Barone died in 1958.

The name *Barone* seemed alive on the page, lifting itself from the very sentence it occupied. I stared at the image of the five men, goose bumps prickling up and down my arms. Who were the three unidentified men? Was one of them Robert Riese, aka Roberto Rienzi? The man identified as Alfonso looked to be in his early thirties; Roberto would be his age. I brought the book over to the window and held it up in the light for a better look.

In the grouping of three, the youngest man stood in the middle, wearing a fedora pushed back on his head. Unlike the others, he was grinning, cocky, and familiar. *So familiar.* There was no doubt in my mind that the man in the fedora was a Rienzi, from his crinkly-eyed smile to his taste in haberdashery. Because in the right light, I might have been looking at a picture of my father. Only he wasn't my father. I knew instinctively that this man was his long-lost, supposedly dead uncle—alive and well in Atlantic City, circa 1948.

Despite the warmth in the children's room, a chill traveled down my spine as the litany of names spelled themselves out in my head: Robert Riese and Roberto Rienzi. Alfonso and Peter Petrocelli. Leo Barone and Richard Barone. Barone was a common enough name, but there were only so many coincidences I was willing to accept. There was a trail here—a cold one, perhaps, but a trail all the same. And it led straight to Richard Barone.

I left the library clutching the three books like a lifeline, and wobbled down Ocean Avenue on my bike through the late-day shore traffic. Without even thinking about it, I headed back to the restaurant. They'd be busy, but I had to find my dad. I tore through the kitchen, ignoring

Tim's confused look, and headed straight for the basement, where I found my dad turning his wine bottles.

"Oh, you are down here! Good," I said breathlessly.

"Everything okay, baby?" He stood up and walked toward me, concern on his face.

"Yeah. I . . ." Some impulse made me duck the book behind my back. I'd come charging over here to show my dad the picture and pepper him with questions, but I hadn't thought it through. For one thing, he told my mother *everything*. And there was no way he'd keep something like this from Nonna, either. If they thought I was snooping into Pete's death, there'd be a hell to pay that even Dante wouldn't recognize. So I took my usual cowardly way out—I stalled for time. "So, how's the latest vintage?"

"Good, I think. People seemed to like it." He frowned as he looked at the racks. "I guess we went through more of my stock than I thought," he said. "Pretty soon I'll need to make another batch." He rubbed his hands together. "Hey, wanna help me, honey?"

"Sure, Dad," I lied. "One of these days." But it wasn't winemaking I needed to learn about; it was the mysterious Robert Riese. "So, listen, I've been doing some research for the new book, and there were some things I was wondering about."

"Sure, honey. What can I help you with?"

"Family stuff, mostly. Okay, so when Grandpa Francesco came over here, he was young, right?"

My father tilted his head and screwed up his face in thought. "It was near the end of World War Two, so I wanna say he was thirteen, fourteen, maybe."

"Do you know where he lived before they came to Oceanside?"

"Somewhere in south Jersey, I think. They had a farm down there and sold produce out of a truck."

"Actually, I remember hearing some of this," I said. "Because Nonna's family already had the restaurant, right? So that was probably how they came into contact with each other."

"Absolutely," my dad said. "Your great-grandpa and my dad delivered produce all over down here. Even to Atlantic City."

My hands tightened on the book. "Really? Atlantic City?"

He nodded. "There was a big Italian community down there—place called Ducktown. But a number of them restaurants were owned by some scary guys, if you know what I mean. After a while, my grandfather just stopped delivering to them. It wasn't worth the risk."

"Yeah, I've heard about Ducktown. And some of the, uh, colorful characters who lived there." *Just a few minutes ago, in fact.* Was it possible that my great-grandfather had crossed paths with the son he thought was dead? Still clutching the book in my now sweaty hand, I asked another question. "Dad, Nonna mentioned that Grandpa had an older brother, Roberto, who died back in Naples. What do you know about him?"

He leaned against the wine shelves, his arms crossed. "Well, I know he was much older than my pop and that he barely remembered him. He mighta been a bit of a wise guy back in the old country, because one day he just up and disappeared. They never talked about him. It was like they were ashamed of him."

"Nonna said the same thing. I just wish I knew more about him. For the book, I mean," I added hastily.

"Not much to know, babe," he said with a shrug. "It's ancient history."

Not so ancient as you think, Dad. "Okay. Well, if you think of anything else about Zio Roberto, let me know, okay?"

"You got it, sweetheart."

I was halfway up the stairs when I heard him call out to me, "Hang on a minute, Vic. There is one more thing. 'Member I said that they never talked about my uncle? Well, that's not completely true. My nonna once told me I looked just like Roberto." He turned to me with a wink. "Musta been a handsome guy, right?"

"I'm sure he was, Dad," I said, suppressing a shiver as I remembered the bold grin so like my father's. "I'm sure he was."

Chapter Ten

Isabella set the grocery sack down on the small table in the kitchen that was shared by three other women—her zia Concetta and her two cousins, Theresa and Lucia. As she was the first one home, it was up to her to begin la cena, or evening meal. As she carefully sliced the fresh bread, she ...

She ... thought about her day? Wondered if she'd ever get out of the garment factory? Cut her finger? I let out a loud sigh.

"What am I going to do with you, Isabella?" I said to the computer screen. "I've got to get you out of the city, out of the garment factory, and away from those awful cousins of yours so you can meet Tomasso and start your produce business. And I've got about forty minutes left on this battery."

I sat back against my plush desk chair, a small luxury I'd allowed myself since moving back to Oceanside. In the three months I'd been here, I hadn't completed nearly enough of the new book. Not to mention that my latest Bernardo Vitali mystery was releasing in little more than a week, and I had a ton of promotion to do. And all the while I had to stop my ears from the siren song of those three library books. I pushed them to the corner of my desk, willing myself not to look at that picture again, at the man I was certain was Zio Roberto.

I'd sat up last night with a flashlight, going back through the books for other mentions of the Barones or Petrocellis, to no avail. Now I only had a few precious minutes left on my computer battery, and I couldn't waste them on ancestry Web sites or Google searches of Leo Barone. In fact, I had a much better idea.

"Sofe," I whispered into the phone, "are you alone?"

"Yes, and why are you whispering?"

"Oh, sorry. I was worried Danny might be there."

"He's on duty till six."

"Great. That gives me plenty of time before I have to go to the restaurant at four. I have some stuff to fill you in on, and I'm heading over right after I take a shower. Oh, can I blow-dry my hair there?"

"Only if you let me do it. I've seen your version of style."

"Deal. See you in a few."

In less than a half hour I was at Sofia's door, hair dripping wet and a large messenger bag over my shoulder.

"What the heck have you got in here?" Sofia took the bag from me and set it down on her kitchen counter.

"Just a few things. Some books. A notebook. My computer and cord. My phone charger. My hair dryer. My shaver."

"Your shaver?"

"It's out of power. I was hoping I could charge it while we talk; you should see my legs. I look like Sasquatch Italian-style."

She held up her hand. "No, thanks. And I don't know why you don't get them waxed like normal people."

I grinned. "You mean like pretty Italian princesses.

Hey, wanna hear another shocker?" I dropped my voice. "I polish my own nails, too."

"Okay, stop giving me crap and tell me what you came over here for. But get in this chair first so I can fix that mess on your head."

Over the sound of the blow dryer, I told her about my Internet research and my trip to the library.

"So, do you think you can pick up with the family tree stuff?" I shouted. "I'll send you a link to the site and we can change the account over."

Sofia nodded and patted her slightly swelled belly. "I've got the perfect excuse." She widened her eyes in a semblance of innocence. "After all, my baby should know all about his heritage, right?"

"Or *her* heritage," I said, crossing my fingers in the air. "I'm still holding out for baby Isabella."

"And I'm still not naming this baby after one of your characters, so don't hold your breath. And sit still so I can finish this, please."

After I was smoothly styled, we sat at her table talking while we sipped decaf espressos.

"Vic," Sofia asked, "are you really convinced that this Riese guy is your great-uncle?"

Instead of answering, I opened the book about Atlantic City, found the photo section, and pointed. Sofia frowned and read the caption aloud, her eyes flicking back to the picture. Her mouth dropped open and she gave a little gasp. "Oh my God," she said. "It's your father. Right down to the hat."

I nodded. "It's eerie, isn't it? And when I asked him about his uncle, he said that his grandmother once told him he looked like Roberto."

She closed the book. "Well, you sold me. But if Roberto was in Atlantic City, he would have been within miles of his parents and younger brother." Sofia shook her head. "To think they believed he was dead and here he was, right in the same state."

"Maybe even the same city. My dad said my grandfather and his parents came here near the end of World War Two, so let's say 1944 or 1945. We know Roberto is already here from the ship's manifest and the 1940 census. The photo is dated 1948, so they definitely overlapped. But even if Roberto somehow knew his family was nearby, my gut's telling me he wanted to stay hidden."

"The name change," Sofia said. "He and Alfonso came over together, but Alfonso kept his Italian name, so why would Roberto have changed his? Unless he pissed off some seriously scary people back in Naples."

I nodded. "It makes sense. He gets in trouble there, so he changes his name and takes off for America, letting his whole family think he's dead."

"To protect them, I bet!" Sofia's voice rose in excitement. "The Italian Mafia—they were called the Black Hand, right? They didn't fool around; they'd go after people's families for revenge."

"Absolutely. That has to be why he took off. And don't forget, it was probably a lot easier to stay hidden in the 1940s, before computers and cell phones. He could blend right in with all the other Italian immigrants in Atlantic City."

"True. But he was still taking a chance."

"Look, the guy was reckless," I said. "He gets here and instead of looking for a legit job, he picks up right where he left off. As Nonna put it, *he got in with criminals*."

"The Barones," Sofia said, tapping the cover of the book. "We need to find out more about Leo Barone."

"It's Richard Barone I'm more interested in."

A wicked grin spread across my sister-in-law's face. "Watch it, or your friend Iris will scratch your eyes out."

"I didn't mean *interested* that way. Though he is a good-looking guy, and you're right: Iris is besotted with him."

Sofia's face was blank. "*Besotted*? Is that good?"

"Actually, no. It means you're so infatuated that your judgment's impaired."

"You mean like how Cher is over Nicolas Cage in *Moonstruck*?"

I laughed. "Something like that."

She raised an eyebrow. "Or how you were about Tim back in the day?"

This one wasn't so funny. "Okay, yes, I was *besotted* with Tim. But it's Iris I'm worried about."

"But what does it matter if she's crazy about Barone?"

"It matters if he's a bad guy."

Sofia pointed with her coffee cup. "All I've ever heard about him is that he's a *good* guy. If I'm following your logic, you think that Pete knew something about Leo Barone—through his brother, Alfonso—that threatened Richard in some way. Am I right?"

"Well, it's possible, isn't it? Barone was at the party. And he could be hiding something about his family's involvement with the mob."

"But what, Vic? He's made no bones about his relative's criminal activities; I read an interview with him once and he was honest about it. Talked about his family's 'unfortunate past' and how it inspired him to do charitable work."

"Even so, what if there was something he didn't want

coming out? Something that would be too serious and too big to overcome by throwing his money around?"

"Such as?"

"Well, that's the question, isn't it? I can't help wondering if Pete had incriminating information about the Barones. You saw that census record. Pete lived with his brother and Robert Riese in Atlantic City; he must have been privy to a lot of stuff."

"Maybe," Sofia said. "But without more to go on, it's a big leap to Richard Barone as a murderer. I just wish we knew more about Robert, Alfonso, and Leo Barone."

"Me, too, Sofe. But I suspect the one person who had that information is dead."

When I got to the Casa Lido later that afternoon, both the restaurant and my father's generator were up and running. Out in the dining room, Lori and Florence were putting clean linens on the tables.

"Hey, girls," I called. "Want me to make setups?"

"Please, hon," Florence said. "Everything's out and ready on the family table."

"So they've got all three of us on tonight," I said as I carefully folded our red-and-white-checked napkins into pockets for the forks and knives. I'd learned to do this as a little girl, and it was my only claim to fame at the Casa Lido.

"Yup," Lori said. "I think everyone in town with an electric stove is coming in for dinner."

"Ya'd think they'd never heard of a grill," Florence mumbled. "My feet can't take this."

"You can go early if it quiets down, Flo," I said. "I'll stay." I looked around the empty dining room. "Do we have any busboys coming in tonight?"

"Just Jason," Florence said. "For all the good he is."

"You really don't like him, do you?" Lori said, snapping a fresh cloth onto the last table.

She shrugged a skinny shoulder. "What's to like? He's just another rude teenager. Like that Alyssa—how come she gets the whole weekend off?"

From the corner of my eye I could see that Flo was still frowning at the thought of our sullen busboy and sorority girl waitress. But it struck me that what came across as Jason's rudeness might have been shyness or insecurity. Whatever it was, he'd better get here soon, or we'd be clearing our own tables tonight.

"Well, girls, these are all done," I said, getting up from the table. "But those veggies ain't gonna prep themselves. See you out here for service in an hour."

In the kitchen, Nando, our line cook, had gotten a start on the vegetables. I watched in wonder as he furiously chopped carrots, turning out perfectly even discs that were all the same size.

"You have mad knife skills, Nando."

He dipped his head and grinned, his knife still moving at double speed. "Thank you, Miss Victor."

"Nando, I've known you fifteen years—don't you think it's time you called me *Victoria*? Or *Vic*? I answer to both."

He shook his head, his long black braid moving from side to side. "I don't think so. It would be too . . . *extraño.*"

"Too strange? Like calling my grandmother by her first name instead of *senora*?"

"*Sì,*" he said, a wide grin on his round face. "Eh-zackly. Oh, she leave you her notes there."

"I'll bet she did." I tied my apron around my waist and pulled the yellow pad closer. Then I groaned. "I have to seed tomatoes? Is she kidding?"

"No, she's not," Tim said as he came in the back door. "It's for my tomato coulis."

"But it all goes in the blender, Tim."

"That doesn't mean I want seeds in it." He went over to the sink to begin the long process of washing up to his elbows. I'd say this for the guy—he ran a clean kitchen.

"Okay," I muttered. "Seeding tomatoes is the first order of the day."

"Nope," Tim said. He dried his hands and pointed to a basket of garden tomatoes. "Blanching and peeling them is."

"It's gonna take me forever," I said, filling a stock pot with water. The tomatoes had to be gently dropped into boiling water, and then shocked in ice water before they could be peeled. And I couldn't do too many at once, so I'd be stuck back here for at least an hour. But maybe it wouldn't be such a waste of time after all. I set the heat on under the pot and covered it, thinking about how to broach the subject that was uppermost in my mind. I filled a bowl with water and ice, trying to keep my tone casual.

"So, that was quite the party on Friday night, huh, guys?"

The only responses were a Spanish-inflected *uh-huh* followed by a grunt I recognized as Tim's. I tried again. "It's great that Frankie's generator is working. It sure kept us going the other night."

"Still is," Tim said. "That water boiling yet, Vic?"

Of course it wasn't, and if Tim thought he was going to distract me, he was dead wrong. "Uh, not yet. So, what did you guys think of Stinky Pete showing up like that? Crazy, huh?"

"God rest his soul," Nando said, shaking his head.

"Yeah, the poor guy," I said. "Hey, did either of you talk to him that night?"

"I jus' tell him he has to go," Nando said with a shrug.

"When was that, Nando?" I asked.

"After your grandmother give him the food. He was still hanging around."

For how long? But before I could ask, Tim was at my shoulder. "Cut it out, Vic," he said in a low voice. "I know what you're doing."

"I don't know what you're talking about," I said.

"Please," he said, shaking his head. "Listen, I need some sun-dried tomatoes."

"In the pantry," I said, knowing he expected me to happily fetch them for him. But I merely pointed the way.

Tim was barely out of the kitchen before I pounced. "So, Nando, did you actually see Pete leave?"

He nodded. "Yes. I see him pass me with the two bags and then he walk toward the boards."

"The boardwalk, you mean? Hang on—did you say *two* bags?"

"*Sì*, two bags. A white plastic one that has the food in it, and another brown one that has the, you know—" He curled his hand into a fist, lifting it as though holding something.

"You mean handles? Like a shopping bag?"

He nodded, grinning. "Yes, *handles.*"

"Did it look like it was heavy?" I asked.

He tilted his head, as though remembering. "I think so. He was walking like this," he said, listing to one side.

"Thanks, Nando," I said, and put a finger to my lips as Tim pushed through the doors. I turned my attention back to the tomatoes, as the water was now boiling. My mind spun as I watched the tomatoes simmer in their hot bath. When I'd seen Pete round the corner of the restaurant, he was only holding the food container—at least that was how it appeared from a distance. When — and where — had he gotten the other bag? More to the point, *who* gave it to him? There had to have been wine in that bag, probably more than one bottle, if he struggled with it — it was the most logical assumption. And whoever had given him that wine had surely contributed to his death. *Please, God, don't let it have been my dad.*

I ladled the tomatoes out of the boiling water and shifted them into the ice, their skins now a bright orange red. I worked mechanically, my mind scurrying from one point to the next, always returning to the same place: If Pete had two bags, one of them heavy, somebody at the party had given him the means to his death. Was it a careless act of intended kindness, or something much more sinister? When Pete said he knew things, were those words the rambling of an incoherent drunk, or did they hold real significance? I shook my head and put the last of the tomatoes into the ice water to cool. And then a thought took hold of me, wrapping itself around me like the tough old grapevines in the garden.

"I'll be right back, guys," I said, and raced out the back door. In the parking lot, I tried to retrace Pete's steps as I remembered them, rounding the corner to the front of the restaurant. I stood with my hands on my hips, studying our striped awnings and gold-lettered sign.

Where had Pete gone? Had he doubled back, and had that been when someone supplied him with the wine? My eye strayed to the alley that separated our building from the hair salon next door. Trash and debris from the storm made it hard to navigate the narrow space, and I picked my way through it slowly. On our side was a door that led to our basement, but it was one we rarely used. I jiggled the knob, finding it locked as I expected. Past the door, the alleyway narrowed and darkened, with climbing plants covering the brick exteriors. I stood against the wall of our building and slid down, my legs bent in front of me. Plenty of room for someone to sit. Plenty of room for someone desperate for a drink to stop and have one. And it had the added benefit of keeping him out of the wind. I hugged my knees, my chin resting on my crossed arms, staring at the assortment of trash all around me. Even in the dim light, I noticed a splash of red near the other building. It wasn't blood, but the sight of it set my heart racing anyway.

I crossed the alley, dropped to my knees, saw the glint of glass half-hidden by a piece of torn cardboard. I lifted it and stared at the object I'd known was there all along. Resting on a wet and dirty red-and-white-checked napkin was a wine bottle that bore a familiar label: Frank's Thursday Chianti.

Chapter Eleven

I got up stiffly and brushed the dirt and grit from my black pants, surveying the scene. Except for the doorknob, I hadn't touched or moved a thing. That bottle was evidence, as was the napkin. The bottle alone was damning enough, but if there was any doubt where it came from, that checked napkin dispelled it. I dropped my head in my hands. I knew what I had to do, and it meant involving the restaurant in Pete's death, and possibly incriminating my father. My doting, charming, life-loving dad, who'd never intentionally hurt a soul. I lifted my face, hoping that by some act of fate the bottle had disappeared. But fate wasn't on my side today, and that bottle and dirty napkin stared back at me in reproach. I took my phone out of my apron pocket and called my brother, knowing exactly what I was setting in motion.

As the uncooperative Fates would have it, the Oceanside PD showed up at exactly the moment my dad's silver Lexus pulled into the parking lot. My mom got out first, holding the door for my grandmother. My father followed, and all three stood rooted to the pavement when they spotted the police cars. I ran to meet them.

"It's okay, guys," I said. "No one's hurt, I promise."

My mother's face drained of color, with only two bright spots of blush on her cheeks. "Honey, why are they here?"

"I found something in the alley and I thought—"

"That's enough, Vic," Danny said. "They might have to make formal statements." His eyes were apologetic, but his expression was grim. "So please don't say anything else." He led them back to the restaurant, but all three of their faces were turned my way—my mother's a study in concern, my dad's full of confusion, and in my grandmother's, a fury so cold I needed a sweater. I followed them back inside at a respectable distance and watched as my brother took my dad aside. Danny's look was serious, questioning. My dad's eyes widened and he shook his head vehemently. I could guess the conversation: *Pop, did you give Pete a bottle of wine? Absolutely not, son, no way.*

But somebody at the party had handed Stinky Pete at least one bottle of wine with a napkin from the dining room. Someone who either knew where the wine was kept or made a good guess at it. But I kept those thoughts to myself when the officers had questioned me, providing only the information for which they'd asked, and no more. Danny, of course, was not part of the investigation—it would be a conflict of interest for him. But he stood on the sidelines, arms crossed, his mouth a tight line of discontent. When I caught his eye, he nodded, his only gesture of encouragement, and a glance that said, *It's okay, sis, but I'm still not happy*.

In the end, the police didn't talk to any of us. They milled about outside while I watched the clock anxiously. Dinner service was scheduled to start at five thirty, and police or no police, my grandmother would make sure the food got out on time. And judging from the line of patrons forming outside our doors, even the presence of two police cruisers didn't dissuade the hungry and powerless, many of whom were carrying their phone chargers and computers.

But they parted easily for my brother, who beckoned me from the doorway. "Listen, sis, you were right to call. And we confiscated the bottle. But I don't think this is going anywhere. So Pop doesn't have to worry and neither do you," he said, emphasizing that last word.

"But, Danny, I think somebody wanted Pete drunk enough to hurt himself or maybe worse—"

He held up a warning hand. "Enough," he said softly. "And be glad Pop's not getting dragged into this." He left through the kitchen, and soon after, we opened our doors to the crowd outside.

After that, the work never let up. Jason called in sick at the last minute, so we had no busboy, causing Flo to grumble long and loud about selfish kids who only thought about themselves. But I was happy to lose myself in the tasks of talking about the specials, taking orders, and serving people who couldn't cook for themselves. From time to time I'd glance over at the rest of the waitstaff, wondering if they were mentally calling me names, with Tattletale and Goody Two-shoes among the kindest. If I'd had even a second to myself during dinner service, I'd have called Sofia, the one person I knew would wholeheartedly support me. Though Lori seemed sympathetic, she had trouble meeting my eye, and I was feeling more foolish by the minute. My parents were thankfully busy out at the bar, and unsure what he might say to me, I stayed away from Tim. Between tables, I busied myself at the coffee station, readying the cappuccino maker and filling the hot water carafe for tea. Flo appeared at my elbow.

"That tea water hot yet?" she said without looking at me.

"I just filled it; probably a couple of minutes, Flo."

"That's just great," she said, letting out a loud huff. "I got a nasty customer back there who don't want to wait."

We stood in silence while the water heated; when it was finally ready, Flo took a cup with shaking hands. Hot water spilled into the saucer and she let out a curse that would have gotten her fired if my grandmother had been in earshot.

"Are you okay?" I asked her.

"Oh, I'm just ducky," she hissed. "The place is crawling with cops; I run my ass off for crappy tips in a place where I have to bus my own tables, and people have a habit of dropping dead when they leave." She set the teacup on her tray and turned to me, her hostility washing over me like an ocean wave. "In fact, I don't need this. I don't need any of this. Consider this my notice, Victoria. After tonight I'm done with the Casa Lido, so take me off the damn schedule."

She pointed her finger at me, and I noticed her chipped nail polish and bitten cuticles. "And while you're at it, you can say buh-bye to that crazy grandmother of yours for me." She narrowed her eyes at me, malice written all over her heavily made-up face. "By the way," she said, "when I was in high school, we had a name for people like you: *narc*. Maybe you've heard of it."

I cringed as though she'd hit me, but before I could answer, she stalked away, hiking up her skirt as she went. So now we were down a waitress, and that was my fault, too.

I better tell Mom and Dad now, I thought as I headed back to the office. *Let them tell my so-called crazy grand-*

mother. Unfortunately, said grandmother was waiting for me in the hallway. Instead of her typical scowl, her expression was as tight and smooth as Italian marble. But there was no masking the anger in her eyes.

She leaned in close to me, her voice harsh. "What were you doing out in that alley, Victoria?"

I looked at her steadily, determined not to flinch. "Though I'm tempted to, I won't lie to you, Nonna. Nando told me that when Pete left the party, he was carrying a shopping bag that looked heavy. I wondered if someone gave him something to drink."

"The only thing I gave him to drink was water!" she rasped.

"I know that, Nonna. But what Nando said got me thinking. I figured if Pete had been given wine, he might have wanted a drink so badly that he wouldn't wait. That he'd find somewhere to have it right away. So I checked the alley on a hunch."

"A *hunch*," she said, her disgust evident. "You think you are a detective, miss, but you are not. So Pete stole a bottle of wine and got drunk. For that you call the police? Do you know the trouble you could have brought on us, on my son—your own father!" Then she used the most powerful weapon in her verbal arsenal: "You have no family feeling, Victoria."

I closed my eyes and took a breath before I answered. "A man is dead, Nonna," I said. "A man you knew. Isn't it important to find out the truth about what happened to him?"

"We know what happened to him, and it was an accident!" She stabbed a finger inches from my face. "What's important is family. Family first, we taught you that."

I closed my hand around hers. "You also taught me

right from wrong. That's why I called Danny. It was Danny who brought the police here, but I don't see you ripping into him."

She pulled her hand from mine and crossed her arms. "*Daniele* was doing his job."

"Right," I said, tasting the bitterness on my tongue. "When it's my brother, it's okay."

"What do you care?" she asked, her eyes narrowing. "For eight years you stayed away. For eight years you could barely be bothered to visit us. Suddenly, you're back. Suddenly, you're interested in the business."

"You know why I stayed away. I couldn't bear to be here," I said, my voice finally breaking.

She shook her head, either in pity or disgust—I couldn't really tell. "Your father should never have hired him back." She pointed back to the kitchen doors, behind which Tim was working in the kitchen. "And he'll hurt you again, Victoria, if you let him. You know he will."

I swiped my eyes with the backs of my hands, and as I watched her walk away, I thought about a line from a poem I'd read in high school. Was it Robert Frost? *Home is the place where, when you go there, they have to take you in.* Well, they'd taken me in. But today the Casa Lido didn't feel very much like home.

I waited until the last diners had cleared out before sneaking out to the parking lot, trying not to give in to the tears that were threatening to overtake me. In the distance, I could see a figure heading toward me, lifting his hand in greeting. I walked toward him slowly, shoulders sagging, wearing my mortification like a sign.

I looked up at him, blinking back the tears. "Oh my God, Cal, it's been such a horrible day."

He folded his arms around me. "Why don't you tell me all about it?"

So I did, and afterward, let myself have a good cry against Cal's chest while he stroked my hair. "Better?" he asked.

"Yes, thanks," I said weakly, still sniffling. "But I'm still embarrassed. And now I got your shirt wet."

"No matter, *cher*. I've had many a worse thing on it." He took a folded blue bandanna from his back pocket and held it up. "It's clean, just so's you know." He blotted the tears from my face and then handed it to me. "Now give her a good blow."

I did as he said, wiped my nose, and held the crumpled cloth in my fist. "You're not getting this back until I wash it."

He pushed a strand of hair from my face and gripped my shoulders. "Listen to me. You did the right thing, Victoria. Even if it did come to nothin.' Don't let anybody tell you otherwise."

I nodded, unconvinced, until I saw my dad emerge from the back door. He wasn't wearing his hat and his face was serious. My stomach sank.

"I heard what Cal said, baby," he said. "And I agree with him. Course you did the right thing. Mommy thinks so, too."

"Daddy, I'm so relieved," I said, letting out a breath. "I've been feeling awful all night."

He put an arm around my shoulders and squeezed me in one of his familiar sideways hugs. "You got nothin' to feel bad about, sweetheart. And I hope you're not worried about your old man. I didn't give Pete that bottle."

But that doesn't mean your prints won't be on it. "I know you didn't," I said.

"And I feel bad about poor old Pete, I really do, but nobody at the restaurant had anything to do with his death. Hey, for all we know, Pete stole that bottle of wine."

And did he steal a napkin, too? Or was that the work of someone else, someone who didn't want to leave fingerprints on the bottle? I glanced at Cal, whose expression was skeptical, but he gave me a quick nod. "You could be right, Dad," I said. "Let's hope, huh?"

"Hope's what I've got plenty of, baby," he said with a wink. "Hope and luck. Now dry those eyes and come back inside." He motioned for us to follow, but just as we opened the door, the lights in the kitchen flickered.

Tim looked up from scrubbing the sink. "What the—?" Before he could finish his question, the vent fan groaned to a stop, and the loud hum of the walk-in fridge was suddenly stilled.

"Oh no," I said, just as every light in the kitchen—in fact, the whole restaurant—went dark. That old generator had finally given up, and it appeared the famous Frank Rienzi luck was about to run out.

Chapter Twelve

*T*he next day, my ever-resourceful family held a giant lunchtime barbecue at the Casa Lido. The minute we lost power, my grandmother divided all the perishable food among those with working refrigerators (keeping a careful inventory, naturally) with orders to bring everything back in the morning. We cooked every vegetable and every piece of meat and fish outside, with Tim, Nando, and even Chef Massi working the outdoor grill. We put a sign outside advertising a prix fixe grilled luncheon, and by eleven thirty we had yet another line of customers outside the Casa Lido doors—one that included our mayor, Ms. Anne McCrae.

"Oh, Victoria," she said, waving me over. "I don't suppose you could find me a table right away? I do need to be back to my office as soon as possible." She flashed me a bright, fake smile. "No rest for the weary!"

"I'll see what I can do, Anne."

"You do that, dear," she called as I hurried away. "And then maybe we can have a chat about that little fool's errand you sent my police force out on."

I skidded to a halt out on the sidewalk. Of course the

mayor would know what the police had confiscated from that alley. And did she plan to use that information against us? I doubled back, a smile plastered on my face. "Anne, why don't you come with me and I'll get you seated now?"

"Why, thank you. That's very kind." She followed me into the dining room, where I led her to a small table in the corner. "Now, this is very cozy," she said as she settled into her seat.

"I'll bring you some water right away," I said. "Would you like something from the bar?"

She sat up straight in her chair. "I'm a city official on duty, dear. Water will be fine. But don't hurry away just yet, Victoria."

I tried to affect a cheery tone. "Well, I'd like to stay and talk, but you saw that line out there."

"This won't take long. Sit," she said in a tone with which there was no arguing. I sat. "Good. First of all, I'd like to say that what you did yesterday was admirable in its way, but it was completely unnecessary."

"You mean when I called the police about the wine bottle?"

"Do keep your voice down, dear," she said through her teeth. "You need to understand something. That man's death was unfortunate, but it was an accident. He was an elderly alcoholic who drank too much and likely drowned in that carousel house. In fact, the sooner we sell that carousel, the sooner we can put all this behind us here in Oceanside Park."

"But—"

She held up a callused palm. "As the Bard once said, *but me no buts.* Consider this a friendly warning, Victoria. Please don't attempt to do any *investigating*"—here she made air quotes—"of your own. It will only bring more trouble to your family." She cocked her head and looked at me steadily. "We've already had one murder in this town. Now, I don't think for a moment that anyone here gave Mr. Petrocelli that bottle of wine; as I said, I firmly believe his death was an accident." Her gray eyes were hard. "But that might not be the perception in town. And such a perception would not be good for the Casa Lido, would it?"

"No," I said quietly. "It wouldn't."

"So we understand each other, then?" She shook open her napkin and spread it across her lap. "Good. Now if you could bring me a diet cola and some rolls, that would be wonderful. Thanks, dear."

"Oh, you're very welcome, Anne," I muttered under my breath. What had I started? What was I bringing down on my family? And for that matter, the town: Calling attention to Pete's death gave Anne the perfect excuse to close down the carousel house. I threw some rolls into a basket with shaking hands; when I looked up, I saw Lori at the drinks station pouring a soda. I waved her over.

"Listen, L.J.," I said, "I'm sorry about bringing the police here yesterday. I'm still kinda mortified about it all."

Lori set the drink down and slipped her arm through mine. "What were you gonna do, pretend that bottle wasn't there? I know you better than that, girlfriend. You wouldn't have been able to sleep at night." She lowered her voice. "And I also know you think somebody offed Pete—am I right?"

I sighed. "I don't know. Maybe. I can't help thinking somebody gave him that wine on purpose."

"You know what? I trust your instincts. But if you're planning to run around asking people questions, be careful, okay?"

"I will be. I'm a wuss, remember?"

She grinned, her round, freckled face full of warmth. "Only when it comes to boardwalk rides. I remember it well."

"Ah yes, our teenage years—when you would try anything once and I would hold your purse while you did it. Thanks for listening, pal." I handed her the basket. "Now would you mind bringing these over to Her Honor and taking her lunch order? I presume the drink is hers?"

"You presume right. She caught me on the way in."

"Of course she did. Okay, time to let in the rest of the hungry hordes. Has Alyssa come in yet?"

Lori nodded. "She was just getting her apron on in the back. But today's her last day, you know. Says she's got to get ready to get back to school."

"And her sorority, no doubt."

"I hear you two girls talking about me!" Alyssa stood with her hands on her hips, a pose that was undercut by her wide smile. "I'm *so* going to miss working with you both. We've had such *fun* this summer!"

Sure we have. Except for that dead guy in the carousel house. But it was hard to be cranky in the face of such perkiness. "Yes, we have," I said.

"It wasn't so much fun yesterday," Lori said. She lifted the basket of rolls. "I better get these over to the mayor."

Alyssa turned to me, her blue eyes wide. "What did she mean? What happened yesterday?"

So there was at least one person in Oceanside Park who hadn't heard about our visit from the police. Well, she'd hear about it at some point today. And if I was the one who told her, I might learn something she knew or remembered from the night of the party. "The police were here," I said. "I, uh, called them when I found a wine bottle in the alley next to the restaurant."

"You called the police for a wine bottle?" Alyssa repeated. "What's the big deal about that? Somebody probably threw it there instead of recycling it." She shook her head. "Some people are so thoughtless."

I shook my head. "It's not that. I actually thought Pete might have had it the night he died."

Alyssa blinked in confusion. "Who's Pete? I don't understand."

"The homeless man they found in the carousel house," I explained.

"You mean that disgusting old man who tried to crash the party?" She wrinkled her nose. "He died?"

"Yeah," I said, "I'm surprised you didn't hear about it."

"Well, I didn't work Saturday or Sunday, so I was kind of out of the loop. And to tell you the truth, I'm *so* busy getting ready for school that I've barely had time to think about anything else."

"Alyssa, did you by any chance see Pete leave that night?"

"Nope. Sorry."

"Did you notice if he came back? Because Nando saw him a bit later, but I'm having trouble pinning down the time."

She frowned. "I don't know why you're so interested in this, Victoria."

I smiled. "Ah, it's probably my overactive writer's imagination at work, but I can't help being curious. We couldn't find you at one point and I just wondered if you'd seen Pete again."

She lifted her shoulder and smiled brightly at me. "It was a busy night. I could have been anywhere. Listen, I have to get back out there, but in case I don't get a chance to see you later on, I just wanted to say it's been a pleasure, Victoria." She held out her hand to me.

"Same here. Come see us next May, okay?"

"You bet! But in the meantime, we've got a party of four at the head of the line, so I hope Table Five is ready," she called as she walked away, her blond ponytail swinging behind her, the picture of innocence. *But are you as innocent as you look, Miss Alyssa? And do you know more than you're willing to say?*

By three thirty, the last of our guests had gone, and my grandmother called us to a meeting at the family table. She sat between my parents, her yellow pad in front of her, the page covered in notes. "First things first," she said. "Is the lunch cleanup completed?"

"The linens are cleared off and bagged for the laundry, Mrs. R," Lori said. "And Alyssa finished busing everything before she left."

"And the dishes are all washed, *senora*," Nando added.

Her face cracked in her closest approximation to a smile. "Thank you, Lori and Nando. We can always count on both of you."

Certain that was intended for me, I kept back a sigh. "Coffee and drink stations are cleaned," I said. "And the machines are unplugged and emptied of water."

Nonna merely nodded and went on to the next item on her list. "Massi, have you canceled the food orders for the rest of the week?"

"No, but I pushed them back by a few days. I can always revise the menu if necessary. And if the power is back and I am needed . . ." He paused here for effect. ". . . I am willing to come in on Saturday." Massi lifted his Roman nose in the air, looking around the table as if for applause for this sacrifice.

"*Grazie*, Chef," my dad interjected. "What else, Ma?"

"Victoria, check the refrigerator for perishables," Nonna said, still looking down at her yellow pad. "Once it's emptied, Tim should clean it with bleach and prop the door open."

"Okay," I said.

"Now, please," she said curtly, and I hopped up from the chair, knocking into Chef Massi, who took my arm to steady me and smiled.

"*Va bene, cara,*" he whispered. "All will be well eventually."

"Thanks, Massi," I whispered back, and relieved to be out from Nonna's harsh glare, I headed to the kitchen, where Tim was crouched in front of the walk-in.

"I hear you're on cleaning patrol," I said. "What did you do wrong?"

"I exist. Hey, you okay?" he asked over his shoulder.

"Yeah, I'm fine. Why do you ask?"

He put the sponge down and straightened up to face me, and yes, my heart did a tiny tarantella when I saw his concern. "Because I know what it cost you to call the cops yesterday," he said. "And to have to face your crazy grandmother afterward."

I smiled. "You're the second person in two days to call her that. Flo was the first, right before she quit."

"Flo quit?"

"Yup. Then she called me a *narc*."

"Ouch," he said, wincing in sympathy. "Sorry about that. Actually, I think Jason quit, too."

"And today was Alyssa's last day; she's getting ready to go back to school."

Tim shrugged. "But it doesn't much matter now, does it? Without power, we can't really stay open, so we don't need the summer help. It was damn lucky your grandmother thought of having us refrigerate all our stuff— hardly anything went to waste."

"So she's crazy like a fox," I said.

"Indeed she is, lass," he said, and I didn't even chide him for his bad Irish brogue. Because as I stood across from him in that kitchen, I was unaccountably happy. He was worried about me. Heck, he had *empathized* with me, and no matter what had happened between us, our friendship, at least, was intact. *He says he's changed, Vic,* said a small, treacherous voice in my head. *Maybe he has.* Right. *And even if he has changed,* I replied to the insistent little voice, *he has a girlfriend. And I have a sort-of boyfriend.*

"Thanks, Tim."

"For what, Vic?"

"For being there. I really appreciate it."

He took a step closer and rested his hands on my shoulders. "I don't want your gratitude. I want—"

The kitchen door swung open, and Tim dropped his hands.

In the doorway stood my mother looking startled, but also a little pleased to see us together. "Oh, sorry. I didn't mean to interrupt anything. I was looking for Victoria."

"Well, you found me," I said, wondering why I felt guilty. "What's up, Mom?"

"Honey, could I speak with you for a moment? C'mon out to the dining room." She motioned me to follow, and we sat at a corner table, far from where the staff was still engaged in an animated discussion.

The minute we sat down, I tried to ease my mother's fears. "Being closed for a couple of days won't kill us, Mom."

"Honey, you know as well as I do that we can't lose our Labor Day business." She glanced at my grandmother, who was still presiding over the staff meeting. "We're already a little behind this year."

"I know," I said, patting her hand. "Because of that mess in the spring. What does the town say about the power situation? It's been almost three days."

"Your brother tells me the utility company is working around the clock. They're *saying* we'll have power back in time for the holiday weekend, but I'm not sure we can count on it. Is it a problem for you at the cottage, hon?"

"Not much. I've got a gas stove and hot water heater. At night, I read with a flashlight. Anyway, I've barely been there with all the work to do here."

She looked around the dining room nervously. "Not for much longer. And even if the power comes back on for Friday, we'll be losing three days of business in the meantime. And it's not just us, but the staff, Lori and Nando especially. They have families."

"They'll be okay, Mom. They know our work is seasonal, and they plan for that. But I know what's really bothering you. You're worried about Daddy because of that bottle." She blinked and nodded, her large dark eyes suddenly brimming, and I grabbed her hand. "Danny said it's not likely to go anywhere. I feel ridiculous for even calling."

"But what if you were right?" she asked in a whisper. "What if somebody gave Pete that bottle deliberately?"

"I think that's possible, Mom." I didn't want to share my theory of Pete "knowing things" about people as a motive. "But it wasn't Daddy."

"Of course it wasn't!" She leaned closer. "But his fin-gerprints will be all over it."

"But you'd expect them to be, right? It's from his own wine cellar. And anyway, that bottle was out in the rain. I can't imagine them getting even one clean print off that bottle." *Partially because of that handy napkin.* But I didn't know this for sure. *So, Bernardo,* I thought, calling upon my fictional sleuth, *what's your take on this—does rain wash away fingerprints?* Not for the first time, I wished my nattily dressed detective would materialize with his special notebook and fountain pen to help me figure out just what the heck was going on.

"I know your father thinks Pete stole that bottle," my mom was saying. "But I don't see how he could have. Your grandmother and I accounted for every bottle out on that bar; we knew how much went out and how much came back in." She let out a sigh. "It had to have come from the basement."

"I agree," I said, lowering my voice. "Because I just remembered something. I was chatting with Dad down there on Saturday afternoon. He was messing with the bottles and said something about going through more of his homemade wine than he thought."

My mom looked at me with desperation in her eyes. "Honey, do you think that Pete could have somehow gotten into the basement?"

"Maybe. But it was locked from the outside when I checked it yesterday." *Unless someone deliberately left it unlocked that night.* But that was a thought I chose not to share.

"What about through the restaurant?" she asked.

"It's possible, I guess. At some point, Nando saw Pete holding *two* bags, one that had food in it and another one that looked heavy. When I saw him leave—or at least when I *thought* he was leaving—he rounded the corner, and I assumed he passed the restaurant. But I guess he could have gone back inside through the front doors."

"He could have," she said, her curls shaking as she nodded. "The front door was unlocked so guests could go inside to use the restrooms."

"Of course; I should have thought of that. But we were all in and out of the dining room and kitchen. I still think one of us would have seen him inside, don't you?" *Or smelled him,* I thought.

She rested her forehead in her hand and groaned. "Who knows? This just gets worse and worse."

"Listen to me," I said. "I know this doesn't look good for the restaurant, but there other possibilities. There are still no autopsy results, Mom. Whether or not someone here deliberately gave him wine, or whether he stole it, he still might have fallen and hit his head and drowned. His death might simply be the accident everyone assumes it is."

My mother lowered her voice and gripped my wrist. "But you don't think so, do you? You think somebody wanted poor Pete to drink himself to death on Friday night." She closed her eyes briefly and took a deep breath. "Honey," she said, "do you think you can . . . look into this? Can you *please* find out what happened to Pete Petrocelli?"

It wasn't like my mother to ask such a thing of me; in fact, she'd begged me not to get involved with the last two murders. But a half hour later, as I packed my computer, the library books, and a few other electronics into the backseat of my blue Honda, I realized how desperate she was to know the truth. And despite the mayor's warning to me, so was I. To find out, I was planning to do something that could backfire on me, but I was willing to risk it. I didn't have any other choice.

Chapter Thirteen

*B*y late Monday afternoon, the weekenders were mostly gone, so it was a quiet ride across town to my brother's house. I'd already called, so I knew he and Sofia were home. I told him I needed to charge my electronics, which was partially true. But I had another reason for coming.

Danny answered the door wearing shorts and flip-flops and holding a beer. "It's always such a relief to see you in normal clothes as opposed to your uniform," I said as I gave him a hug. I stepped back and looked into his face. "Are you mad at me?"

"How could you even ask me that? C'mon." He opened the door and let me go ahead of him into the living room. "You can plug your stuff in right there," he said, pointing to a power strip on the floor.

I took my computer and phone from my bag and plugged them in. "Would you have done what I did? Even though you think it isn't significant?" I asked over my shoulder.

"You mean call in the troops if I found that bottle? Probably." He rubbed a hand over his chin and flashed a grin at me. "I wouldn't have wanted to take a chance. Now, if our grandmother had found it—"

"She'd have tossed it into our Dumpster."

"Not ours," Danny said, "but the one next door. On second thought, she'd have chucked it into the ocean."

We were both laughing when Sofia emerged from the kitchen with a tray. "C'mon," she said, "let's go into the family room and then you can tell me what's so funny."

"Our grandmother," I said as I settled down on the couch while Danny and Sofia sat on a love seat across from me.

Sofia handed me a glass of white wine. "Funny as in *amusing*?"

"You could say that," Danny said. "We were talking about what she woulda done if she'd found that bottle."

"Dug a pit and buried it," Sofia said. "And then spread lime over the spot."

"It's not a body, Sofe." I took a sip of wine, grateful for its small kick at the end of a long day. I held up the glass. "Thank you for this; I needed it today. Things have been a little . . . awkward at the restaurant."

She nodded. "Your brother filled me in. But think about this, Vic—any one of those guests might have left a bottle out there. If I was a defense lawyer, that's the angle I would play."

Danny took a swig of beer and shook his head. "You're assuming somebody needs defending, babe. And I just don't think that's the case here."

"But, Dan, don't you think the napkin is damning?" I asked.

"Could be. But so far there's no proof Pete was in that alley. Yes, the bottle and the napkin are from the restaurant, but that night there was a big party of what, forty, fifty people? Like Sofia said, anybody could have thrown that stuff out there."

"But who would throw a cloth napkin away?" I persisted.

"A lazy person," Sofia said, "or a careless one. Remember how quick everybody had to get inside, Vic. You've got a guest with an empty bottle and a dirty napkin who's in a hurry to get out of the weather, so he just pitches the stuff."

"But think about it, guys—that person would need to walk to the other side of the property to put the stuff in that alley. Why not just dump it in the garden? And there weren't bottles out on the tables; Dad was pouring glasses at the bar."

Danny shrugged. "Doesn't mean somebody might not have taken a bottle off the bar."

"Mom said that she and Nonna had accounted for all the bottles that went out and how many came back." I shook my head. "No, I think that bottle came from the basement." I looked my brother in the eye. "And I think somebody deliberately gave it to Pete, maybe with the promise of more where that came from."

"You might be right, sis," Danny said, "but unless there's clear forensic evidence linking Pete to that alley, or another person to Pete, none of this is solid. I still think we're looking at an accidental death, plain and simple."

"Dan," I said, "I'm assuming the police combed that alley. Might I also assume they haven't found anything else from the restaurant—say a food container—or you'd be more worried?"

"You can assume anything you want, Vic," Danny said with a grin. "But I won't corroborate it."

"Yeah, yeah, I know the drill. You can't talk. Not even about the autopsy results, I guess?" I asked, trying to keep the eagerness out of my tone.

"We're still waiting on those," he said.

"I'm betting his blood alcohol levels were through the roof," I said.

"But they might be anyway, right? The man liked his *vino*." Danny raised his beer bottle in a toast. "Me, I prefer hops to the grape."

I studied my brother's relaxed expression. "You're really not too concerned about this, are you? I mean, that Pete died after leaving the restaurant. You'd be much more serious and grim."

"How could you tell?" Sofia said, punching her husband lightly in the arm.

"That's cute, babe," he said.

"Seriously, hon," Sofia said, "I'm with you on the wine bottle, but for me there's a larger question: What was Pete doing in the carousel house in the first place?"

"Shelter—what else?"

"But that's problematic for a couple of reasons," Sofia said. "One, there were probably other places he could have sheltered much closer to the restaurant."

"Like the alley," I added.

"Two," Sofia continued, "once the weather got threatening, they would have closed the rides pier, right? So how'd he get in there?"

"That is something OPPD will follow up on if there is any reason to think there's foul play behind Pete's death," Danny said, adopting his professional tone. "I mean, c'mon, why kill Pete? Not for money, that's for damn sure."

"What if it was to keep him quiet?" I asked. "What if he knew something that could hurt someone?"

"Maybe," Danny conceded. "But what would give you that idea?"

"Pete himself," I said. "Back in early August, he told me he 'knew things,' but I didn't take it seriously."

"'Cause the guy's a drunk, sis." He looked from his wife back to me. "Please don't tell me you two are getting ideas again."

"Not exactly," Sofia said. "But Vic found something you should see."

"I know we've, um, kind of gone behind your back a couple of times," I said. "And I want things to be aboveboard between us."

"Completely," Sofia said, nodding.

"So I wanted to show you this, because I think there could be a connection here to Pete's death." I held up the book for him to see.

"In a book about Atlantic City?" He took it from me and began leafing through its pages.

"Look at the page I marked, Dan. There's a sticky note on one of the pictures."

I watched the different expressions cross my brother's face—a frown of concentration, then his raised eyebrows, and finally a look of clear understanding.

"Holy . . . ," he began. "That's Pop. I mean, that's his face. Even the hat."

Sofia leaned over his shoulder. "Kinda looks like you, too. Except you don't smirk like that."

I laughed. "No, Danny's the other side of this guy's coin. And it's not Dad, as you could probably tell by the year."

"But he's gotta be a relative," my brother said.

I nodded. "I'm pretty sure it's his uncle Roberto, our great-uncle and Nonna's brother-in-law."

He frowned again. "Isn't that the guy who died back in Italy?"

"Maybe not." I explained about our Internet searches and the ancestry database, including the ship's manifest and the census that had Robert Riese and the Petrocelli brothers in the same building in Atlantic City. I told him my theory about his name change and pointed to the caption under the 1948 photo. "Pete's older brother is clearly identified, as is Leo Barone. If Riese is really 'Rienzi,' as it looks like, then we've got a clear connection to the past. Think about it, Danny—the last time a Petrocelli, a Barone, and a Rienzi were all in the same place was on Friday night, at the Casa Lido party. And who's the link? Stinky Pete, who ends up dead."

Sofia rubbed her bare arms. "Oh, I'm all goose-bumpy. Tell him what your father said, Vic."

"Dad confirmed the resemblance to his uncle; he said his grandmother mentioned it once. He also said his family actually delivered produce to Atlantic City. There are just so many ties to the past here."

"So I'm guessing you like Richard Barone for this," Danny said. "With that whole Mafia thing in his background. You think Barone had something big to hide that Pete knew about."

"It's possible, isn't it?" I looked from Danny to Sofia.

"I wasn't sure at first," Sofia said slowly, "but you've got me wondering if there is something there."

But Danny was skeptical. "We don't even know the family relationship between Leo and Richard Barone."

"That's true," I said, making a mental note to find out.

"Please keep a couple of things in mind," Danny said. "As yet, there is no formal investigation going on. And even if there was, whether there's enough to indict somebody is for the county prosecutor to decide. We're a long way from that." He closed the book and handed it back to me. "And here's the other thing: Barone has a ton of power and money behind him. I do *not* want you two messing with this."

"It can't hurt to keep researching our family, though, hon," Sofia said, bestowing a wide smile on her husband and resting her hand on her belly. She was good; I'd say that for her.

Danny tightened his arm around her and kissed her temple. "You can do all the family research you want, right from the safety of this house."

"Speaking of family," I said, "I'd like to hold off mentioning our possible family history to Mom and Dad just yet. Until we actually confirm that this guy is really our great-uncle. And on that happy note," I added, getting to my feet, "I will collect my newly charged stuff and get going. That power's gotta come back on soon. The novelty of reading by flashlight is beginning to wear off."

"Since when?" Danny asked as he walked me out. "You spent your whole childhood doin' that."

"I know. I'm a dork." I gave him a quick kiss and packed my bag. "But think about what I said, will you?"

"You think about what *I* said. Stay away from Barone. No investigating, Nancy Drew."

I hid my irritation behind a smile. "You got it, bro. Talk to you soon."

I was only a couple of blocks away when Sofia's name appeared on my phone screen.

I pulled over to answer. "Hey," I said. "What's up?"

"I can't talk long," Sofia whispered into the phone. "But I just overheard your brother talking to somebody at the precinct about Pete's autopsy. There was definitely water in his lungs."

"So he drowned."

"Yup. But you were right about his blood alcohol. I heard Danny say his levels were .27. Do have any idea how high that is? I looked it up: He drank the equivalent of more than two bottles of wine that night. That's enough to kill somebody, especially an old man whose liver was probably shot anyway."

"Wow. So he had at least another bottle to drink, probably more—the question is, did they all come from Frankie's cellar? Thanks for telling me, Sofe. I appreciate it. But we've already broken our word to Danny about keeping him in the loop."

"We haven't really broken it. Maybe stretched it a little."

After we ended the call, I sat for a moment staring at my phone and made a decision, one that went completely against my brother's warning to me. It was close to five, so I didn't have much time. After a quick Internet search, I found the number I was seeking.

"May I help you?" asked the female voice on the line.

"Yes, thank you," I said. "My name is Victoria Rienzi, and I'd like to make an appointment with Mr. Barone. As soon as possible, please."

Chapter Fourteen

While I was concerned about the Casa Lido's future, it was still nice to have a couple of days off. I could get back to my book and maybe do some digging into the Barone family. My appointment with Richard was for later in the afternoon, so I had the morning to myself. And I knew just how I wanted to spend it. I woke early, threw on some clothes, and headed out my back door to the beach.

I relished the view of the cloudless blue sky and the sun's silvery reflection on the water. I kicked off my flip-flops and walked along the water's edge, savoring the warmth of the August surf. My life back in Manhattan seemed miles away, and I realized with a start that I didn't miss it. Work at the restaurant was taxing, demanding, often tedious, but I felt productive there. I was learning to work with Tim, and to put our past together into some kind of perspective. I dug my toes into the wet sand as the waves crashed and receded around me. Though I might have a better understanding of my relationship with Tim, Cal remained a bit of a mystery, both the man himself as well as my feelings for him.

What might those feelings be if Tim were not in the picture? If he were not literally at my side nearly every day in the kitchen? It was hard to say. But I simply didn't know enough about Cal to commit to more than a dating relationship. Maybe I was overly cautious. Or maybe I just didn't want to be hurt again.

I made my way to the rock jetty, picking my way carefully over the black, slick rocks. I walked out to its edge, remembering a story that Nonna had told me about a desperate person on the edge. That story had come to a sad conclusion a month ago, partly because of my involvement in it. Should I have left it well enough alone then? And what about now? There was still time to cancel my appointment with Barone. The police were unconvinced that Pete was murdered. There was no obvious motive. *He drank too much and drowned, Vic. Leave it at that.* Why? Because he was old and homeless and a drunk? Did his life matter any less? I looked out at the vastness of the ocean and I had my answer.

As I approached my cottage, I saw a lean figure sitting out on my deck, legs stretched out in front of him, his face turned to the sun: none other than Calvin Lockhart, the very subject of some of my recent thoughts.

"Mornin', *cher*," he said with a wave. "You interested in some breakfast?"

"I'm always interested in breakfast. Did you bring some?"

He lifted a bag. "Brought the makings."

"Well, then, you are certainly welcome to come in." He followed me inside, and looked around with an amused glance. The mismatched furniture, old-school Venetian blinds, and rag rug were a stark contrast to his white walls and minimalist decor. I met his eye. "You act like you haven't seen the place. Is it that bad?"

"Not at all," he said. "I didn't get a real good look at the place the other morning. But it looks like you."

"Does it smell like me, too? Seashore musty?"

"Nah, you know what I mean. It's a little old-fashioned, but I think you like that," he said, setting the grocery bag down on the table. He reached for my hand and dropped a kiss on my knuckles. "After all, you're kind of an old-fashioned girl."

"I will try to take that as a compliment." I peeked into the bag. "Oh my God, is that cinnamon bread?" I sniffed. "And there's coffee in here, too." I looked up at him and grinned. "How did you know I needed sugar, white flour, and caffeine?"

"Just a guess, *cher*. You got some plates for us?"

"I'll get them; you sit down. Just don't get between me and that coffee."

We ate and chatted about the power outage, the restaurant being closed, and the possible loss of Labor Day revenue. "What about you?" I asked. "Do you have other work until we open again?"

"I've always got some kind of project going on. I keep busy."

I eyed him over the top of my coffee cup. "Doing what, particularly?"

"You know. This 'n' that."

"That's just it, Cal. I *don't* know. For example, you disappear for a week at a time, work a few days at the restaurant, and then go away again."

"Your daddy lets me make my own hours," he said with a grin.

"Well, I'm not as trusting as my daddy. And sometimes I feel as though I don't know you at all. For instance, what happened to that fancy black James Bond BMW you took me out in a while ago?"

"That's easy," he said, still smiling. "Lease came up and I didn't renew. Don't see what's so strange about it."

"Because that car didn't *look* like you. And neither does your apartment. Earlier you said that my house looks like me, but I have to say that your apartment doesn't in any way reflect the warm, funny person you are. Actually, it doesn't reflect much of anything." *Except for that yellow room, of course.* But I wasn't sure I was ready to ask him about that.

He shrugged. "Place came furnished. That's easier for me 'cause I move around a lot."

I looked him straight in the eye. "Why is that, Cal?"

"After the storm in '05, I lost my home base. My foundation, I guess— in every sense of the word. So I packed up what I could save, got in the truck, and just drove." He looked down at his now-empty coffee cup.

"And you ended up here?"

"Among other places."

I stood up, pushed in my chair, and brought my plate to the sink. "You know, Cal," I said over my shoulder, "I feel like with you I'm on a need-to-know basis." I turned toward him, leaning against the sink. "God knows, I come from a family of oversharers, so maybe my definition of what's private isn't the same as yours. But there's a difference between privacy and secrecy." I looked straight into his eyes. "And I think you are a man with secrets."

"Listen to me, *cher*," he said, getting up from his chair. He took my hands in his. "I'm not dangerous. I haven't done anything illegal." One side of his mouth curved in a grin. "I'm not a spy or an escaped criminal. I guess you could say I'm kind of a loner."

"Tell me something I don't know. I get that from your apartment."

"What do you want to know about me, Victoria? Just ask."

"Okay," I said, taking a breath. "Tell me about the yellow room."

He dropped my hands and stepped back. "There's nothin' to tell."

"Oh, I think there is," I said quietly. "It's the only room in your apartment with any color. It's got a homey quilt on the bed. And then there's the Velveteen Rabbit I found under the bed."

He stood still, his arms at his sides, looking much as he did the night of the storm as he looked up at that tree. The lines around his eyes looked deeper, sadder. His sigh was barely audible. "That is something I just can't talk about. I'm sorry. Can you accept that?"

"That's a little difficult for me. Because until—or unless—you can be more honest with me about who you are and about your past, I just don't see us going anywhere."

"And I respect that, I really do, but that doesn't mean we can't spend time together." His voice was husky and warm, and that quickly, he was back to his old self. He slid his arms around me, pulling me against him. He was fresh out of the shower, the ends of his hair still wet, and he smelled more delicious than the cinnamon bread.

I rested my hands on his chest, partly to keep him at bay and partly because it felt nice. "When a grown man and woman spend time together," I said, "that generally leads to, shall we say, a certain *closeness*. I'm attracted to you, but as you may have noticed, I'm not the hooking-up type."

"I have noticed, Victoria, but that only adds to your charm." He kissed my forehead. "Like I said, you're an old-fashioned girl. And I've told you I'm patient."

"That may be so," I said, crossing my arms. "But even platonic friends are honest with each other. And while I don't believe you have out-and-out lied to me, I suspect there's a whole lot about your life I don't know."

He took my hands again and gently uncrossed my arms. "Give me a little time, okay?" he asked. "I need to square a few things away. I'm in a place in my life where . . . where things are kinda uncertain. And I didn't expect to meet a woman like you." He leaned down and whispered in my ear, "You've thrown me for a loop, girl."

"That old bayou charm isn't working on me at the moment, Mr. Lockhart. And I won't wait forever."

"Wouldn't expect you to, *cher*," he said as he turned to go. "But a man can hope, can't he?"

Cal had just pulled out of my driveway when I heard a knock at my front door. "Geez, it's like Grand Central here today," I grumbled, and peeked through my side window. And I was more than a little surprised to see who was behind my door.

"Hi, Lacey," I said as I opened it. "What brings you here?"

She took off her sunglasses and I could see that she'd been crying. *Trouble in paradise, perhaps?* But I banished the thought as quickly as I could. "Could we talk for a minute, Victoria?" she asked.

"Sure. C'mon in. I do have an appointment in less than an hour, though."

"This won't take long. Cute place," she said, looking around at the tiny living room.

"Thanks," I said. "But I picked it more for its location than its ambiance." I moved my bag from the couch. "Sit down, please."

"First, can I ask you not to tell Tim I was here?"

"Um, okay," I said, wondering what the heck was coming next.

Lacey twisted her hands in her lap, apparently having trouble looking me in the eye. "This is a little awkward," she began.

God, I thought, *maybe they're engaged and those are tears of joy.* I strained to smile at her. "It wouldn't be the first awkward conversation we've had, though."

"No, it wouldn't. So I think I should just say it." She took a shuddery breath and finally looked me in the eye. "I'm not sure where things are going with Tim, and I'm very conflicted about my feelings right now."

I wanted to yell at my heart, to tell it to stop leaping around joyfully in my chest. "Okay," I said, wondering if she could hear its thumping across the room. "Why come and tell me about it? It's your business, yours and Tim's."

She smiled slightly and a knowing look crossed her face. "That's not completely true, is it? I mean, there's still a pretty strong bond between the two of you."

This wasn't the first time that Lacey had made this observation. Was the trouble with Tim because she sensed he still had feelings for me? "Of course there's a bond between us," I said. "We've known each other for half our lives. But we were over a long time ago; I've already told you that."

"Victoria, I know you *think* you believe that. And maybe you do." She tilted her head, studying my expression. "But I know something about having a past, too. Do you remember when I told you that I'd had a broken engagement?"

"Yes. And I felt for you, having had my own heart broken."

"Ah," she said. "You assumed that *he* was the one who hurt me. I can't blame you, I guess. I've got *Good Girl* written all over me."

"Takes one to know one," I said, and we both laughed. "Let me get this straight, then—your former fiancé is not a scoundrel or a cad?"

"Far from it." She shook her head slowly, her eyes filling with tears. "He's a great guy. One of the best." She pushed her hair back from her forehead and sighed. "I was the one who messed up. He was pushing to get married and I wasn't really ready. Instead of being a woman about it, and being honest with him, I got involved with someone else."

"Oh." I had a little trouble meeting her eye.

"*Oh* is right." She dabbed at her eye with a crumpled tissue. "Once he found out, it was all over. That was a year ago. Tim is the first guy I dated in all that time, and I like him, I really do. I thought we might have a real chance."

"But not now?"

"I'm not sure. Mark—he was my fiancé—called me last night. He wants to meet and talk. The minute I heard his voice, I knew what I wanted."

"You mean *who* you wanted. And it's not Tim."

She shook her head. "It's not that cut-and-dried. Even if Mark is willing to forgive me, that doesn't mean he'll take me back. But it's not fair to keep Tim in the background like some kind of romantic insurance policy. Things aren't easy between us anyway right now, partly because of my work hours and partly because . . . well, let's face it, he never stopped loving you."

My cheeks burned, and I let out a small breath. "Even if that's true, I still don't understand why you're telling me all this."

She smiled slightly, her eyes dry now. "Because you care about Tim, and if things go south with us, he'll need a friend. I also thought it was important that you heard my story."

"Why?"

She reached over and closed her hand around my arm. "Because people make mistakes, Victoria. And if they're lucky, they learn from them. And if they're *really* lucky, they find forgiveness." She stood up and slung her purse over her shoulder. "I'm not sure what Tim did to hurt you, but I'm sure of this: He's sorry for it. And I think he deserves another chance."

After she left, I stood holding on to the sides of the doorframe, just the way you do in an earthquake—so when things come crashing down around you, you'll still be on your feet.

The Barone Foundation's offices were located right outside Oceanside Park, and I got there quickly, giving me time to compose myself after those two disconcerting conversations. Determined to put them from my mind, I mentally rehearsed the ostensible reason for my presence: In doing research for my book, I'd stumbled across a connection between his family and my own, and was hoping he could answer some questions for me. All in the service of my novel, of course. I'd even brought the Atlantic City book with me, partly to make my excuse legit, but mostly to see his reaction to that photo.

Barone's plush offices had plenty of power; the air-conditioning blew hard and cold across my bare legs. In the waiting room, I spent my time studying a brochure that detailed the various Barone charities. He'd established scholarships for needy high school and college students; founded an organization dedicated to helping the widows and children of police and firefighters; headed up a clean water initiative for the bay shore; created an Italian-American heritage association of which he was president ("Dedicated to fighting stereotypes and spreading awareness of Italian contributions to American life") and built a newly dedicated pediatric wing at Shore Regional Hospital. Was there no good deed this guy left undone?

Learning about his work made it difficult to imagine him a murderer. If his goal had been to overcome his family's criminal past, it appeared he'd achieved it. I stuffed the brochure into my purse and stood up, fully prepared to leave when his secretary came out from her office.

"He's ready for you, Ms. Rienzi. I've scheduled a twenty-minute block—will that be sufficient?"

"More than sufficient, thank you," I said, and followed her to Barone's office, my stomach fluttering. This was a powerful man, and he would make a powerful enemy. Remembering my brother's words, I decided to tread carefully.

"Victoria, how are you?" Richard Barone said, stepping out from behind his desk to take my hand. He gestured to his secretary. "I was pleasantly surprised when Debbie told me you had called."

"May I get you something?" she asked before leaving. "Coffee or water?"

"No, I'm fine. Thank you." I waited until the door closed to continue. "I won't take much of your time, Richard. Thank you for seeing me on such short notice."

"Not at all," he said. "And please sit, won't you?"

I sat, glancing at the pictures on the wall behind Barone's desk. In one, he was standing on a vast green lawn in front of a familiar white building, shaking hands with a slender, attractive man whose hair was graying at the edges. And who happened to be the leader of the free world. I swallowed nervously and asked an obvious question. "Uh, is that you with the president?"

"Yes, it is," he said, affecting a modest tone. "I made a small contribution to his campaign and I was honored to be able to meet him."

Small contribution, my eyeballs. "Wow," I said, and took my notebook and a pen from my purse.

Barone sat forward, his hands clasped in front of him, giving me his full attention. "Now, how can I help you? Something to do with your book, Debbie said."

I sat up a little straighter in the plush office chair. "Well, as your secretary mentioned, I'm doing research for a historical novel that's loosely based on my family history."

"This is not one of your mysteries?"

"No, it's a departure, one I've wanted to make for some time." And that, at least, was the truth. "I've begun doing some research on an ancestry site, and found something very interesting—I think there may be a connection between our two families."

"Is that so?" He still had a smile on his face, but did I imagine that it had tightened a bit?

"I'm fairly sure," I said. "But before we go any further, I have to ask: Is Leo Barone an ancestor of yours?"

"Yes, I regret to say. He was my great-grandfather. Please understand that I have no illusions about who he was or how he made his money. And I've never hidden the connection." He wasn't smiling anymore, and I gathered this was a sore subject.

"I understand. Would you mind telling me a bit about him?"

He looked as though he *would* mind, but he nodded anyway. "Well, like other Italian immigrants who turned to crime, his family was desperately poor." From that beginning, Richard Barone told the tale of a tough boy with a difficult life who ended up wealthy from a career of Atlantic City bootlegging and gambling operations. It sounded carefully rehearsed and well learned—a story he'd told many times before. And there wasn't much in it I hadn't already learned from the book and the Internet, but I couldn't just plunge in with questions about Robert Riese. At least not yet.

"And that, Victoria," Richard concluded, "is the story of my unfortunate relation. The best I can say of him is that he never killed anyone."

"We all have those folks somewhere in our family trees, though, don't we?" I said. I slipped my hand back into my purse and brought out the library book. "In fact, the man I'm researching—a man I think may be my great-uncle—was a pretty unsavory character himself." I opened the book to the photo and turned it so he could see it. Showing this to Barone was risky, particularly if he connected Alfonso Petrocelli with Stinky Pete. But I had to see his reaction. "If you'll look at the photo where I have a sticky note, and read the caption, please."

Richard drew his dark brows together, his eyes flicking from the picture to the caption and then back again.

He frowned more deeply and peered at the page. When he lifted his head, his expression was wary. "I recognize my great-grandfather, of course," he said, "but none of the other men." He tilted his head, his eyes watchful. "Should I?"

"Would you look again at the man in the fedora?"

"Is he the bad apple in your family tree?" he asked. He glanced back down at the page and then back at me. "I suppose he could be related to your father or brother. There's a surface resemblance."

I nodded. "I think he's the man our family knew as Roberto Rienzi. We'd always believed he died back in Naples. But I've found evidence of someone using an Anglicized version of the name—a Robert Riese, spelled R-I-E-S-E, who closely fits the profile of my great-uncle."

He grew quiet and still, so much so that I could hear the ticking of the expensive clock on his desk. "Robert Riese, you say?" he asked, his tone carefully neutral.

"Yes, do you recognize the name?" I held my pen poised over the notebook, ready to catch anything Barone might have been willing to share.

He closed the book and pushed it back across the desk. "No, I'm sorry, but I don't."

But I was willing to bet every bottle of wine in my father's cellar that he did.

Chapter Fifteen

"So that's all he said?" Sofia, who'd just polished off a dinner of local bay scallops, garlic mashed potatoes, and a pile of steamed vegetables, eyed my plate, more interested in my dinner than in my interview with Barone. "Do you plan to eat those carrots?"

"*Yes* to the first question and *no* to the second. Here." I pushed my plate toward her and watched her dig in. "Someone has gotten her appetite back." We were at the Shell Café, a Casa Lido competitor. But they had a great chef and plenty of electricity.

She nodded, her mouth full, and held up a finger while she chewed and swallowed (in a ladylike way, of course). "Once that morning sickness stopped, I just wanted to eat everything in sight." She winked. "But enough about me. Finish telling me about Barone."

"There's not much more to tell. Like I said, he gave me the party line about his great-grandfather, talked about living down his family's past, stressed the fact that Leo hadn't killed anyone, and then denied knowing the name Robert Riese. But he got very, very quiet after I asked him. Like his wheels were turning. I think I caught him off guard—whatever he thought I was going to ask, that wasn't it."

"Vic, you showed him the picture, right? Do you think he might have connected Alfonso with Pete?"

"I honestly don't know. If he did, he's one cool customer."

"But if he's the one who gave Pete that wine—"

"Assuming Pete didn't steal it," I interrupted. "The restaurant was open, after all."

"Please," she said, rolling her eyes. "You don't believe that for a minute. But you know what I'm getting at. If Barone is our guy, seeing the name Petrocelli would have set off alarms in his head."

I nodded. "True. For some reason, he might have been prepared for that, though. But I still say he wasn't prepared for Riese. By the way, have you found anything else out about our mysterious great-uncle?"

She finished the rest of my carrots and took a roll from the bread basket. "Yes and no. I dug up the 1950 census for Atlantic City; Pete and Alfonso were at a different address by that time, still living together, but Riese wasn't with them." She split open a roll and slathered on some butter. "You know, I was thinking about Roberto and the name change. *Reese* is a common name, but not with the I-E spelling. I think it's possible he might have used the double-E version or maybe switched between the two, especially if he wanted to blend into the background. What do you think?"

"Hmm. You might be onto something there, Sofe. This is a guy who didn't want to be found—which of course makes our job harder. There had to be a ton of Reeses in Atlantic City. He might have changed his first name, too, for that matter."

"Here's what I think," she said, gesturing with her butter knife. "There were probably any number of guys named Reese in that city. But there was only one Leo Barone. If Riese or Reese is in fact the guy in the picture, and if he *is* Zio Roberto, he was connected to Barone in some way. That's the way to go—we dig up everything we can on Barone and hope it leads to your missing uncle."

"You're right, but there's only so far we can go on the Internet. I think we're looking at hours in a library with microfiche machines or whatever they use to scan and preserve old documents these days. Maybe Gale Spaulding can help us."

She brushed the bread crumbs from her fingers and grinned. "Maybe. But I think we need a trip to AC. We need to go down there for our research."

"For research or to play the slots?"

She grinned. "A little of both."

"Well," I said, "the restaurant's closed until the power comes back." I held out my hand to her. "Road trip?"

She shook it heartily. "Road trip it is, SIL."

"By the way," I said, "in case you thought my visit to Barone was the most interesting part of my day, wait till you hear about the rest of it. My love life is growing ever more complicated."

She held up her hand. "Save it. It'll give us something to talk about on the ride."

The next day was rainy, and we made our way slowly down Garden State Parkway South. Sofia was driving a sedate fifty-five miles an hour; the red folder sat on the seat between us. I had filled her in on both my conversations of the day before, and she looked thoughtful as she drove.

"You know," she said, "regarding Cal—on the one hand,

you don't want to get involved with a guy who seems less than honest. But on the other, isn't he entitled to some privacy?"

"I know," I said. "I feel the same way. But clearly, the guy's got some baggage, and for all I know there's a kid hidden in one of those suitcases. It makes me hesitant to get more involved with him."

She sent me a knowing look. "Sweetheart, you're hesitant anyway. You're so cautious there should be an amber light blinking over your head at all times."

"Thanks for that. Though it's true, I guess." I made a face as I remembered Cal calling me an "old-fashioned girl," and wondered if that was merely code for *boring*.

"Actually," Sofia said, "I'm more interested in your little chat with Lacey. You knew she'd had a broken engagement, yes?"

"I did. But I jumped to the conclusion that she was the one who'd had her heart broken."

"It makes sense you would think that, though, right? I mean, that's what happened to you."

"Again, thank you, Sofia, for reminding me that Tim dumped me for somebody else eight years ago."

She raised an eyebrow in my direction, but managed to keep her eyes on the road. "Yeah, and look how well that turned out for him. That girl was one big bucket of crazy."

"Small consolation," I said, and we were both quiet for a few minutes.

"Hey, Vic?" Sofia asked, breaking the silence. "Have you thought enough about your feelings for Tim? I mean, taken a really good look at them, without flinching—you know what I mean, right?"

I nodded. "I know what you mean. When Lacey told me she was having her doubts about Tim, my heart was beating like mad. I'm not sure I even understand the reaction."

"Is that so?"

"Honestly, I really don't. But I will say that watching him with Lacey makes me feel old and wallflowerish. Kind of like Anne Eliot when Captain Wentworth is cavorting with the Musgrove sisters."

Sofia frowned. "Who's Anne Eliot?"

"Geez, Sofe, what good are you if you don't even get my literary allusions? I'm talking about *Persuasion*. You know, by Jane Austen? Only the second-best novel ever written. My company is wasted on you."

"Tell ya what," she said. "You read up on some Nora Roberts and we'll talk. In the meantime, the expressway comes up in a couple of miles. We'll be in AC before you know it."

Once inside the library, my research partner and I found side-by-side study carrels and got to work. By the end of an hour, Sofia and I had become experts on the topic of Leo Barone. From his beginnings as a young bootlegger to his "retirement" in the late 1950s, Barone's life was well documented. His inner circle included Alfonso Petrocelli and two other younger men: Louis "Lou Lou" Bellafante and Gerardo Domenica, aka Gerry Sunday. Though their specialty was illegal gambling, they also dabbled in prostitution and drug trafficking. Apparently, Barone and his cronies prided themselves on having a "bloodless" organization, which seemed to be borne out by Richard's assertion that his great-grandfather hadn't killed anyone. *That we know of,* I thought.

As the rain pattered against the library windows, we

worked in silence, with me taking notes on paper while my sister-in-law typed into her phone. I was startled when she poked her head around her study carrel.

"Vic," she whispered, her voice urgent. "You need to look at this." She handed me an old-fashioned photostat of a newspaper article dated 1949. It featured a picture of a man, his face partially hidden by his hat, being led away from a courthouse in handcuffs. Next to that was his mug shot. I stared at it and seemed to be looking into the eyes of my father and brother. But the man's hairline had receded, and there were now lines and shadows on his face that spoke of a hard life. Gone was the cocky grin, and his glittery gaze was pained and unfocused.

"Look at his eyes," I said in a low voice. "Drugs, I think. Or possibly alcohol. But whatever it is, he looks like he's in withdrawal from it." I felt a pang of pity as I stared into the face of the man who might well be my grandfather's lost brother. *What happened to you, Roberto?*

"Read the article," Sofia urged, just as though she had heard my unspoken question.

Trenton, November 12, 1949

Robert Reese, aka Robert Riese, of Atlantic City was convicted of second-degree murder today in the death of Nino Mancini, known racketeer and lieutenant in the Caprio crime family. Mancini was found in his car in the Pine Barrens, dead of gunshot wounds. Reese was remanded to Trenton State Prison, where he awaits sentencing.

I raised my head slowly, meeting Sofia's eyes, nearly as wide as my own.

"Do you get it now?" she asked. "That's why Robert Riese wasn't living with Alfonso and Pete in 1950. He already had another address—a great big stone house in Trenton."

Chapter Sixteen

On the ride home, Sofia and I debriefed, pooling our knowledge of Leo Barone and Riese's involvement with him. We had spent another hour in the library searching him out, but the trail went cold with Riese's conviction.

"What do you think happened to Robert Riese?" I asked as we headed north on the highway.

"I think he probably died in prison. Don't you? There must be some way we can get ahold of those records. Was he ever up for parole, for example?"

"What kind of prisoner was he?" I added. "And did he kick his drug habit?" I stared at the strained face in the grainy copy I'd made of the article. He looked ill, as though he'd lived a dissipated life. But he didn't look dangerous. I studied the picture a little longer before I had a thought. "Hey, Sofe?" I asked. "Have you ever heard of Richard the Third?"

"I think so. Isn't he that English king they dug up in a parking lot in London? I saw a *National Geographic* special about it." She frowned. "What does he have to do with your missing great-uncle?"

"Their faces. For years people believed that Richard

the Third had murdered his little nephews so he could gain the throne. But when you look at his likeness, he just doesn't look like a murderer." I held up the clipping. "And neither does Robert Riese. You know, Bernardo is a good reader of faces. We could use him right now."

Sofia raised an eyebrow. "Hate to break it to ya, Vic, but Bernardo the Annoying Detective doesn't exist outside your imagination."

"I wonder . . ."

"You wonder what?"

"Well, did Riese really do it? Murder the Mancini guy, I mean?"

"He was convicted, wasn't he? But you think he was framed by Barone, don't you? And maybe Pete knew that from his brother and was holding it over Richard Barone's head?"

"I don't know what to think." I looked out my side window and watched the mile markers roll by, my mood as dark as the gray sky. The rain had stopped, but it was damp and chilly, and I didn't much relish the thought of another night in my cottage with only flashlights and candles. I let out a loud sigh. "Even if he *was* framed, how would we know after all these years? I'm beginning to think we should just drop this whole thing."

"If nothing else, Vic, don't you want to know if Riese is really your great-uncle?"

"Sure, but how do we confirm it? Dig him up and test his DNA?"

"There's a thought," Sofia said. "I wonder how hard it is to get an exhumation order."

"Please. Let's not get carried away, okay? Hey, what were the names of the Barone cronies again?"

"Bellafante and Domenica. But they've got to be dead by now."

"True. But maybe there are relatives—kids or grand-kids who know something about their pasts. It's worth a try." I pulled my notebook from my purse and began writing. "Barone's enemy was named Caprio, right?"

"That was the other crime family, yeah." She glanced over at me as we slowed for a toll. "None of those names are that common; it might not be hard to find somebody in one of those families who knows something. In the meantime, I'll work on Danny and see if he can get hold of those old prison records. Is it okay with you if I tell him what we found out today?"

"Please do. I hate keeping stuff from him. But more than that, we need his help. Without him, we'll never find out what happened to Robert Riese."

After a stop at a Chinese restaurant that still had power, I arrived at my cottage clutching my notes, my newspaper clipping, and a pint of General Tso's chicken. I sat out on my deck in the fading light of dusk, shivering in my old Rutgers sweatshirt. Between bites of chicken and red pepper, I mulled over what we knew so far. Most of it was supposition—what did I really have to go on beyond the words of an elderly alcoholic and a photo from the 1940s? I swallowed the last of my chicken, trying to sort out the different threads that ran through a story that started long before I was born. Essentially, there were two mysteries to solve: Was Robert Riese really Zio Roberto? And was Stinky Pete a true threat to someone or just an old man who wanted some attention? Once I had answers to those two questions, then I could investigate the connection between them. If Pete's death had been murder, the motive might lie in the past. Or it might not.

But there *was* somebody who might be able answer at least one of those questions. I took out my phone and made a call.

"I appreciate your taking the time to see me, Father Tom."

"It's delightful to see you, Victoria." He raised a thick eyebrow. "In fact, I'd like to see more of you on Sundays."

His tone was kind, and he was smiling, but I still squirmed a little in my seat in the rectory office. "I tend to go to Saturday evening Mass. Well, when I *do* go," I added hastily. *Great, Vic, lying to a priest. There's probably a special section of hell reserved just for you.* "Did you enjoy the party Friday night?" I asked, desperate to move the conversation away from my church attendance.

He nodded. "I did. And I was gratified to see that my special fresh sauce was on the menu. I picked up the recipe on a trip to Sicily."

"That was your recipe? You must rate high with Nonna. It was delicious, by the way—the arugula gives it a nice bite." I hesitated. "But much as I enjoy chatting about food, I'm here for a different reason. I'd like to talk to you about Pete."

His face was unsurprised, perhaps because he'd heard of my recent adventures in amateur detection. "Of course," he said. "I'll help in any way I can. I'm hoping to have a memorial for him as soon as they release the body." He shook his head. "Pietro was a bit of a lost soul. And sadly, his death reflects his life."

I leaned forward in my chair. "Father, do you believe Pete's death was an accident?"

"I'm not sure what I believe, to tell you the truth. I know he was troubled; that's partly why he turned to drink." He looked steadily at me. "Why do you ask, Victoria?"

"Because several weeks ago he told me he 'knew things.' That he had stories to tell me for my mysteries. And I wonder if something he knew might have been a threat to someone."

Father Tom's expression didn't change. "I can't really speak to that," he said.

"But you're not surprised, are you? You either sensed— or know for sure—that Pete had information, information he may have planned to use in some way."

He pressed his palms together and crossed his thumbs, as though he was about to pray. "I *cannot* speak to that," he said again.

It took me a minute, but I finally connected the dots. "Oh," I said. "Confession."

His answer was one syllable. "Yes."

"All right," I said, taking a breath. "Might I ask some things about his life? Where he would go for shelter, for example?"

His shoulders relaxed and he nodded. "Well, he would come here whenever we sheltered the homeless, which is about once a month for several days. During the cold months, he would sometimes travel to the county shelter and stay there for weeks at a time. On occasion, he would rent rooms, but he never lasted long."

Given his hygiene, I thought, *it was a miracle he lasted anywhere.* "Did he go to hotels?" I asked. "I wouldn't think he could afford them."

"No," he said, "but one of our parishioners, Mrs. Ferraro, would sometimes rent him a room in her basement. She lives in an old house over on Eighth."

"That's near my parents," I said, scribbling the name in my notebook. I would definitely be paying her a visit. "Father," I asked, "if you think about the route between the restaurant and the rides pier, can you think of places he might have sheltered the night of the storm?"

He tilted his head in thought. "I assumed he wandered into the carousel house to get out of the storm. That was the direction he was heading when I last saw him."

"I'm pretty sure it would have been closed. In fact, that's one of my big questions: What was he doing there?"

"Have you tried to trace his movements?"

I nodded. "Unfortunately, I found one of my father's wine bottles and a dinner napkin from the restaurant in the alley next door. I think that was his first stop. And our line cook, Nando, told me he saw Pete carrying a shopping bag with something heavy in it."

"And you think more wine was in that bag?" He spoke slowly, weighing his words. "Are you saying that you believe someone at the restaurant deliberately gave Pete wine, perhaps to cause him to drink himself into a stupor—or worse?"

"Yes. Call it a gut feeling, but I can't shake it. His blood alcohol was unusually high, even for a heavy drinker."

Father Tom released a sigh. "Poor Pete. Out there alone in the storm like a drunken King Lear. What a sad end."

"It's that, Father, for sure, but it might also be a deliberate one."

He put his hand on my arm. "Victoria, you know there are things I can't tell you about him. But if you're asking me whether someone might have had a motive to take Pete's life, the answer is yes. I'll say this much: Through

his own bad choices—through his own sins, if you will—
he made himself vulnerable to someone's evil designs."

Someone's evil designs. The phrase repeated itself over
and over as I left the rectory. While the priest's words
might have been a bit melodramatic, their meaning was
clear. Pete wasn't lying when he said he knew things. But
what did he do with that information? Or *intend* to do?
On impulse, I pulled over, dug my phone out of my purse,
and searched for a Ferraro in Oceanside Park on Eighth
Street. There was just one—Lillian—and it appeared she
was the only person in her household. I had about an hour
of daylight left and decided to take a chance. I couldn't
show up at an old lady's door in the dark, but if I hurried,
I just might get the information I needed.

The ramshackle Colonial at the end of the block loomed
over the tidy Cape Cods and bungalows that lined the
street. A nondescript shade of brown with black trim, the
house was badly in need of paint. One window shutter hung
crookedly, and the brick steps were in disrepair. There was
an air of poverty about the place; it was no wonder Lillian
Ferraro was willing to rent her basement to Stinky Pete.

I hesitated at the front door, wondering what I would
say. *Try the truth, Vic, for once.* I rang the doorbell and held
my breath. The tiny woman who opened it frowned at me.

"May I help you?" she said. "I don't want any reli-
gious magazines if that's what you're selling. I have my
own church."

"Are you Mrs. Ferraro?" I asked.

"That's Miss Ferraro. Who are you?"

I held out my hand. "I'm Victoria Rienzi. My family
owns the Casa Lido. In fact, my parents live one block
over on Seventh."

Her face creased into a smile as she took my hand. "I know your grandmother from church. Sometimes we go to bingo together." She opened the door wider. "Would you like to come in?"

I followed her into a living room that looked like a 1970s time capsule. The furniture was good quality but shabby, done in a neo-Colonial style that featured lots of eagles and crossed rifles on the upholstery fabric. She led me to the kitchen and motioned me to sit down.

"Call me Lillian, please." She settled into the small chair across from me. "What can I help you with?"

"Miss Ferraro—Lillian—did you sometimes rent your basement to Pete Petrocelli?"

She nodded. "Yes, now and then. I felt sorry for him." She lifted a thin shoulder. "And to tell the truth, I could use the money. I heard what happened the night of the storm. They say he drank himself to death. Is that true?" She blinked behind her thick glasses, her watery blue eyes magnified.

"I don't think they know yet how he died. In fact, that's something I'm trying to find out. He was at our restaurant that night, and we're all wondering what happened to him."

She nodded again as I spoke. "It's only natural," she said. "To want to know, I mean. But I hadn't seen him for about a month. He came in June and left at the end of July."

"Did he leave because he couldn't pay you?" I asked.

"No, he always paid. And always in cash." She shook her head. "But I asked him to leave. He was *scifoso*," she said, using Italian slang for a dirty person. Despite her old appliances and speckled linoleum floor, Lillian's kitchen was immaculate; it smelled of the fresh basil and marigolds she had in pots along the counter. No matter how much she needed the money, it must have taken a lot for her to allow Stinky Pete into her home. And that raised another question: How did Pete afford to pay rent?

"You say he always paid?" I asked. "Where do you think he got the money?"

She shrugged. "Me, I don't ask."

But I do. "I know this is an imposition," I began, "but would you mind letting me see where he stayed? Maybe I can get some idea of how he died."

She opened a door off her kitchen and pointed down a narrow flight of steps. "You can look. I don't mind. But I don't like to take them steps if I can help it, so I can't go showing you around." She lifted her chin as though challenging me to argue with her. "I've got the arthritis, you know."

"Please, don't trouble yourself," I said, starting down the stairs, feeling lucky and relieved to be on my own to look around. "I'll be fine."

She switched a light on behind me and called out, "The room is on the right side. Has its own entrance. I didn't want him in my kitchen."

Even in late summer, the basement room was chilly, the stone walls unfinished and damp with moisture. An old-fashioned camp bed stood in a corner, covered with a thin cotton blanket in a faded shade of blue. There was a small table with a lamp, and a ratty braided rug on the floor, but that was all. I switched on the lamp and surveyed the space. There was no indication that anyone had even been here. I leaned close to the bed and sniffed, but smelled only laundry detergent. Mrs. Ferraro had probably washed all the bedding thoroughly.

Dropping to my knees next to the bed, I slid my hand

under the mattress and pulled out a flat object, a navy blue billfold that looked like a passport. But when I opened it and saw what was inside, I knew. It wasn't a passport, but a pass*book*, from First Savings Oceanside Park. A book that showed small deposits of cash, rarely more than a hundred dollars at a time. I looked at the machine-stamped dates. Two years previous there had been a balance of less than fifty dollars. The last deposit, made only two weeks ago, brought the balance to nearly ten thousand. While I knelt in that musty, dark room, the truth struck me. Small deposits, all in different amounts, spaced at fairly regular intervals. An account that grew from a few dollars to several thousand.

I tucked the bankbook back under the mattress, wondering if I'd just discovered a motive for murder. Was Stinky Pete, who'd boasted of knowing things, more than just a harmless alcoholic or an unwashed bum? Was he also a petty blackmailer? If so, maybe someone had finally gotten tired of paying him off.

Chapter Seventeen

Isabella peered from her window at the two men on the stoop below. The younger of the two wore his cap pulled low over his eyes; he stood with his shoulders hunched, his movements furtive and frightened. The older man was broader and thickset, wearing an expensive suit.

And not like the ones made in her garment shop, but cut and tailored to order. Even from the window, she could see his fine shoes of Italian leather. He held out his palm and the younger man placed something in it. Money. A payoff, she thought. Isabella had heard of such men in the neighborhood . . .

I looked back at the words and sighed; it was clear that the details of the case of Stinky's Pete's death and my great-uncle's history were seeping into my work. *Okay, Isabella, I've got about an hour left on this computer. Help me figure out what to do with you that doesn't involve gangsters or other disreputable types.* I sat at my desk, the cursor blinking on the screen; I knew I wouldn't do any more writing this morning, and I might as well save the battery. It was time to catch up with my partner in crime-solving.

*   *   *

"So, the question is," Sofia said as we sat in her office, "what exactly did Pete know?"

"And not just what, but who—he had the goods on somebody, possibly more than one person. At least that's how it looked. Where else would he get the money for rent and regular bank deposits?"

Sofia held up her thumb and fingers and began counting off. "Social Security. Pension checks. Help from a family member we don't know about. Even panhandling if he was good at it. Any number of places."

I shook my head. "No, Sofe, they were small payments, under a hundred bucks in cash on a fairly regular basis. The last deposit was only made a couple of weeks ago."

"How much did he have in total?"

"Over nine thousand."

"That's not a lot of money, Vic."

"Relatively speaking, it is. This guy everyone assumes is a homeless drunk has nearly ten grand in the bank."

Sofia still looked doubtful. "I don't know. If he really was blackmailing somebody, wouldn't you expect him to have more than that?"

"Maybe. But such small amounts wouldn't raise suspicion. And I think this was more about having some power and control than it was about the money. When he told me he knew things about people, he was almost—I don't know—*gleeful*."

"And Father Tom confirmed that Pete had put himself in a dangerous position with at least one person, maybe more." Sofia opened the red folder and took out a pad and pen. "There's only one thing to do, Vic. Time to make our list." She pointed her pen at me. "It had to be some-body at the party, right?"

"I think that's a safe assumption. So let's start with Rich-ard Barone. At least we have an implied motive there."

She nodded and scribbled on the pad. "The connec-tion to Robert Riese. I wonder if it had to do with Riese's murder arrest?"

"Certainly possible. Hey, Sofe, let's make a note to dig into that one a little more. We need to find out how much time he served. Again, I wonder if he died in jail. If noth-ing else, I'd like to be able to tell my dad and my grand-mother the truth about Zio Roberto."

"Okay, but let's not get sidetracked," Sofia said. "So we've got Barone. Who else?"

"Strictly speaking, any and all the guests and waitstaff could be suspects, right?" I asked.

"True," she said, "but for now let's go with the likeli-est, starting with the guests. What about Iris?"

"Iris?" I frowned. "She's, like, the gentlest human be-ing on earth. Why would she want to hurt Pete?"

"You said yourself that she's crazy about Barone. What if Pete was blackmailing him and he shared it with her? She might have wanted to protect him."

"Put her name down, but I'm not buying her as a mur-derer. Anne McCrae is a more likely fit. She's obsessive about this town and her role as its leader. What if Pete knew something about her?"

"Certainly possible," Sofia said. "And she's a slippery one. How about Gale Spaulding?'

"The librarian?" My voice rose with incredulity. "Are you kidding me?"

Sofia shrugged. "I'm not counting anybody out. In

fact, I'm adding Father Tom," she said as she wrote his name out carefully.

"Okay, I draw the line at our parish priest, Sofe. He was concerned about Pete. Why would he deliberately draw attention to Pete walking toward the rides pier?"

Sofia tapped her temple with a forefinger. "A shrewd move to deflect suspicion."

"How did you get so cynical? You're not even thirty years old, for gosh sakes!"

"I'm not a cynic, I'm a realist. We can't rule anybody out. In fact, we should probably get the full guest list from your mother."

"I'll work on that. In the meantime, what about staff?"

"You tell me," Sofia said. "We got the Casa Lido regulars and all the summer help."

"I know we're not supposed to be ruling anybody out, but I don't see Lori or Chef Massi knocking off poor old Pete. Florence, on the other hand, has a vicious streak."

"Okay, so Florence DeCarlo goes on the list. What about the kid? The busboy with the scars on his face? Poor kid," she added.

"Listen to you," I said, "showing sympathy for a suspect."

"Well, he can't help his bad skin. But he's not a very friendly type, is he?"

"An understatement if I ever heard one. No, he's sullen and kind of withdrawn. His name's Jason Connors, by the way."

Sofia made note of the two names. "Any other summer hires? What about the blond with the ponytail? I caught her checking Danny out when she was serving the appetizers."

"Alyssa? Miss Sorority Girl? Your imagination's working overtime on that one. She's a kid—maybe twenty or twenty-one."

Sofia raised a perfectly arched eyebrow. "And you think twenty's too young to give an older man the eye? Please."

"We're not talking about flirting here; we're talking about murder. What possible reason would Alyssa Mayer have for wanting Pete dead?"

"What reason would *any* of them have, Vic? He had something on them. Think about it. This is a guy who sleeps out, who roams all over this small town. He's in the perfect position to observe things about people—things they think they're keeping private. And if you're right about those deposits, he was using that information to make money off them."

I sighed. "And I was feeling so sorry for him. But Pete sure isn't the innocent we had him pegged for. Father Tom even said it—he put himself into danger."

Sofia nodded. "He pissed somebody off big-time."

"Oh, I just had a thought," I said. "What about the temporary guys we hired for the party? I think there were at least six extra servers here that night."

"Let's not worry about them right now," she said, still making notes. "We'll start with the likeliest guest first."

"Unfortunately, I think I know who that is," I said. "Richard Barone."

"You've talked to him once," Sofia said. "We don't want to raise his suspicion."

"I think I already did that, but you're right. We'll hold off on him for a bit. Where should we start?" I asked. "Or I should say, *with whom*?"

"I think it's better if I focus on the restaurant staff," she said. "You ruffled some feathers with that wine bottle. Put me down for Florence DeCarlo, Jason Connors, and Alyssa Mayer—can you get me addresses on them?"

"What are you gonna do—show up at their doors?"

"Heck no. I'll be parked down the street, practicing my stakeout skills."

"Not again," I said with a groan. "I thought you gave up on the whole private investigator thing."

"No way." She patted her belly. "It's just on hold for a while."

"Sofia, if you do anything to put yourself or that baby in danger—"

"Give me a little credit, will you? All I plan to do is check out where these people live and watch their comings and goings for a bit. In the meantime, I think you need to tackle the other party guests—start with Iris Harrington and Anne McCrae."

"I don't mind grilling Anne, but I like Iris. She's a friend."

Sofia wagged her finger at me. "There are no 'friends' in our investigations, only suspects."

"If you say so," I said with a sigh. "When do you plan to do these stakeouts, by the way?"

She glanced at her phone for the time. "ASAP. I don't have another class until after lunch. I can close the studio for a couple hours and follow up on those three. We can meet back here later this afternoon. Text me the addresses as soon as you can, okay?"

"Will do. And you'll be careful, right?"

She rolled her eyes at me. "Yes, Nervous Nellie. You sound just like your mother."

"Thanks loads. I'll be touch," I called as I headed out the door.

After a quick call to my mom, I sent Sofia the three

addresses. Florence and Jason both lived close to Ocean-side; Alyssa lived in Westwood, a few miles inland. Wishing I could ride shotgun with Sofia instead, I reluctantly drove to the Seaside Apothecary to see Iris, hoping to get that interview over with before I tackled our snarky mayor.

Her store appeared quiet, and I jumped as the bell over the door rang when I opened it. Iris came forward, today wearing a sheath dress in a floral print; the faint scent of patchouli wafted my way.

"Hi, Victoria," she said, without her usual friendliness. In fact, her manner was wary. "Anything I can help you with?"

You can tell me if your boyfriend's a murderer. "Yes," I said, my forced smile making my face ache. "I'm out of those probiotics I bought last month."

"Oh, of course. They're over here with the vitamins."

Did I imagine the relief I heard in her voice? I followed her down the aisle, and she handed me a plastic bottle. "There are ninety in this size. Is that okay?"

"Perfect, thanks." We stood across from each other among the rows vitamins, both of us silent for a moment. "So, how are you and Richard doing?" I asked, my voice unnaturally loud in the quiet store.

This time there was no question about it; her attitude shifted as swiftly as the winds across the bay. "I know you went to see him," she said coldly. "He told me all about it."

"Right," I said. "I was doing research for my new book and—"

"Oh, please, Victoria. I know you better than that. You think I forgot that you came here in May with questions about toxic herbs? That was supposed to be *research*, too, wasn't it? And now you're at it again."

I tried to approximate a look of confusion. "Iris, truly, I had questions about an ancestor of mine that I thought Richard could answer."

"Don't you dare insult my intelligence." She crossed her arms. "I know why you went to Richard's offices. As if he would have anything to do with the death of that disgusting old man."

"I never suggested that."

"But you're thinking it," she said, pointing at me accusingly. "Why else would you have gone to see him? You can't help yourself, can you? You've snooped around twice before. It's become a habit with you." Her voice was harsh, her eyes angry. I was unprepared for this side of the gentle, hippie Iris I thought I knew.

She stepped closer to me, her patchouli scent overwhelming. "Stay away from him. I finally have some happiness, and if you think I'm going to let you—or anyone—get in the way of that, you're dead wrong. Now please leave my store. And find somewhere else to buy your vitamins." She spun around and stalked to the back of the store while I stared after her, my mouth gaping.

Iris Harrington wasn't just in love with Barone; she was obsessed with him. And who knew how far she might go to protect him? Because there was only one word for the look in her eyes as she stared me down: *murderous*.

Chapter Eighteen

Still shaken from my encounter with Iris, I was relieved to learn that Mayor McCrae wasn't in her office; I wasn't up for another confrontation. I was sitting in my car, pondering my next step, when my sister-in-law called.

"Guess where I am," she said, but didn't wait for me to answer. "I'm down the block from Alyssa Mayer's house, where her mom and dad are busily packing their SUV with boxes and clothes. Meanwhile, the princess is standing in the driveway directing them."

"I think she goes to school in Boston," I said. "Her classes probably start right after Labor Day. And if they're leaving today or tomorrow, I don't see how we're going to get much from her."

"We might have gotten something already," she said. "About a half hour ago she scooted down the street, acting very much like somebody who didn't want to be seen. But you could see that blond ponytail from a block away."

"What was she doing?" I asked.

"Meeting somebody. A guy in a red Dodge Charger—not a very subtle car to be driving around in. It had vintage plates on it, too. She got in the car and they talked for a few minutes. Then they kissed for a while—and man, did that get boring—and next thing I know, she's out of the car, fixing her hair, and hightailing it back home."

"Did you get a look at him?"

"Yup. He drove right past me. He's no college kid, that's for sure. Looks closer to thirty. His hair was super short, like it had been shaved and it's growing back in. Fair skin and I think light eyes, but I didn't see the exact color."

"Except for the red car, he could be any number of guys out there, though, Sofe."

"That's where you're wrong, Vic," she said, unable to keep the satisfaction out of her voice. "He had tats up both arms. Talk about identifying characteristics."

Even in my warm car, I felt a chill up both arms. "I think I've seen that guy," I said. "He was one of the extra waiters we hired."

"He was at the party? Oh, this is better than I thought," Sofia said, and I could imagine her rubbing her hands together with glee. "Somebody to add to the list. Now, did Miss Alyssa know him beforehand or did she meet him that night?"

"She might have suggested him for the job, but I wonder if that even matters," I said. "Or if *he* even matters."

"Talk to your mom anyway, Vic. Find out his name."

"I'm writing it down right now. Listen, he didn't see you, did he?"

She let out a huff. "You have no faith in me, SIL. Of course he didn't see me."

"Okay, but I think you should get out of there now. I shudder at the thought of what my brother might do if he found out you and the *bambino* were out on a stakeout."

"You let me worry about Danny. I'm heading back to Oceanside now anyway to track down Jason and Florence. I'll let you know what I find out. Hey, how did you do with Iris and McCrae?"

"Not great. Her Honor's not in her office and I'm not sure Iris is speaking to me." I explained Iris's suspicion and her heated words. "She's very protective of Barone," I said.

"Sure sounds it," Sofia said. "And it makes you wonder how far she'd go for him. So, who's next on your list?"

I sighed. "I guess I'll go see Gale Spaulding at the library. She might remember something from the party, but I hardly see her as a murderer."

"Remember what I said, Vic."

"Yes, I know—nobody's a friend. Everybody's a suspect. Even the librarian."

When I got to the library, the parking lot was pretty full, even on a beautiful August day. With power still out on my side of town, the library provided electricity, a wireless network, and lots of diversion. I found Gale in her office attempting to eat a quiet lunch. She motioned me inside.

"Need to charge up or do some research?" she asked.

"A little of both, Gale. But I was hoping you had a minute to talk."

"Sure. Have a seat. Is this for your book?"

"Yes and no." Mostly no, if I were to be honest. "I've been thinking a lot about Pete Petrocelli's death, and there are some things I'm wondering about."

"Really?" she asked with a frown. "I would think it was pretty straightforward. He was elderly, he was an alcoholic, and he was out in that terrible storm. I assumed it was an accident. I mean, doesn't everyone think that?"

"I think the police are still looking into it. Maybe it's just my mystery-writer brain working overtime, but I was wondering if you noticed anything the night of the party—say around the time that Pete showed up?"

She set her sandwich down and leaned forward in her chair. "Do you think someone killed him?" she asked in a hushed voice.

"Oh no," I said, realizing I'd just tipped my hand to a possible suspect, no matter how unlikely she might be. "I mean, who would want to kill Pete?" *Besides the people he was blackmailing, of course.* "No, I meant I was curious about the events that led him to the carousel house."

"I'm not sure I can help you with that," Gale said. "I mean, I remember Pete making quite an entrance at the party. He was already a couple sheets to the wind."

"You're right. He was swaying and stumbling when he got there." *So it might not have taken that much wine to push him over, after all.* "Gale, did you notice him talking to anybody?"

She frowned in concentration. "I saw him heading to the table your dad had set up as a bar. And I remember your grandmother going to intercept him."

"What about after that?"

She shook her head. "I'm not—hang on a minute. I did see him talking to someone else. A woman. I was wondering if he was bothering her."

A woman? "Was it Iris?" I asked, struggling to keep the excitement out of my voice. "The woman who owns Seaside Apothecary?"

Gale's expression was confused. "The woman who owns Seaside Apothecary has long salt-and-pepper hair. This woman had short dark hair. I remembered her because she was wearing such a pretty dress."

"With purple flowers on it?" I asked. "In fact, they were irises."

"Yes, of course! Oh, I should have put that together — the irises, I mean. But she's changed so much I didn't recognize her."

"She certainly has," I said. How much had Iris changed? Enough to kill — or help kill — a man who was a threat to her new relationship? "Thanks, Gale. You've been a big help."

After I left Gale's office, I found an open study carrel with an outlet and got my laptop and phone plugged in. I clicked open my e-mail, dismayed by the number of entries in bold. When was the last time I'd checked these? There were two from Josh Silverman, my agent, and one from my editor, Sylvie Banks. The next Bernardo mystery was releasing right after Labor Day, and Sylvie's message was a reminder to call the publicist about possible book events. I had every intention of returning those e-mails until my phone dinged with a picture message from Sofia. The text read:

Look who I just saw leaving Florence DeCarlo's house

I squinted at the image and enlarged it with my fingers. On the front steps of Florence's house was a pixelated but still recognizable Jason Connors. What was Jason doing at Florence's? A kid she couldn't stand and for whom she had little patience? One plausible reason might be that she had cash for him from her last night at the restaurant. But the waitresses generally settled up with the cleanup staff at the end of the shift. *There's definitely something weird about this,* I thought. Just then another text from Sofia came through:

Check yr email

I refreshed the page to see a new e-mail from Sofia; there was no message, but only a link to an archived edition of the *Oceanside Chronicle* from late June. I clicked on it, wondering what could possibly be of interest in an article about the graduates of Oceanside High. Scrolling down through the various senior portraits of smiling boys and girls, I stopped the cursor on a dark face with an even darker expression. There was Jason Connors, wearing a too-big jacket, a blue tie, and a scowl. Next to his picture was a description of his achievements: National Honor Society, awards in chemistry and computer programming, leader of a robotics team, with perfect SAT scores in math, chemistry, and physics. I shook my head in disbelief. But the kicker came at the end of the piece. "Connors will be attending MIT on a full scholarship in the fall."

One thing was clear: This kid was a genius. And he certainly wasn't the Jason I knew. The monosyllabic boy who claimed he was going to county college was, in actuality, something of a prodigy who was heading to one of the most prestigious schools in the country. On a full ride, no less. So why pretend to be something else? Why hide who he truly was? Was he merely being modest? Or secretive? I thought about what a scholarship to MIT would mean to a working-class kid like Jason. His was a future that most kids dreamed of.

But what if something threatened to jeopardize that future? Something that Stinky Pete knew or saw? I immediately got busy searching *Jason Connors + Oceanside Park*. He seemed to have a lower social media profile than most kids his age; there was no Facebook or

Twitter account. I went back to the *Chronicle*'s archives and searched his name, coming up with an article about his robotics team. I scanned it quickly, skipping over the scientific details. Several members of the team were quoted, as were their parents. And there it was, in the last line of the piece. A quote from Jason's mother expressing her pride in her son and her wish for his bright future. Her name leaped from the screen; without thinking, I shut down the computer and mechanically packed up my things. I had a visit to make. Before I could leave, however, a final text from Sofia appeared on my screen:

He's got a lot to lose, doesn't he???

He sure does, I thought. But enough to kill for? There was only one way to find out.

It wasn't long before I was heading to a small garden apartment complex just outside Oceanside Park. Judging from the lights on in a few windows, this building and its twin next door had power. I found the apartment number I was looking for and climbed the crumbling brick steps Jason Connors had stood on just an hour before. I rang the buzzer; when nobody came I knocked and continued knocking until the harried and furious lady of the house finally answered the door.

"Hello, Florence," I said cheerfully. "I was hoping to have a chat with you and your son."

"I don't know what you're talking about," she said, her voice on edge. She stood blocking the opening of the door. "I live alone."

"Give it up, Ma," said a male voice from behind her. "She knows. Just let her in."

"I don't work for you anymore," she said. "And I don't need you harassing me."

"I'm not trying to harass you, but I think I have a right to know why you lied to me and my family." I deliberately raised my voice. "Why did you hide the fact that you and Jason are mother and son?"

Florence stuck her face close to mine, close enough for me to see her smeared mascara and smell her cigarette breath. "I don't have to answer your damn questions."

"You could always let me in. Unless you want the neighbors to hear all about what a fraud you are."

"Will you let her in, for Chrissakes?" Jason roared, and jerked the front door open, nearly knocking his mother over in the process. Florence turned without a word and I followed her inside.

I stepped into a small living room, most of which was taken up by a long computer table. On it was an expensive-looking desktop computer, two laptops, and what appeared to be a small robotic car. "You're quite the whiz, aren't you, Jason?" I pointed to the cluttered table. He merely grunted, cleared some newspapers from the couch, and sat looking at me expectantly while Florence hovered at his side. As I looked from one to the other, I searched for a resemblance that wasn't there, part of the reason they'd gotten away with their masquerade.

"I don't get it," I said. "Why the whole act about hating Jason? What was the big deal about letting us know that he's your son?"

Her voice was petulant. "We didn't think you'd hire us both. Some places have policies against it. We needed the work."

"So you never thought of just asking my father or grandmother?"

She let out a snort. "That crazy old hag. She never woulda let us work together."

While I wasn't above calling my grandmother a variety of names—privately, of course—it was quite another thing to hear someone else do it. My Italian blood was rising, and I answered her through my teeth. "In the first place, don't ever speak about my grandmother that way again. In the second, if you didn't ask, how would you even know what our policies are? But I think you had a different reason for hiding his identity."

Jason looked up at me through a lank strand of dark hair and frowned. "What are you even *talking* about?" His voice had that eye-rolling tone that teenagers often take with adults, and my temper flared again. Too angry to worry whether these two might be dangerous, I plowed on.

"I'm talking about Pete Petrocelli, Jason. I'm talking about you and your mother taking a job at the Casa Lido because you knew he hung around the restaurant." I paused and looked from mother to son, both of whom were wearing frozen expressions. "I'm talking about opportunity. You're a very smart boy—do I really have to spell it out for you?"

He jumped to his feet, his face dark with anger. "Get out of here, you b—"

Florence grabbed his arm. "Sit down, Jason. And shut up. I wanna hear what else she has to say." She glared at me. "I'm not as smart as my son, so maybe you should spell it out for *me*, then."

"Okay," I said. "I think one or both of you gave Pete wine the night he died. His blood alcohol was dangerously high."

"He was an old drunk," Florence snapped. "And he

probably fell and hit his head or something." She frowned at me. "What do you care, anyway? What's he to you?"

"I care about the restaurant. And as you so sweetly reminded me, he died after leaving the Casa Lido. I have a stake in knowing what happened to him."

Florence plopped down on the couch next to her son and crossed her arms. "We can't help ya with that. So you can go now." Her eyes darted to Jason, who ignored her. He was busy staring at his computer table, clearly itching to get back to it.

"I'll go after I get some answers." I looked at Jason, who stared back at me with a bored expression. "By the way, congratulations. MIT on a full scholarship. Well done. Guess you won't be attending county after all."

"It's none of your business where I go to school."

"Maybe not. But what happens at the restaurant is my business. Which of you gave Pete that wine?"

Jason shrugged. "I don't know what you're talking about."

Florence, who remained silent, fidgeted on the couch. She eyed an open cigarette pack on a table next to her but didn't take one. I wasn't getting very far with these two, so I took a chance and went with a lie. "By the way, the police know Pete was a petty blackmailer. Did he have something on one of you?"

Florence's eyes widened and she stood up. "I gave him the wine. Not Jason. It was me."

"She's lying," Jason said. "I was the one who gave him the wine. But it was just to get rid of him, that's all. He stunk and I didn't want him around. Last time I checked, it's not a crime to give an old drunk a bottle of wine."

"It might be if he dies as a result. So which of you was it?" I asked.

"Me," they said in unison. Mother and son glared at each other and I sighed.

"Look," I said, "I'm not trying to make trouble for either of you. But that empty wine bottle in the alley could be damning for the restaurant." I paused. "Unless of course your prints were lifted from it."

Florence swallowed audibly, her expression terrified, and I couldn't help feeling sorry for her. She was clearly protecting her son, but from what? I tried another tack. "You must be proud of him, Florence. He's really talented. Most kids would . . . give anything to get into a school like MIT." I'd nearly said *most kids would kill to get into that school.*

"You're damn right," she said, her bottom lip trembling. "And I'm not gonna let anything get in the way of that. Jason was not involved with—"

"Shut up, Ma!" her son screamed. "What the eff is wrong with you?"

She grabbed his arm. "Don't talk like that, Jason. Please, honey. It's gonna be fine, really." She turned to me, her face a deep red. "You get the hell outta my house now. You stay away from us, do you hear me?"

"I don't think you meant any harm, Florence," I said. "You just want the best for your son, right?"

"Get out!" she screamed. "Get out before I kick your skinny ass!"

I held up both hands. "Okay, I'm leaving." I backed out of the room, unwilling to turn my back on either of them. I hurried down the front steps, but doubled back along the side of the building and stood under an open window where I could hear snatches of conversation. Florence mentioned that they were packed and then I heard something about them leaving tonight. To bring

Jason to school, of course. His voice was a deep rumble, but he seemed to be disagreeing with her. Then Florence's voice rang out clearly:

"...guy is gone. You don't have anything to worry about."

After that, they moved to another room, and I walked back to my car. Was Stinky Pete "the guy" Florence meant? What did she mean by *Jason was not involved*? Jason was not involved in Pete's death? Or in something Pete saw and was holding over both their heads?

Chapter Nineteen

As I headed home, I thought about what I'd learned. The big reveal, of course, was that Florence and Jason were mother and son. A mother and son who were clearly protecting each other when it came to the question of who gave Pete the wine. Then there was the mysterious reference to a guy being gone. It seemed natural to assume she meant Pete, but it still didn't give me much to go on.

By now Sofia would be at the studio, so I was on my own for a while. Back at my cottage, I sat at my desk upstairs, hesitant to use up the two hours of power I had on my computer. As I looked out at the beach from my tiny bedroom window, I mulled over what we'd found out so far. A dead man with ties to my own family's past as well as to the Barones. A likely blackmailer who might have had a hold on any number of guests at the Casa Lido party, particularly Barone, Iris, Jason, and Florence. Iris in particular, as she was seen talking to Pete. Where did Alyssa fit in? And who was the tattooed man? Odds were that the man Sofia had seen her kissing was the same guy who'd worked the party. It was time to put in a call to my mom.

"Are you guys keeping busy with the restaurant closed?" I asked her.

"Well," she answered, "your grandmother is cooking up a storm in preparation for reopening. Your father is busy making wine. And I'm spending time in the garden, harvesting the last of the herbs and tomatoes." She sighed. "And trying hard to forget that tomorrow is the official start of Labor Day weekend."

"The power will be back on in time, Mom. Don't worry."

"Right. Might as well tell me not to breathe."

"Well, maybe I can at least distract you. I have a couple of questions about the night of the party."

"This is about Pete's death, isn't it?" she asked, lowering her voice. "What do you need to know?"

"Who were the extra servers for the party? Did you interview them or did Nonna?"

"I interviewed them. There were six. Three of them were Nando's cousins from Asbury Park—three brothers. We've used them before."

Despite what Sofia had said about everyone being a suspect, Nando's cousins were from out of town. It seemed likely that if Pete knew something about someone, it would be a person he'd seen around Oceanside. So we could probably rule out the Ortiz relatives.

"What about the other three guys, Mom? Were any of them from town?"

"In fact, they weren't, but again, we'd used them before."

"Did any of them have tattoos on their arms?"

My mother sounded puzzled. "Tattoos? No."

"Are you sure? Because there was a guy in black pants and a black shirt helping stack tables when the storm hit; he had tattoos on both arms. Images of plants and animals. This doesn't ring a bell?"

"Honey, I think I'd remember somebody with animals tattooed on his arms. And I can tell you unequivocally that we did *not* hire anyone fitting that description. Could he have been a guest who just pitched in to help?"

"Maybe." My mind turned over the possibilities. A helpful guest wearing the uniform of a server who just happened to be Alyssa's boyfriend? Had she allowed him to slip in to make some extra money from tips? And then I remembered: She *had* asked me about splitting tips that night.

"Victoria? Are you there, honey?"

"I'm here, Mom. Sorry. Listen, could I have the names of the extra hires?" I probably shouldn't leave any stone unturned, but I doubted any one of these guys was a murderer. After taking down the info and promising my mother I'd keep her posted, I realized our head waitress might also know something about the extra servers that evening. I shot my friend Lori a text:

Hey, girlfriend, how many extra guys were helping to serve and clear last Friday night?

In less than a minute, she got back to me:

Seven. Does Nonna have you doing payroll now?

So Lori's count was seven. But my mom had only interviewed six. I absentmindedly sent her back a smiley face, and thought again about the people at the party, particularly the one who seemed to have no good reason for being there: The Guy with the Animal Tattoos.

*   *   *

"I agree," Sofia was saying, "that we can probably rule out the Ortiz cousins." We were back in Sofia's office, red folder at the ready, the desktop computer already powering on.

"But not our parish priest? Or the town librarian?"

"Not just yet. And not Miss Iris, either, now that we know she had contact with Pete that night." She made herself comfortable in her desk chair and reached into a bag of trail mix on her desk. "But Tattooed Guy—we'll call him TG for short—interests me. We've got him on the scene and we've got him with a connection to a Casa Lido employee. Maybe him and that Elle Woods wannabe are in it together."

"Maybe, but my gut tells me he was using her to get access to the restaurant."

"In the hopes he could get access to Pete."

"Exactly. It was pretty well known around town that Pete hung around the Casa Lido." I stopped to consider an unpleasant thought. "You know what, Sofe? It kind of freaks me out that our party provided an opportunity for someone."

She shrugged. "If somebody wanted him out of the way, Vic, they would've found a way to do it. If we only knew *who* Pete was blackmailing," she said, her nails tapping the computer keys.

"We don't even know for sure he *was* a blackmailer or that he was even murdered," I said. "Everything we're coming up with is based on circumstantial evidence— Pete's boasts, an old bankbook, and an empty bottle of wine. Not much to build a case on." I helped myself to a few almonds from Sofia's bag.

Sofia poked her head around her screen to look at me. "You're forgetting something there, SIL. Our instincts. Both of us sense that something is off here."

"But the police don't. And we haven't had any visits from County Prosecutor Sutton." Twice recently I'd run afoul of Regina Sutton, a woman nearly as formidable as my grandmother. After the discovery of the wine bottle, I'd half expected her to summon me to her office for questioning, but thus far I'd heard nothing. "We need to ask Danny if there's been an official cause of death yet," I said. "And when they plan to release the body."

"I've been asking," she said, "but he hasn't been answering. I'll keep working on it, but I want to go back to the conversation you heard outside Florence's window. Tell me again what you heard."

"Well, there was some garbled talk, a lot of yelling, and then Florence's voice came through pretty clearly. She said something like 'The guy's gone. You don't have anything to worry about.' I assumed *the guy* was Pete. What do you think?"

"Well, that's the obvious choice," Sofia said. "And I'll definitely make a note of it. But I don't think we should jump to any conclusions."

"You're sounding like me," I said. "But you didn't see their reactions when I mentioned Pete's name and asked about the wine bottle."

Sofia nodded. "No doubt they're protecting each other. Tell me again how they acted when you accused them of giving Pete the wine."

"*She* was terrified. But Jason, not so much. He just seemed impatient and angry. You know, I don't know what to make of that kid."

"He seems hard to read," Sofia said. "You'd think he'd be happier, considering he's got an opportunity most kids would kill for."

"Funny, I almost slipped and used those exact words when I was talking to him. The question is: *Did* he kill for it?" I paused, straining to remember the conversation I'd had with Florence and Jason. "You know, Sofe," I said slowly, "as a mother—and probably a single mother, as far as I could tell—Florence would be as heavily invested in her son's future as he is. She actually said something to the effect of 'I won't let anybody stand in his way.' Then she said 'Jason was not involved.' With what? I wonder."

"Pete's death," Sofia said promptly. "Or something Pete saw."

"Exactly." I thought for a moment. "Florence said the guy was 'gone.' *Gone* can mean a lot of things."

"Right. It could mean *gone* like Pete is gone. As in dead," Sofia explained unnecessarily.

"Yeah, I get that. But it could also mean *gone* as in 'has left.' What if they weren't talking about Pete, but about somebody who's alive and well?"

"What do you mean?"

"Think about it. It's almost Labor Day. Who leaves here around the first week in September?"

"Summer people," she answered promptly. "And college kids like Miss Alyssa."

"Absolutely," I said, nodding. "If *the guy* isn't Pete, he could be any number of people. That's the problem. Without resorting to the needle-in-a-haystack cliché—"

"God forbid the famous writer should lower herself to such depths," Sofia interrupted. "But I will: You think we don't have a snowball's chance in hell of finding the person Florence was talking about."

"And you *do*?" I shook my head and groaned. "It's another dead end."

"Not necessarily. Maybe our focus should be on the *event* itself and not the mysterious guy—whatever it was that Florence insisted Jason wasn't involved in."

"Okay," I said, "but I'm not sure where to start."

She leaned across her desk and patted my arm. "You'll figure it out. I have faith in you." She turned her eyes back to the screen. "In the meantime, I think we need to work on the Barone angle a bit more. We've got two names of men who were in Leo Barone's inner circle back in the day—Bellafante and Domenica. I'm gonna look for relatives; I'll let you know what I find."

I said my good-byes and left feeling much less optimistic than my sister-in-law. I didn't give voice to my doubts: that trying to find out what Jason Connors had gotten himself into would be difficult and identifying the mysterious "guy" nearly impossible. And behind it all was the nagging worry that somebody would end up getting away with murder.

It was already dusk by the time I got back to my cottage that evening. I pulled into my driveway, wondering what I could scrounge from my cabinets for dinner, only to find Tim standing on my porch holding a cooler. He held it out to me with a grin.

"You hungry?"

"This must be my week for visitors," I said. *And men feeding me.* But I didn't elaborate. I didn't want to break Lacey's confidence, and my relationship with Cal (or lack thereof) wasn't any of Tim's business. "Where's your girlfriend tonight?"

"She's got a wedding this weekend. Funny, I finally get some time and she gets busy."

So Lacey was still hanging in there with Tim. I tried to ignore the tiny pang of disappointment that seemed to be tapping at my shoulder for attention. "Ah, I get it, Tim. You're on your own, so you come and see good ol' Vic, is that it?"

"Cut it out," he said good-naturedly. "With the restaurant closed, I have to cook for somebody. Hey, if you're not interested in hand-cut tagliatelle with my famous Bolognese sauce—"

"You mean Nonna's Bolognese sauce, don't you?"

"Okay," he conceded. "It's her recipe. But I made it." He held the cooler close to my face. "It's still warm. Can't you smell it? C'mon, you know you want it."

"I'm no match for a good Bolognese," I said. "So you might as well come in." I opened the door, and he followed me into the kitchen. I took down a couple of plates and two wineglasses. "Here," I said, handing him the plates. "You dish and I'll pour."

Tim set the plate in front of me with a flourish, and I stared down at it. If I had to choose my last taste of something before I died, it would be pasta à la Bolognese. Bright dices of carrot studded the pale orange glaze; chunks of fragrant meat nestled among the eggy pasta. I leaned closer and breathed it all in, my olfactory nerves registering each separate ingredient: sweet onion, garden tomatoes, the rich blend of beef, pork, and veal, a touch of cream, and the faint notes of cinnamon and clove. And behind it all were notes of spicy pancetta. "Oh God," I groaned, my nose practically in the plate.

Tim looked up, startled. My eyes met his, a smoky gray in the candlelight. As we stared, the air seemed charged, and my face reddened. "Sorry," he said, "it's just that it sounded like . . ."

I held up my palm. "I know how it sounded. Good food has that effect on me."

He raised an eyebrow, his voice sly. "I remember."

"Me, too. But that doesn't mean we make that trip down Memory Lane." I held up my wineglass. *"Saluté."*

"Saluté," he said, lifting his glass. "Go ahead. Try it. Tell me what you think."

I took a forkful of pasta, scooped up some of the meat and vegetables, and placed it in my mouth. Then tried not to groan again; it was that good. I followed up with a mouthful of Chianti and my life was complete. "Do not ever breathe this to my grandmother," I whispered. "But I can't tell the difference between yours and hers."

Tim sat back in his chair and smiled broadly. "I knew it."

I shook my fork at him. "Don't let it go to your head, Trouvare. Hey, why aren't you eating?"

"I was savoring your reaction for a minute. It was worth the time I put in for that *ragu*," he said, using the Italian word for *sauce*. He dug in, and for a while the only sound was the scrape of silverware.

I pushed my empty plate toward him. "More, please."

He took my plate and filled it and then replenished my wine. After serving me, he took seconds for himself, and we chatted companionably about the possible sale of the boardwalk carousel and the rumor that power would be back on tomorrow. I was tempted to ask him if he remembered the tattooed server at the party, but I wasn't up for a lecture about amateur murder investigations. When we were finished, Tim cleaned up the dishes and refilled our wineglasses.

"You know," I said, "I kind of like you waiting on me."

"Is that so?" He looked down at the table, a stray curl

falling over one eye. "I didn't think you liked much about me these days."

I put my hand over his. "Hey. Look at me for a minute, will you?"

"Yes, Victoria," he said in an obedient tone, but his eyes held their old spark.

"No matter what's happened between us," I said, "first, last, and always we are friends. Right?"

He clinked his glass against mine. "You bet," he said. "Friends for always." But his tone was hollow, almost disappointed. He stood and gathered his things, put his clean serving dish in the cooler, and gave me a quick kiss on the cheek.

"Bye, Vic," he said. "See you soon."

The tables have turned, I thought as I watched him go. It was clear that Tim still cared about me, and I didn't know whether to be delighted or terrified at the prospect. I trudged up to my room with my trusty flashlight and sat at my desk. I suddenly knew how I wanted Isabella to meet Tomasso, and I probably had just enough battery power to write it:

Isabella opened the door, looked from the older man to the younger one. The boy's hands were plunged into his pockets, his eyes on the floor. Were they father and son? Or perhaps uncle and nephew? The older man clutched a bottle of homemade wine; his broad smile revealed missing teeth. He spoke in a strange dialect, but she grasped that they were neighbors.

The younger man pulled the cap from his head slowly, still looking down at his shoes. His thick dark hair was in a tumble; he ran a hand through it hastily, but the curls would not obey, and Isabella smiled behind her hand. At that moment, he lifted his head, and she looked into the most re-

*markable eyes she'd ever seen. She had never been to
Venice, but she thought,* This must be what it looks like.
His eyes are like the sky over Venice, a blue like no other.

*For a moment they simply stared, until he reached out
his hand.* "Tomasso," *he said in a whisper.*

"Isabella." *She rested the tips of her fingers in his warm
palm, and their eyes met in the shock of recognition. She'd
heard the women in her village speak about it—*un colpo
di fulmine, *the lightning bolt that strikes, the moment of
illumination when the world becomes bright and clear.
When the answer is in front of you.*

Here he is, *she thought,* and here I am. *We have been
waiting for each other, and now we are home.*

I sat back, smiling in the darkness, satisfied with what
I had written. So Isabella, at least, would get her happy
ending.

If only I could write my own so easily.

Chapter Twenty

It had been a week since the Casa Lido party and the hurricane that crashed it like an unwanted guest. Our side of town was still without power; the rides pier was still closed, as was our restaurant and a number of other businesses in our neighborhood. I doubted if we'd see the same influx of guests today as we did on every other Labor Day weekend. I also found myself missing the restaurant—the camaraderie of the staff, the bustle and just plain hard work of cooking and serving people every day. And frankly, the romance of my Cottage by Candlelight was wearing thin. I wanted the lights back on.

But the lights back on meant I would be back at work, with much less time to focus on what had happened to cause Pete's death. It didn't help that the possibilities went in two disparate directions—to the past, and to a circle of criminals who were long dead. And to the present, in which there were any number of people who'd crossed a moral or legal line. Did one of them deliberately cause Pete's death?

Still in my pajamas, I climbed back onto my bed to think more comfortably. My mind went back to my visit to Florence and Jason, and their panicked responses to my questions. What could Jason have done that was so bad it needed to be kept hidden? Something that would have jeopardized his admission to MIT? *Well, what kinds of things get teenagers in trouble?* I thought. Drinking and driving. Using drugs. Hazing or bullying of other kids. Then, of course, there were academic crimes like cheating or plagiarizing.

If Jason Connors had broken the law, though, that information would have landed in the media, even if it were only on the police blotter section of the *Oceanside Chronicle*. And Jason was eighteen; his name would have been made public. But when I'd searched those archives, his name came up only in relation to his schoolwork. I shifted on the bed, stuffing my pillows behind my back. I concentrated on what Florence had actually said— *Jason wasn't involved.*

Involved suggested the presence of another person or persons. Was there something that a *group* of kids had done? A group that Jason might have associated with, one that did something that perhaps Pete had witnessed?

Without Internet access, I couldn't do any more digging, but I could make some calls. I scrolled through my contacts. My brother could look up arrest records, but whether he *would* was another story. Hmm. There *was* somebody who just might have the information I needed, but I wasn't looking forward to speaking to her. *Put on your big-girl panties and just do it, Vic.* Resigned, I searched the history of incoming calls for the number I needed. Just my luck, she picked up on the first ring.

"Victoria!" Nina LaGuardia trilled in my ear. "To what do I owe this honor, darling? Do you have some murderous little tidbit for me? Hmm?"

I winced. Twice now Nina, a television journalist, had been hot on my trail for interviews, both times in connection to murders. I'd given in the first time, but since then had evaded her calls and visits. I took a deep breath and spoke. "No, Nina, not this time. Actually, I have a question for you. Do you know of any incidents in the last couple of years that involved local teenagers breaking the law?"

Her laugh was tinny and artificial as it came through the phone. "Good God, darling, that list must be a mile long. Do you really think I bother myself with stories about juvenile delinquents?" Her tone sharpened and lost its fake-friendly quality. "Why? What do you know? Are you sniffing around some corpse again?"

I sighed. If I weren't careful, Nina would connect the dots on this one. She'd reported on Pete's death last week, but he was portrayed as a storm victim. I couldn't tip my hand that his death might be more complicated than accidental drowning.

"Actually," I said, sticking as close to the truth as I dared, "I'm looking into the background of one of our summer hires. I'd heard rumors about him and I want to protect the restaurant's reputation."

"Right. So you come to me for information? When that handsome big brother of yours has access to arrest records? Something smells about this, Victoria, and it's not my Gucci perfume. What are you really up to?"

"Nothing," I said, staring down at my crossed fingers. "I'd just like some information. Do you recognize the name Jason Connors?"

"No, I do not, so you can just stop bothering me about this." No longer curious, but merely exasperated, Nina droned on. "I mean, for goodness' sake, if you want to know about teenagers, go find some high school kid to gossip with. I have better things to do."

"I know, but . . . ," I began to say, but stopped dead, the phone frozen to my ear. *Go find some high school kid to gossip with.* "Thanks, Nina. Gotta go!" I said, ending the call with one hand and dragging off my pajamas with the other. I hopped around on one foot to untangle them from my ankles while I placed another call.

"Sofia, listen, I think I've got a lead. Or I'm about to get one. Just wanted to let you know before I head out." I kicked off the pajamas and tugged open a dresser drawer, pawing through it for a pair of jeans, the phone clamped between my neck and shoulder.

"Wait, where are you going?" Sofia's voice was distant as the phone slipped onto the floor.

"The one place that probably has the answer to the Jason Connors mystery," I shouted. "I'm going back to school."

I pulled into the parking lot at Oceanside Park High School and was immediately flooded with memories: Lori and me sneaking out at lunch to go to the beach; following our soccer team to matches with our big rival in Belmont Beach; the smell and din of the school cafeteria, and days and evenings spent working on the school newspaper, the *Cormorant*, on which I'd been a features editor for two years. Our paper was a weekly, and each Labor Day weekend the editors and adviser would show up on Friday morning to begin work on the first issue. Rather than resenting the loss of the last weekend of summer, kids on staff found it a badge of honor to come in to work on the paper. It was likely that this year's group would already be inside, and if there was anybody who could tell me what Jason Connors had been involved in, it would be a student journalist.

The front door of the school was open, and as I walked inside, the fifteen years I'd been gone seemed to fall away. The sound of excited voices filled the hallway, getting louder as I approached the journalism room. The same inscription from Dante still hung over the newspaper room door: ABANDON HOPE, ALL YE WHO ENTER HERE. I stepped inside and the chatter stopped as one by one, the kids' heads turned to look at the stranger who'd crossed their threshold.

"Ms. Rienzi!" boomed a familiar voice. "What brings you back to this heart of darkness, pray tell?" I looked up into the looming face of my old adviser, Allan ("Only my monogram gets As") Ainsley, and grinned. He was still here, still teaching British lit and journalism, and still inspiring terror in the hearts of his students. Standing six-five in his loafers, he was built like a linebacker but spoke like an Oxford don. Or at least his idea of an Oxford don. Without waiting for me to answer, he gestured grandly in my direction.

"Students, meet Ms. Victoria Rienzi, former features editor on the *Cormorant* and current purveyor of popular fiction." The way he said *purveyor* made me feel as though I walked around wearing a sandwich board to advertise my mysteries. But I was used to Mr. Ainsley–isms and fairly immune to them now.

"Hey, guys," I said. "First day back, right?"

They waved and nodded, and after a few polite hellos, they quickly resumed their work behind a bank of sleek computers, the only real change to the classroom I remembered. There were still the same shaky worktables and on the walls the same dog-eared posters for various productions of *Macbeth*, a play with which my former teacher was obsessed, as he claimed James I as an ancestor. I pointed. "I see you're still a *Macbeth* fan." *Oh no*. The word was out of my mouth before I had time to think about what I'd just said.

"Ms. Rienzi!" he thundered. "Have I taught you nothing?" He pointed to the doorway. "You know the consequences. Now you must suffer them."

I backed out the door and stood in the hallway, making a halfhearted attempt to neutralize the curse with more Shakespeare. " 'Angels and ministers of grace defend us,' " I quoted.

"Once more, Victoria. This time with feeling."

By now the kids were laughing, no doubt relieved they weren't the ones suffering the Curse of the Scottish Play. Resisting the urge to remind him that the bad luck only happened in theaters, not high school classrooms, I gave it one more try from the hallway. " 'Angels and ministers of grace defend us!' "

"You may return," he said grandly. "Now, that will teach you never to speak the name of the Scottish Play in my classroom."

"Yes, Mr. A," I said, feeling like a sophomore again. "Uh, do you have a couple of minutes to chat?"

"Certainly. Come pull up a chair." He sat down at his cluttered desk and I sat in a low-seated chair intended for someone much younger and shorter. I opened my mouth to start, but Mr. A got there ahead of me.

"So you *are* still writing your little mysteries, are you not, Victoria?" he asked. "Any chance you'll write a real book soon?" He clutched both hands into fists. "You know what I mean by a real book, don't you? One with meat. One with heft." He shook his large fists at me again. "You know what I mean by *heft*, right?"

I knew exactly what he meant. Some highbrow literary tome that I couldn't have written to save my life. My old teacher had expected me to become a critical darling, but I'd ended up writing beach books instead. Which was fine by me, but a bit of a disappointment to him.

"C'mon, Mr. Ainsley," I said, "you of all people know that my true talent lies in commercial fiction."

At this he grumbled something indecipherable, but I did make out the word *crap*. He crossed his arms and glowered down at me in my little chair. "So I hope you have a valid reason for interrupting our labors here today."

As Mr. A was notoriously short of patience, I jumped right in. "I need some information about a former student."

Mr. Ainsley raised one bushy, triangular eyebrow. "Is that so?"

I nodded. "Did you have Jason Connors by any chance? He graduated last June."

He frowned. "No. He wasn't one of my students. But a high achiever, nonetheless. Quite talented, but . . ."

"But what?"

He shifted in his chair and it gave out a loud creak under his bulk. Picking up a small bust of Shakespeare from the top of his desk, he stared down at it as though the Bard might provide an answer to my question.

"What about him, Mr. A?" I persisted.

He held up a broad palm. "Heaven forfend I should criticize one of our young scholars, but Mr. Connors got up a lot of people's noses."

"By *people* you mean staff, I take it."

"Staff, students, the custodians, the cafeteria workers, you name it," he said, waving his hand. He leaned toward me, dropping his voice. "Look, the kid's brilliant. Not a word I use lightly, Victoria. But he knew it. And he lorded it over the other students and even his teachers. There was a . . . ruthlessness about him." Almost involuntarily, he glanced up at the *Macbeth* poster and then back at me. "Anyway, once he got into MIT, he was insufferable."

"Okay," I said, "I already know he's not the most personable boy. But I'm wondering if he did something wrong—possibly even illegal—"

"To what do these questions pertain, Ms. Rienzi?" he interrupted.

Several of the kids' heads lifted at the sound of Mr. Ainsley's sharp tone. One ponytailed girl in wire-rimmed glasses was standing a little apart from the other kids. Though she appeared to be working, it was clear she was listening to our conversation.

I turned my attention back to my old teacher and tried an approximation of the truth. "Jason worked for the restaurant this summer and there was some trouble. I'm trying to ascertain whether he might have had something to do with it."

"Trouble, eh? Would that be like the *trouble* last May when that producer was found dead behind your family's restaurant? Did you think I didn't know about that?"

I sighed. "I think there's very little you and the *Cormorant* staff don't know, Mr. A. That's why I'm here. Can you please tell me if Jason Connors got mixed up in something illegal when he was at Oceanside High?"

He slapped his palm down on his cluttered desk.

"That I cannot speak to," he said, echoing Father Tom's words about Pete. "I won't speculate about a situation that is based merely upon rumor and innuendo."

"So there was something?"

He glanced over at his students; the girl with the ponytail and glasses was holding marked-up article copy and making suggestions to a boy working at a computer. Though she seemed engrossed in her work, I knew she had her ears trained on us. He scowled at her and her cheeks reddened.

He looked back at me and lowered his voice again. "Last fall, the online grading system was hacked. Whoever did it didn't change any grades. They only used the comment function to leave stupid messages. It was a malicious prank—nothing more. The school kept it in house and out of the media. The kids were never caught."

"Kids?" I asked. "There was more than one? And Jason was one of them?"

He shook his large, shaggy head, looking like an intelligent dog. "There is no proof that he did it. But he had the skills for it, as did any number of kids in this building."

"You said it was kept out of the media. But did the *Cormorant* report on it?"

"We did," he said, nodding. "It was a straightforward news piece. We indicated that the perpetrators were unknown, featured some bland quotes from administrators, and that was that."

I glanced over at the busy staff. "I remember how you trained us, Mr. A. Those kids did some digging, didn't they? But if they had names, they wouldn't have shared that information with you."

"No, because I'd be legally bound to turn those names

over to the authorities." He shook his head. "We're not in the business of ruining lives here. Certainly not for a stupid prank that ended up hurting no one." He jabbed his forefinger in my direction. "And what did I teach you fifteen years ago?"

"That we have to balance truth with harm," I said with a sigh. "But prank or not, Mr. A — what they did was illegal. And if a college got wind of such activities, isn't it possible it would rescind that student's admission?"

"Of course. That's why, if my staff had information about who hacked into the system, they weren't sharing it with me. Nor would I want them to." He stood up, a clear signal that our conversation had ended.

"Thanks, Mr. A. I'll let you get back to it." I stood up and held out my hand, wincing as Mr. Ainsley crushed it in his large paw.

"Nice seeing you again, Ms. Rienzi. And remember what I said: I want to see a real book from you one of these days!"

I walked down the hallway mulling over my conversation with Mr. A. Was the grading system hack truly a victimless crime? Was it merely a prank perpetrated by very smart kids just to prove they could do it? In Mr. A's place, would I have also turned a blind eye? But why wouldn't the school have worked harder to find out who was behind it? And just as I reached the door to the parking lot, it struck me: Jason Connors was a classic success story. The son of a working-class single mother who wins academic awards, gets a full ride to a prestigious institution, and brings lots of positive attention to the school that fostered his talents. Even if the school suspected he was behind the system hack, they would be reluctant to call him out on it. *Geez, Vic, you're getting cynical in your old age. Maybe Jason—or whoever did this—just covered his tracks too well to be caught.*

I was opening my car door when I heard a breathless voice behind me. "Miss Reed?"

Not expecting to hear my pen name, I turned, a little puzzled. The girl with the ponytail and glasses held out a pen and a battered copy of *Molto Murder*, one of my early Bernardo Vitali mysteries. "Would you mind signing this for me?" she asked a little shyly.

"Sure. What's your name?"

"Kelly," she said, peering over my shoulder. "I recognized you from the back cover."

I scribbled our names on the title page and handed it back to her. "How do you like working on the paper?" I asked her.

"I love it," she said. "It's so cool getting that first byline. But it's nothing like having a real book out with your name on the cover."

"Yeah, it is. How do you think I started? With bylines on the school paper." She seemed in no hurry to leave, and I knew that she had not followed me out here just to have me sign her book. "Can I ask you something, Kelly?"

Her blue eyes gleamed behind her glasses. "Sure." Her expression was expectant, almost excited.

"I think you overheard some of what I was talking about with Mr. A," I said. "The system hack that you guys reported on last year."

"We wanted to do an investigative piece on it, but he wouldn't let us." She rolled her eyes. "So much for hard-hitting journalism." She shrugged. "In the end, though, nothing we got could be substantiated. But we all knew who did it."

"Was it Jason Connors?"

She nodded. "And someone else from the robotics team. Here's the thing: People didn't really like Jason that much, but there's nobody who doesn't like Guy. So nobody would, like, run and tell about the hacking."

I frowned. "I'm sorry, I don't understand. You said no one liked Jason, but then you indicated that everybody liked the guy. Which is it?"

She shook her head. "I said everybody liked *Guy*. Guy St. Vincent. I guess you could say he was Jason's accomplice."

Chapter Twenty-one

*O*f course. *Guy is gone* was what Florence had said, not *that guy is gone*. I'd had the name all along, without even knowing it. "Kelly, where is Guy St. Vincent now?"

"At school, I guess, like they all are."

College kids make terrible suspects, I thought. *Especially in September.* I crossed my fingers and sent up a small prayer to the Holy Mother. "Do you know where he goes to school?"

She frowned slightly. "Why do you want to know? Are you gonna make trouble for him?"

"No, really, I'm just looking for information. I won't get him in trouble. I give you my word."

"Okay," she said with a sigh. "He's at Rutgers."

"New Brunswick?" I could barely contain my excitement. Aside from being my alma mater, Rutgers was a relatively short hop along Route 18; I could be there in under an hour.

She nodded. "Look, he's a really nice kid. He made a stupid mistake by following Jason. Please don't tell anyone about what they did, okay?"

I wanted to be able to promise Kelly that I would keep my mouth shut. But that would depend on what I learned and whether I needed to bring the information back to the police or the county prosecutor. "I'll do my best, truly." I held out my hand. "Thanks for the information. It was nice meeting you, Kelly. You better get back inside before Mr. A has to hunt you down."

"I'm not afraid of him," she said, but her hurried gait said otherwise. "Thanks for signing my book," she called.

I hopped in the Honda, turned on the ignition, and checked the gas gauge. Plenty to get me to New Brunswick and back. It was time for my next class reunion.

I had barely gotten onto the highway when I realized that I only had a name—Guy St. Vincent. He was one student out of thousands. Heck, tens of thousands. I didn't know his dorm; I didn't even know if he lived on the main campus. The Rutgers campus sprawled over several miles and a couple of towns. Where would I even start? College Avenue seemed the natural choice, but did they even house freshmen there these days? *Think, Vic. Think.* I considered calling the university and pretending to be his mother, but what kind of mother forgets where her own kid is housed? It was Friday of the holiday weekend—did I really think some helpful administrative assistant would pick up her phone and just hand me the info I needed?

This wild goose I was chasing was likely to leave me with nothing but an empty gas tank and a heap of frustration. I turned off the highway into a strip mall and parked my car. I took a swig of warm water from the bottle in my cup holder and tried not to think about how old it was. I fished my phone out of my purse and stared at it, as if for answers. And it gave me one, in the form of a tiny "F" that appeared among my apps. Gotta love Facebook. And uncommon names.

Unlike Jason, Guy St. Vincent had a Facebook page. And Rutgers, New Brunswick, was listed as his college destination, but there was no mention of his dorm. He had posted on his timeline this morning, though: *Move-in day at RU!!!* So he was on campus, as Kelly had said. I scanned his page, spreading my fingers across the window to zoom. And then I saw it—a link to a Twitter account.

One quick tap and I had what I needed because Guy St. Vincent was live-tweeting his move-in day for all the world to see:

> Last trip in the elevator to the top of Hardenburgh. Whew.

So the wild goose wasn't so elusive after all. He was living in one of the freshman dorms—in fact, it was *my* old freshman dorm. I started the car and got back onto Highway 18, taking the same route I'd driven more than a decade ago, with almost the same sense of excitement and adventure.

In another thirty minutes I turned onto College Avenue. With a little shock of recognition I took in the student center, the library, and the three river dorms that stood sentinel over the Raritan. And it was all much more crowded and busy than I remembered. I parked in a lot near the dorm (illegally, I was sure) and took a minute to orient myself. These were not the shabby 1950s high-rises I remembered. *Wow. They sure have spruced these up.*

I walked to the back of Hardenburgh, where a lone

young man in a ripped black T-shirt stood smoking against one of the cement columns. As I got closer, I noticed his eyeliner and black nail polish.

"Excuse me," I said a little breathlessly, "but I'm looking for Guy."

He slid his eyes my way and blew smoke at me in a world-weary fashion. "Get in line, sister," he said. "We're all looking for a guy."

"No, not *a guy*. Guy is his first name. Guy St. Vincent. He's a freshman."

"Cool name." Black Nail Polish narrowed his eyes at me. "You're too young to be his mother and too old to be his girlfriend. Are you a creeper?"

I smiled in what I hoped was a reassuring, as opposed to creepy, way. "No. I'm an alum, actually, and I have some information for him."

He raised one penciled eyebrow, took another drag on his cigarette, and waited.

"Really," I said. "I need to see him about, uh . . . a scholarship."

"Right. The Cougar Award, no doubt." He stamped out his cigarette and pointed to his left. "I think that door's open, though." One side of his mouth twisted in a lopsided grin. "Good luck finding your Guy."

Thanks, kid. But I took his advice. Inside the dorm, small knots of students stood talking, holding boxes and bags. A little rush of nostalgia came over me as I remembered my own first day at college; I felt ancient as I listened to their chatter and laughter. I moved from group to group, but no one knew Guy or recognized the name; I had likely come all this way for nothing. I was heading out the door when I spotted a gangly boy with blond curls in the parking lot. He was holding a duffel bag in front of his chest; as he shifted it, I saw his T-shirt: SAVE THE CAROUSEL, OCEANSIDE PARK, NEW JERSEY.

"Excuse me," I said, hurrying toward him. "Are you from Oceanside? And is your name Guy, by any chance?" *And please don't think I'm a creeper.*

He frowned, more out of curiosity than dismay. "Yeah. It's actually pronounced Gee, 'cause I'm French, but everybody says 'Guy.' Do I know you?"

I held out my hand. "I'm Victoria Rienzi. My family owns the Casa Lido Restaurant in town. Jason Connors worked for us this summer and—"

He held out both hands in front of him, his duffel bag sliding to the ground. "I don't know who you are or why you showed up here, but I don't want to talk to you." He scooped up his bag and tried to push past me, but I stepped in front of him.

"Wait, Guy, please. I'm not here to cause trouble for you, I promise. I need five minutes of your time and then I'll go, okay? My questions are about Jason, not you."

His shoulders sagged, and when he looked at me I saw the worry in his face. "Five minutes?" he asked in a low voice.

"Absolutely. We can stand right out here and talk if that's okay, and then I'll go."

Guy nodded, but looked unhappy. "What do you want to know?"

"Look," I said quietly, "you probably know this is about hacking the school computer system. I would never ask you to incriminate yourself in any way—do you believe me?"

"I guess." He looked at me, his pale blue eyes filling with tears. "I thought that crap was behind me. I'm starting college, for God's sake!"

"I know. I'm not here to rake it up, but I need some information. You can just nod or shake your head, okay? Was it Jason's idea to hack the system?"

He nodded without hesitation and I sensed that he was being truthful. "I don't want to know details," I said. "But could someone have seen you near or in the school?"

He shook his head and then spoke. "When Jason and I . . . hung out, we were usually at his house. If we, uh, *played computer games*, we played them on our own desktops."

"Got it. Did his mom know you guys were 'playing computer games'?"

"Afterward, she knew."

"Okay. In terms of playing these games, did you guys *talk* about the games first? I mean, there had to have been some planning involved, right?"

He nodded, looking more miserable by the minute, but stayed silent. "Did you do this talking at his house or at your house?" I asked.

"His. But if his mom was home, we'd talk somewhere else in town."

"In a public place?" My pulse picked up its pace. "Such as?"

Guy shrugged. "Usually outside somewhere. The park. The boardwalk."

The park. The boardwalk. Two places Stinky Pete frequented, and two places that offered areas to hide. My heart raced as I asked Guy my next question. "Do you know if anyone ever saw or heard you talking about the, uh, computer games?"

Guy swallowed hard, his Adam's apple prominent in his thin neck. "There was a homeless guy," he whispered. "He was asleep under the boardwalk one night. Jason said we shouldn't worry about it. That the guy was a drunk and wouldn't have understood what we were talking about anyway."

"Thank you." I held out my hand again and Guy took it reluctantly. "I promise you that this conversation never happened," I said.

And I meant it. Even if I had to bring information to the authorities, there was no way I would mention this boy's name. I pointed to the building behind him. "I lived there my freshman year. It was great. In the winter we'd steal trays from the dining hall and slide around on the frozen river."

He smiled, though he still looked as though he wanted to cry. "I don't think you can do that anymore," he said, pointing. "There's a big fence up now."

"Yeah, well, that was back in the day. I loved it here. And you will, too."

I watched his figure grow smaller as I drove away, grateful that Guy St. Vincent had taken the risk to talk to me. Because another tiny thread had just been woven into the fabric of the mystery of Pete's death—maybe soon a true pattern would take shape.

Chapter Twenty-two

*B*idding my college alma mater a fond farewell, I popped in my earbuds and called Sofia on the ride home to fill her in.

"So, are we pretty sure that Pete overheard Jason and Guy talking about hacking the school computer system?" she asked.

"Yes," I said. "I think Guy was telling the truth. The poor kid was terrified that I was there to drag it all up again. I promised him I'd try to keep him out of it."

"I think you'll be able to keep that promise, Vic."

"What do you mean?"

"Pete's death was officially declared an accident. Danny found out this morning. And after he told me, he sweetly reminded me that you and I should stop 'digging around,' as he put it."

"But Danny doesn't have all the information we do," I insisted. "He doesn't know Pete was probably a black-mailer. He doesn't know about Iris or Tattoo Guy and the Alyssa connection or that Jason Connors and his mother had something big to hide that Pete probably knew about."

"Hey, you don't have to convince me," Sofia said. "But you know your brother."

I did know my brother, and it was time to have a conversation with him. "Is he working today?" I asked.

"No, he's down at the marina. But you better hurry if you want to catch him. Once he's out on the boat, he's gone for hours."

"I'll try. What about you? Anything new on the Zio Roberto side of things?"

"I did find something promising, but I'm still looking into it. I'll tell you when I know more. Good luck in talking to Danny, by the way."

"Right," I said. "I'm gonna need it."

Despite having grown up around water, I wasn't too fond of boats. I stepped gingerly onto the deck of Danny's boat, the *Bella Napoli*, feeling queasy the moment it shifted under my feet. I found my brother out on deck, inspecting his cooler full of smelly bait. He was in his fishing uniform—tattered shorts and T-shirt, ball cap, and wraparound sunglasses.

I wrinkled my nose at the smell. "I don't know how you can handle that stuff," I said with a shudder. "It's gross."

"Can't catch fish without it, sis." He crossed his arms and assumed a wide-legged cop stance. Not a good sign. "What are you doing here? I know it's not to go fishing." He cocked his head. "Or maybe it is."

"Believe it or not, I'm not here to get information. I'm here to *give* it. I heard that Pete's death was ruled an accident and I'm not so sure that's the case."

"*You're* not so sure? And what makes you an expert in law enforcement? I would think you'd be relieved after the wine bottle incident."

"Lose the attitude, would you, Danny? There are things you don't know—things the county prosecutor might find relevant. Will you hear me out or not?"

He sighed. "I won't be able to leave dock until I do. What have you got?"

I filled him in on Barone and Iris, Florence and Jason, and Alyssa and her tattooed boyfriend. I reminded him of the Leo Barone and Zio Roberto connection, and also of Pete's boast of knowing things.

Danny pushed his ball cap to the back of his head and took off his sunglasses, a sign he was taking seriously what I had to say. "I'm listening, Vic," he said. "But I'm not convinced. What makes you so sure Pete was black-mailing anybody?"

Here was the tricky part. Did I admit to my brother that I'd talked myself into Mrs. Ferraro's house and snooped around Pete's room? That I'd found his bank-book? I hadn't involved Sofia, but what I'd done, while legal, wasn't exactly ethical. I took a deep breath, hating myself. "Let's call it a gut instinct, Dan."

My brother settled his cap on his head and squinted at me from under the brim. "Is that so? Your gut's telling you that Stinky Pete was blackmailing people with infor-mation he'd overheard?"

I nodded, and grasped at one last straw. "There's also my conversation with Father Tom. Obviously, Father Tom had to keep some things confidential, but he implied—strongly—that Pete had put himself in danger in some way."

"I don't know," he said, shaking his head. "You've got me thinking." He pointed at me in warning. "But just thinking, you hear me? Don't get carried away, Vic."

"I'll try not to. In the meantime, Dan, can I ask a favor? Do you think you can use your contacts in law enforcement to find out what happened to Robert Riese, aka Zio Roberto? I'm thinking he probably died in prison, but I'd like some proof."

"Sofia already asked me, but I didn't follow up on it because we still don't know for sure that Riese was Pop's uncle." He shook his head and put his sunglasses back on, probably in the hopes that I would get the hint and go. But as stubbornness runs in the Rienzi family, I didn't move.

"Okay," he said with a huff. "I'll do it. I'll check the state databases and use my contacts in corrections to ask about this Riese character. If only to get you two broads off my back."

"Thanks, Danny. Oh, and one last thing—do you know if your brothers in blue were able to lift any prints from that wine bottle?"

"If you are asking me *can* prints be lifted from the bottle, yes, they can."

"You know what I was asking you, but let's keep it theoretical. How do they do it?"

He grinned. "With glue, believe it or not. They put the wine bottle in a water tank, open a glue packet, and drop it in. The fumes from the glue react with the acids in the prints and harden them in place."

"That's so cool," I said. "I totally need to use that in the next Bernardo mystery."

"Cool or not, sis, that bottle—the one you're concerned with—is a no go."

Did my brother mean that no prints were found or that an empty wine bottle did not constitute evidence of murder? But even if he was drunk when he arrived at the party, there had to have been at least one other bottle for

Pete's blood alcohol to have been that high. Was that what he was carrying in the bag Nando had seen him holding? I would probably not get an answer, but I had to ask.

"But what about *another* bottle, Dan? Like perhaps one that might have been found in the carousel house?"

My brother rested two heavy hands on my shoulders and lowered his head so that it was level with my own. "There *is* no other bottle. Or anything else that suggests foul play. That carousel house was swept clean. And except for your 'gut instinct' about Pete being a black-mailer and some ancient mob history, there's nothing there, Vic. Nothing."

"Maybe. Or maybe not." I gave him a quick peck on the cheek. "Listen, I'll keep you posted." I stepped back onto the dock, relieved to have something firm under my cowardly feet.

"Wait . . . posted about what?" he called as I hurried away. "You leave this alone, Vic—do you hear me?"

Oh, I heard him all right. Whether I was listening was, well, another kettle of fish.

After a quick stop for lunch, I headed back to my cottage, where I was greeted by a strange sound from my basement—the steady chugging of my new sump pump. Could it be? I reached for the light switch, and lo, the basement was flooded with light. (And still some water, but the smell was improving.) When I got downstairs, there was another scrawled note from my dad:

> *Hey, sweetheart, your new pump is up and running. Also, I did some cleanup down here with bleach. Don't think you'll have trouble with mold.*
> *Your Pop*

You had to love the guy, though I did wonder how he'd gotten into my house both times. I wouldn't put it past my parents to have a duplicate key to the cottage. Note to self—have locks changed, *subito*.

Up in my bedroom, I plugged in my computer, charged my shaver, and ran my blow dryer just because I could. Still reveling in my restored power, I was about to charge my phone when I noticed the voice mail icon. My mother's cheerful tones rang out across the room:

"Hi, darling! In case you're not aware, the power is back on. Plan to come in early tomorrow morning for food prep so that we can open for Saturday lunch. See you bright and early!"

While I was glad the restaurant wouldn't be losing any more business, my window of time to work on the Mystery of Stinky Pete was shrinking. I'd be tied up at the Casa Lido all weekend long, right through Labor Day. In the meantime, Jason would be on his way to school, with his mother probably right behind him. Alyssa was already gone, and who knew where Tattoo Guy might be? Barone would retreat behind his protective wall of money, and meanwhile, this trail was growing ever colder. I had a sense of urgency I couldn't ignore, but did I have enough evidence to convince County Prosecutor Sutton to initiate a murder investigation? I'd barely convinced my brother that there was more to Pete's death than it appeared. Once Pete's body was released and the official cause of his death made public, it might be too late.

Or would it? I sat at my desk, gazing out my small bedroom window at the ocean in the late-afternoon sun. Maybe if the murderer—or murderers—thought they were safe, they—or he or she—might get careless and give something away. My thoughts were interrupted by a dinging sound from my phone. A text and a link from Sofia:

Have you seen this?

I followed the link to today's *Oceanside Chronicle*, which bore this headline: "Richard Barone Pledges to Save Carousel, Financier/Philanthropist to Purchase Historic Ride."

I scanned the article avidly, taking in the important details. In it, Barone offered to buy the carousel and provide funding for its yearly maintenance. The article included quotes from Barone, some boardwalk business owners, and Mayor McCrae, who could barely muster any gratitude. *Guess you've been foiled again, Annie,* I thought. But the most interesting part was the article update, posted only hours before:

> *With the restoration of power to the eastern end of town, there will be a ribbon-cutting ceremony tonight out on the pier at 8:00. The carousel house will be open and all rides functioning. The event is open to the public.*

For the first time since Pete's death, the carousel house would be opening its doors to the public. To the families who now had their weekend restored. And to the curious who wondered about the body that had been found inside. Would the guilty party be among them? This was exactly the kind of scene I would imagine for my fictional detective, Bernardo. He would show up in his linen suit and Panama hat, closely observe all the suspects, trap one of them into a confession, and have the mystery solved by the end of the chapter. *If only*.

I texted Sofia back:

I'm going. You?

What do you think? she replied. Dinner first? How about Louie's at 7? I'm craving sausage sandwiches.

See you there, sister, I texted back.

Because come hell or high seawater, I would be out on that pier tonight. And I would finally get inside that carousel house—the scene of the crime.

Chapter Twenty-three

Sofia and I sat at our favorite table at Louie's on the boardwalk, out on the upper deck facing the ocean. I looked at my sister-in-law's plate, where she had carefully piled the onions from her sandwich.

"Since when don't you like onions?" I asked.

"Since I got pregnant. I should clarify—I like them but they no longer like me." She turned her plate in my direction. "Want them?"

"Sure." I heaped more of the sweetened, caramelized onion on my sandwich. "It's not like I have a date or anything." I grinned. "I can just breathe all over you instead."

"Thanks. So—wanna hear what I found out about Leo Barone's cronies?"

"Mmmph," I said through a mouthful of grilled sausage and sweet red pepper.

"I'll take that as a *yes*." Sofia carefully cut into her sandwich, putting one small bite at a time in her mouth. "Okay, so the two guys in Barone's inner circle were Louis Bellafante and Gerry Domenica. Bellafante was a dead end, but there's a Gerald Domenica Jr. living in Somers Point."

"Wait," I said. "Somers Point is right near—"

"Atlantic City," she said. "Within ten miles or so. I looked it up."

"I wonder if it's possible that he's related somehow."

Sofia nodded. "It definitely is. According to People-Search, he's around eighty. The age is right for him to be Domenica's son. *And* he's listed with a *junior* after his name. I think he's our guy, Vic."

"What do we do? Just show up in Somers Point and track him down?"

"Why not? We've done it before."

"It's not that. When do we get there? The Casa Lido reopens tomorrow. I'll be tied up all day." I took another bite of sandwich and wiped my dripping chin.

Sofia tapped her nails on the tabletop. "Let's think about it for a minute." Her eyes widened. "Wait, I totally got this. You know what a germophobe Tim is—what if you get 'sick' while you're prepping? One good sneeze and he'll kick your butt out the door."

"I don't know, Sofe. I would feel guilty faking sick when they need every hand there tomorrow. No, I'll appeal to my mom with the truth. And I'll offer to come back for dinner service."

"You're too conscientious," she said, dismissing me with a wave. "They work you to death there anyway." She leaned across the table, her eyes bright. "Don't even try to tell me you're not curious. This might be the one way to find out the truth about Zio Roberto."

"Okay, you got me. Can you get away from the studio by two?"

She nodded and pointed to my empty plate. "I take it you're finished. Because we have to get going."

After a quick trip to the ladies' room, Sofia and I

headed down the boardwalk to the rides pier. It was dusk, and on the bay side, the sun was setting in a bright array of oranges and blues. I let out a happy sigh. "I love the beach at this time of day, don't you?"

"Yup," Sofia said. "And I like it even better after all the tourists are gone."

"Hey, let's be happy the boardwalk is crowded." I looked around at the families, their arms full of stuffed animals and balloons, their kids eating custards and taffy. "It's good for business and good for the town."

"Anne McCrae must be in her glory," Sofia said as we approached the rides pier. It was packed with people; clearly, they weren't squeamish about the idea of a body being found here. Maybe they were curious. Or maybe the death of a homeless alcoholic a week ago was already old news. At one end of the pier, the Ferris wheel was in motion, its colorful lights twinkling with each turn. My stomach lurched as I looked up at the giant wheel, remembering a recent ride on it with Cal. The dome of the carousel house, decorated with strings of white lights, rose into view. As we got closer I admired the green patina of the oxidized copper and the building's fanciful circular windows.

"I assume Her Honor will be here tonight, right?" I asked.

"Are you kidding me? Even though she wanted to sell off the carousel, she'd never miss a photo op. I bet you anything she tries to take credit for saving it, too."

"Probably," I said as we made our way through the crowd. "This is some turnout, huh? I hope we can get inside."

"We will," she said, "but first we have to get past that guy."

I followed her gaze to the open door of the carousel

house, where a familiar figure in a blue uniform stood guard. My heart sank. "I thought you said Danny had to work tonight."

"Exactly. He's working. Wonder how we're gonna play this one off."

"Geez," I grumbled. "You'd think the Oceanside PD would have a better use for a skilled detective than assigning him to a ribbon-cutting ceremony. I wonder if there's a back way into this place."

"Too late, Vic," she said out of the side of her mouth. "He's seen us." She broke into a blinding smile and lifted her arm in a wave. "Hey, babe," she called. "Fancy meeting you here."

My brother's face was expressionless, though his eyes brightened at the sight of his wife. "Hi, honey," he said in an overly sweet tone. "I don't believe you mentioned you were coming to the festivities this evening."

She linked her arm through his, still smiling up at him. "It was kind of a last-minute thing. Vic wanted some company."

He turned to me and I shrugged. "C'mon, Dan. Did you think we'd really stay away?"

He shook his head without a word, but merely ushered us inside, with me trailing Sofia.

"Hurry up, would you?" she asked.

"Sorry. I'm busy extricating myself from the wheels of the bus under which you just threw me. Nice one, Sofe."

"He won't bother us. And anyway, aren't you glad he's here? Just in case the suspects start showing up." She lifted her chin in the direction of the old pinball machines along the circular periphery of the building. "Speaking of which."

"What do you know—Florence and Jason. I guess he

hasn't left for school yet. Wonder why he's sticking around."

Just then Sofia gripped my arm. "Look," she whispered. "Behind the carousel."

And there, arms crossed in a watchful pose, was a formidable figure with a closely shaved head and intense eyes—The Guy with the Animal Tattoos.

"What the heck is he doing here?" I hissed.

"He's kinda creepy up close," Sofia said. "What does little Alyssa see in him, I wonder."

"Some girls just love those bad boys. Hopefully, she'll meet some nice college boy to spend her time with at school." I peered around the crowd to get a better look at him. "What do you think he's doing behind the merry-go-round?"

"I don't know," Sofia said. "Lurking?"

"Clearly—but for what reason?"

Just then a low murmur went through the crowd and it parted behind us. "Excuse us, please," said a familiar baritone voice, and I exchanged a look with Sofia.

"Barone," she whispered. "With Iris right behind him and Mayor McCrae pulling up the rear."

"Make sure you duck when Iris starts throwing daggers my way," I said.

"She looks great, though," Sofia noted. "At least she'll kill you in style."

"Funny. Hey, they're starting."

Richard Barone stood at the carousel's entrance gate, now tied with a bright red ribbon. To his left was Iris, to his right Anne McCrae, who was holding the biggest pair of shears I'd ever seen. She stepped forward to speak.

"First, let me say how wonderful it is to see the boardwalk humming with so many of you this evening. Now that the power is back on—" Here Anne was interrupted by cheers and whistles from the crowd and she smiled broadly. "The rides pier is officially open for business!"

At those words, the lights of the carousel blazed on, and the crowd applauded wildly. Anne signaled for them to quiet, but she was clearly enjoying the crowd's enthusiastic response. "Right now," she said, "it's my pleasure to welcome Mr. Richard Barone, a longtime summer resident of Oceanside Park and well-known philanthropist. It is our good luck that Richard has extended his spirit of giving to save our historical carousel, with its hand-carved animals and beautiful nineteenth-century design."

"Like she cares," Sofia muttered. "She's only interested in the bucks."

Someone tittered behind us and I shot Sofia a look, putting my finger across my lips.

"Mr. Barone has also generously offered to maintain the carousel each season," Anne continued, "allowing our town to enjoy its beloved icon for many years to come." She handed Barone the giant scissors. "Richard, would you do us the honor?"

"It's my pleasure, Anne," he said. "You should all know that this beautiful machine behind me was imported from Italy more than one hundred years ago. It is an exceptional example of Venetian craftsmanship." He pointed toward the top of the carousel. "If you look up as you ride, you will see painted scenes of Venice. The animals are hand-carved and decorated, and inside resides its original Wurlitzer organ. As a side note, you might be interested to know that the word *carousel* originates from a contest of horsemanship called *il carosello*, which is Italian for *little war*."

Did I imagine that Richard Barone's eyes rested momentarily on my own? Was that glance a declaration of our own "little war"? Richard flashed his charming white grin and held up the shears. "I hereby open the Oceanside Park Carousel," he shouted, snipping the red ribbon in half. "Rides will be free this evening, by the way."

He nodded to the double line of visitors, mostly children, already standing at the gate. And then he turned my way and smiled directly at me. "Ladies and gentlemen, we have a famous resident among us this evening, our very own local author, Victoria Rienzi, who writes mysteries under the pen name Vick Reed."

My cheeks burned and my stomach did a flip-flop. Why was he calling attention to me? Sofia was digging her elbow into my ribs and Iris was glaring a hole in my forehead. Richard held out his hand. "Come up here, Victoria, will you? I think you should take the first ride."

Sofia elbowed me again. "Get up there!" she whispered. "Don't make him more suspicious than he already is."

But my shoes seemed to have filled with lead. My knees were locked in place. "I can't," I whispered back. "I have a stomach full of sausage and onions. What if I get sick?"

Her only response was to give me a shove in Barone's direction. Without a word, he took my hand and led me to the ride platform; his grip tightened as we stepped together onto the ride. "There you go, Victoria," he said quietly. "Now go pick out a nice horse."

I walked self-consciously across the wooden platform; avoiding the horses, I sat in one of the chariots along the inside of the ride and pulled the worn leather belt across my lap. Behind the ride stood the tattooed man, his arms crossed as though he was waiting. But for what? As the ride filled with eager kids and more than a few adults, he watched intently.

Richard Barone's voice cut through the noise of the crowd. "Let 'er go!" he shouted.

At Barone's signal, the tattooed man heaved a giant wooden lever, looking on impassively as he set the ride in motion and the organ music began its slow, piping sound. *He's the ride operator,* I thought wildly. *Was he here the night Pete died? Did he let him into the locked carousel house and to his death?* The ride sped up; I gripped the sides of the carved chair as it made its second turn. The lights spun in circles around me, and one by one I could make out the faces of Florence, Jason, Barone, and Iris. Florence, standing protectively in front of her son. Had she provided Pete with enough wine to kill himself? Or had it been Jason, now scowling and restless, wishing he were anywhere but inside this carousel house? Or was it Barone, standing with his arms crossed, keeping his eyes on me with every revolution of the ride? Did he have something to hide that Pete was privy to? And was Iris desperate enough to serve as his accomplice? Or something worse? Round and round their faces circled dizzily across my line of vision; the music reached a crazy pitch while I begged silently in my head, *Please don't get sick, please don't get sick, please don't get sick . . .*

Out in the crowd I could see Sofia's worried face; Danny stood behind her and the relief washed over me like a wave. My brother was here; I would be okay. *As long as I don't puke all over a nineteenth-century work of art.* As the ride came to a stop, I unlatched the leather strap and sat to catch my breath before I stood up. My legs rubbery, my stomach queasy, I took a hesitant step to the edge of the platform, only to have the ride operator reach out his arm to me. He smiled knowingly, much in the same way Barone had when he'd invited me to ride. I didn't have a choice; if I didn't have a hand to steady me, I'd end up facedown on the cement, just like poor Pete. He took my hand gently, his intense eyes looking straight into my own. If he recognized me from the party, he didn't let on.

"That's it, miss. You're fine. Step right there. You got it," he said kindly. I let go of his hand, and for the first time had a clear look at the animals on his left arm. There were jungle beasts and mythological creatures, framed by bright green vines and red flowers. In the center of the design, just below his elbow, was a prancing yellow lion wearing a crown. Dragging my gaze from the vivid images, I met his eyes. There were a pale golden brown, almost feline in their shape and color. *Like a lion's eyes,* I thought, *and just as dangerous.*

I muttered a hasty thanks and hurried to Sofia and Danny as fast as my wobbly legs could carry me. Suddenly, I didn't care if Pete had been murdered—I just knew I had to get out of there.

My brother took my elbow and steered the two of us through the crowd. "C'mon, you two," he said. "There's nothing to see here."

"Do they teach you to say that at cop school?" I asked when we were out in the fresh air again. "I'm surprised you didn't tell us to move along."

"And I'm surprised you're still nosing around a case that's been closed," he said sharply. "Vic, I meant it when I said there was nothing to see."

"I wouldn't be so sure about that, hon," Sofia said. "There are still plenty of unanswered questions about Pete's death."

"Even so," Danny said through his teeth, "it is not your job—or my sister's—to find those answers."

"I don't know," I said with a sigh. "I'm almost ready to agree with you. Look, I got a little spooked in there; I'm not gonna lie. Right now all I want to do is head to my cottage and curl up in my bed to read, with every light on in the house!"

"You okay to walk?" Danny asked.

"Absolutely. I'd like to clear my head, not to mention settle my stomach. But I have a question, big brother: The guy who operated the carousel—the one with all the tattoos—do you have any idea who he is?"

He glanced back inside the building and frowned. "No, but I can tell you one thing: The guy's done time. He's got all the signs. The shaved head. The tats. The jacked arms and chest."

Goose bumps prickled up and down my arms as I remembered the expression on the tattooed guy's face. "So you're saying—"

"I'm saying," my brother said, "that I know an ex-con when I see one."

Chapter Twenty-four

*I*n the bright sunshine of the next morning, my night in the carousel house took on a dreamlike quality, and a sense of unreality permeated my thoughts about the case. Pete's death had been ruled an accident, after all. And it was likely that alcohol would have killed him in the end anyway. But I hadn't imagined Pete's own words or his bankbook; I hadn't dreamed up motives where they didn't exist, and I hadn't invented the family history that Sofia and I had uncovered. Or Florence's fury and fear. There *was* something more to Pete's death, and I was sure that a visit to Gerry Domenica would tell us more.

After a hasty shower, I threw on my white blouse and black pants and biked over to the restaurant. Now that all of Oceanside had power, the town was humming with beachgoers. We would have a busy day at the Casa Lido, and I wondered how I would escape in time to meet Sofia for our trip to find Gerry Domenica.

But when I got to work, my frazzled-looking mother greeted me at the back door, took my arm, and steered me straight to her office. She pointed to her desktop computer, which showed only a dark blue screen and a blinking cursor.

"I thought it was updating," she said. "Then I got the blue screen—you know, the one that indicates your computer has crashed—so I tried to restart it, but this is what I keep getting. I can't access any of my files, including the payroll spread sheets." She shook her head. "This is the last thing we need today, Victoria."

My heart sank. How would I ever get out of here now? "Try turning it off and on."

"I tried that," she said with a sigh. "And so did Nando."

"And he's better with computers than I am. But everything's backed up, right?"

She nodded. "But it's on an external hard drive at home." She looked at me hopefully. "I don't suppose you have your laptop?"

"Sorry, Mom."

"S'cuse me, Mrs. R?" Nando appeared at the office door, his face worried. "The software on the register isn't working. I keep getting a black screen."

Not long ago, my parents had switched over to a software program that allowed us to have digital floor diagrams, menus, records of food tickets, and just about every other kind of information that you need to run a restaurant. Without it, we'd be forced to go back to the chalkboard and scraps of paper. And of course the timing couldn't be worse—this was the busiest weekend of our summer.

Nando turned to go and then looked back at us. "Is too bad Jason is gone. He is good with computers."

Jason. My mouth dropped open and I felt a small shiver. Maybe he wasn't gone. Maybe he was the one who'd gotten in here and messed with our system as a warning to me.

But at least I knew he hadn't left for school yet, that he was still lurking around town. *The spiteful little sneak,* I thought. He was smart enough not to have crashed the whole system, but he'd certainly done some damage. Dealing with customers all weekend with nothing but paper and pencil would make our work much harder.

"Thanks for trying, Nando," my mom said. "It must be some kind of glitch in the whole system."

Yeah, a glitch named Jason Connors. But I held off sharing my theory with my mother. "We can still take credit cards, though, right?" I asked.

My mom held up her smartphone. "I have the card reader attachment." She smiled. "Your father, the least techy guy on earth, actually bought one for me."

"Frankie saves the day again," I said. "My basement's nice and dry thanks to his sump pump."

"We can always count on your dad." Her smile faded as she glanced out at the hallway. "He's gone to pick up Nonna. I dread telling them about this."

"Nonna ran this place for years without computers. We'll muddle through. Hey, do we still have that stand with the big pin in it? We used to stick the food tickets on it."

"No, we do *not*," she said with a frown. "I used to worry that you or Daniel would get hurt on that thing." She stood up and pushed in her chair. "We'll use a binder clip for the tickets and I'll keep paper records until we can have somebody come in and look at the system. Grab your apron, honey. There's a lot to do."

"Um, could I talk to you about that, Mom?" I followed her out to the dining room.

"Sure, hon." But her face was already in the reservation book, which I suspected was pretty full.

"Listen, I'll stay and prep all morning and serve for

most of lunch. But would you mind very much if I took off for a little while in the lull between lunch and dinner? I'll come back and do the whole dinner shift and even help the guys with cleanup. I'll close, in fact."

She sighed. "I assume you have a good reason for asking?"

"Actually, I'm doing what you asked of me. I'm going to talk to somebody who might know something about Pete's death."

She snapped the book closed. "Yes, I asked you to look into it, but that was before his death was officially ruled an accident." Her voice was terse, and her face held the same disapproving expression I'd come to know quite well in my teens.

"Listen, Mom—Dad and Nonna will be here any minute. Can you please cover for me on this? I'll slip out after the lunch rush and be back for dinner service." I took her hand. "I'm not doing anything dangerous, I promise. At the very least, I might find out more about Zio Roberto." I grinned at her. "Now, this is where you let out a great big Nicolina sigh and say *yes*."

"Don't be smart, young lady. If I have to wait a few tables this afternoon, so be it." Her eyes narrowed. "But you owe me." Her mouth curved in a manner that did not suggest mirth. "And we'll see how much you like closing up at eleven tonight."

She went back to her office and I made a beeline for the espresso pot. It was going to be a long day. And an even longer night.

"Whose idea was it to travel south on the Garden State Parkway on Saturday of Labor Day weekend?" I asked my sister-in-law, who was happily ignoring me from the passenger seat of my car. She was scrolling through baby names in her phone, impervious to the traffic all around us.

"What do you think of *Marietta* if it's a girl?" she asked.

"Here's what I think: At this rate, Marietta will arrive well before we get to that club." Sofia's digging had led us to the Atlantic City Country Club, where Domenica worked.

"Now, don't be cranky, Auntie Vic."

Auntie Vic? I didn't want to hurt Sofia's feelings, but that appellation made me feel about sixty years old. "Hey, could we maybe come up with something else for the baby to call me? At least *Aunt Victoria* has a dignified sound."

"I don't know. That's a mouthful for a little kid."

I glared at her. "She'll learn. Which is more than I can say for her mother or her aunt sitting here in this traffic. I hope we can catch this guy."

She nodded. "We will. He should be there until four."

"Wait, did you call him directly?"

"Heck no. I just called the club to confirm he worked there."

"So we're showing up unannounced?"

"I suppose you could say that."

"And our excuse for seeing him?"

She tucked her phone into her purse and looked at me with impatience. "Haven't we been over this? We're doing what you always say to do—we're sticking as close to the truth as possible. We show up, we make nice and blind him with our charm. Then we mention your long-lost uncle and ask if he or his father knew him. And we get some answers. Simple."

"Sofe, it's never simple. What if he gets suspicious?"

She opened her palms and shrugged. "So what? We only want some information."

"Right," I said. "So we come right out and ask the guy if his father was mobbed up and if he knew my drug addict uncle—"

"Your drug addict *great*-uncle. Get it straight, Vic."

I stared over the top of my steering wheel at the endless line of cars in front of us. "Well, at least we have time to plan what we're going to say. And I've got the Atlantic City book from the library; I'd like to show him the picture and gauge his reaction. I'm just not sure what we're going to learn from this, though. I don't think Domenica will want to talk about his father's involvement with Leo Barone. He carries his father's name; he's probably been trying to live it down all this years, don't you think?"

"You never know," Sofia said, shaking her head. "Some of these guys wear the mob thing like a badge of honor."

"Not Richard Barone," I said. "It makes me wonder to what lengths he'd go to distance himself from his family's criminal past."

Sofia looked across at me, her face thoughtful. "Why do you think he made such a point of singling you out last night?"

"I'm not sure. Iris might have told him about my visit to the store. She saw right through my questions. Maybe he's warning me. You know, *I've got my eye on you, so don't mess.*"

"Ha!" She let out a snort. "And here we are, messin' anyway."

"True," I said with a sigh. "And we still don't know much about Tattoo Guy. Except for the Alyssa connection and Danny's hunch that he's served time."

"Even if he did, it doesn't seem fair to judge him for that, Vic."

I looked over at her and grinned. "Listen to you. Since when are you so softhearted? Have we suddenly reversed roles or something?"

"God forbid," she said. "I just think we shouldn't jump to any conclusions about the guy because he's got some ink on his arms."

"But it's more than that, Sofe, and you know it. What was he doing with Alyssa, a kid ten years younger than he is? And why did he show up at the party and masquerade as a server? More significantly, was he in the carousel house the night Pete stumbled in?"

"I thought we established that it was closed the night of the storm."

"But think about it: If he worked the rides out on the pier, he might have had access to the carousel house. We've been wondering all along how Pete got in, and I think the answer's pretty clear. It had to be Tattoo Guy."

"Maybe. But we have other people to consider, Vic, including Barone, Florence, and Jason. Especially after what you told me about the computer crash at the restaurant. And let's not leave out Crazy Iris."

"Actually, we need the answer to a pretty basic question: past or present? Is Pete's death tied to something he did a year ago or fifty years ago?"

Sofia nodded. "Or maybe both." She fished her phone back out of her purse and checked the screen. "The club's off Exit 36, and we just passed the exit for Long Beach Island. Less than thirty miles to go. With any luck, we'll be there in a half hour."

As it turned out, our luck held, and we got to the Atlantic City Country Club by three.

"Wow," I said, taking in the velvety greens and stately clubhouse. "Will you look at this place?"

"Almost makes me want to take up golf," Sofia said. "My dad played here, and apparently lots of famous people played here. It's old school, but cool."

We found Gerry Domenica behind the counter at the pro shop. At first I had wondered at an eighty-year-old who was still working, but one look at Domenica told me he was hale and healthy. Though he was no more than five-six, he had the broad shoulders and compact frame of a much younger man. He still had a head full of silver hair, slicked back in a style of two generations earlier. As we approached him, I picked up the distinct scent of Old Spice.

"Can I help you girls?" he asked with a smile, and I tried not to bristle. *He's of another era,* I told myself. *So to him we're girls.*

Sofia trained her most blinding smile at him. "Mr. Domenica, we're sorry to bother you at work, but we're doing some family research and thought you might be able to help us." She held out her hand. "I'm Sofia Rienzi, and this is my sister-in-law, Victoria. We're trying to track down a Rienzi relative of my husband's, and we think it's possible your father might have known him back in Atlantic City."

"That so?" he asked. He was still smiling, but there was wariness in his voice. "I'm not sure I can help, but I'll try." He tapped the side of his head. "The memory's not what it used to be."

Ha, I thought. *You're still sharp as a tack, Gerry Domenica. And for some reason you're on your guard.* I reached out my hand. "Nice to meet you, sir. I appreciate your seeing us."

"Why don't you girls come and sit down out on the terrace for a minute? I'll bring us some nice lemonade." He led us to a table in a shady spot outside the clubhouse, and the two of us sat down.

"Does he seem suspicious to you?" I asked as soon as he was gone.

Sofia rolled her eyes. "I met him, like, a minute ago. And by *suspicious*, do you mean is he sketchy?"

"More like does he suspect *us*?"

"Probably. We need to disarm him."

"I'll leave that to you, Miss Congeniality," I said. "Here he comes."

Domenica set a tray of drinks down on the table. "Help yourselves, please." He sat across from us, resting his elbows on the table, his hands clasped. "How can I help you?"

I told him what I had learned about Zio Roberto, both my family's version and what I'd been able to piece together about Robert Riese or Reese. When I was finished, I opened the book to the photo of Barone, Domenica, Alfonso, and the unidentified Robert Riese. When Domenica reached for the book, his shirtsleeve hiked up, revealing an old tattoo in faded blue ink. He pointed to the picture and grinned as I tried not to stare at his left arm.

"There's my dad," he said. "*Gerry Sunday*, they called him. Man, they knew how to dress in them days, didn't they?" He traced his finger across the page. "And there's Mr. Leo." He looked up at us. "That's how I always referred to him. He was my godfather." He smiled broadly, providing a glimpse of a gold tooth. "For real, I mean. He christened me."

"Do you know the other men in the picture?" Sofia asked, turning on a high-watt smile.

"Sure," he said. "That's Alfie. I don't remember his last name." He pointed to the man who bore such a marked resemblance to my father. "And that's Robbie. Sometimes we called him Roberto. I tell ya, he was a pistol." He looked at me with narrowed eyes. "He's the guy in your family you're tryin' to track down, right?"

"Yes," I said, a little startled. "How did you know?"

"It ain't that hard, miss," he said. "For one thing, you're too pretty to be related to a Petrocelli, and for another, your eyes are just like Robbie's."

"It's my dad who really looks like him," I said. "We think he went by the name Robert Riese. Does that sound familiar?"

"Mighta been the name. Don't really remember."

"Well, can you tell me what you do know about Roberto?"

"A little bit. He was one for the ladies, that's for sure. Well, until the drugs got hold of him."

"Was he involved with drugs?" Sofia asked.

"Was he?" Domenica let out a snort. "You kids think you invented marijuana, but it's been around for years. That's how Robbie started. He hung around those jazz clubs. But after that, he went on to harder stuff."

Great. So Zio Roberto was a pothead, and probably worse. I might have to tell Nonna and my dad a sanitized version of this particular chapter of Rienzi family history. "I'm sorry to hear that," I said.

"Yup, it was a real shame. He was a smart guy. Coulda rose in the ranks if he'd wanted. But Mr. Leo didn't like anybody in the organization messin' with drugs. Absolutely forbade it. He did *not* approve, no, sir."

Sofia and I exchanged a glance. We both knew that

Barone's organization was only too happy to traffic in drugs. "Mr. Domenica—" I began.

"Please, call me Gerry, honey."

Okay, Gerry honey. I so wanted to say it out loud, but instead I smiled. "Thank you . . . Gerry. I was wondering if you knew what eventually happened to Robert."

He shut the book and slid it across the table to me. "Sorry, I don't. Wish I could be more help." He stood to go. "Now, if you girls don't mind, I have to get back to work."

As I watched him go, an insistent question pounded in my ears—*the past or the present? The past or the present?* Where did the answer to Pete's death lie?

Chapter Twenty-five

We had barely fastened our seat belts when I turned to Sofia. I started the car, but left it in park. "Did you notice the tattoo that showed from under Domenica's left shirtsleeve?"

"No. You were sitting on that side of him. Why?"

"The image was faded and blurred, but I'm sure it was a lion. I tried to see the rest of it through the fabric, but it was too dark."

"A tattoo of a lion? Wait a minute," Sofia said. "Are you telling me—?"

"You bet I am. I think Gerry Domenica has a tattoo of a prancing lion on his arm, similar to the one that Tattoo Guy has. That's got to be more than a coincidence, don't you think? I wonder if they're connected somehow."

"To each other? Or to—?" She stopped suddenly, her mouth dropping open to form a pink, glossy O. She turned to me with a look of triumph. "Okay, Miss Writer. Think: Why is a lion significant?"

I frowned. "I don't know. King of the jungle? A representation of courage?"

Sofia clapped her hands, her tone gleeful. "I can't believe I got this ahead of you. Think horoscopes. Think DiCaprio."

"Oh my God, I'm an idiot. *Leo*. Leo Barone! Of course." I put out my fist for a bump from Sofia. "Good catch, SIL. I wonder if the tattoo signified loyalty or something." My mind was racing through the possibilities. "It might make sense for Gerry Domenica to have a tattoo related to the Barones, but why the carousel operator?"

"I guess we can't rule out coincidence," Sofia said, but didn't sound convincing.

"True," I agreed, "but for the sake of argument, let's assume there's a connection."

Sofia pawed through her purse and pulled out a pack of sticky notes and a pen. "So back in the day, Gerry Jr. gets a lion tattoo." She stopped, her pen poised over the paper. "But why, Vic? His *father* was part of Barone's inner circle, not him."

"Right. Okay, let's think about this. We think that Domenica Jr. is eightyish, right?" I did some quick mental math. "That would have put him in his teens and twenties at the height of Barone's operation in Atlantic City. He certainly could have been involved. You heard him talking about it today—he had this gleam in his eye."

"Like he was proud of it," Sofia said.

"Exactly. And he identified Roberto and Alfonso; he talked about them as though he knew them." I pulled out of the parking lot and onto the main road, hoping Sofia would help me navigate. Even with a GPS, I had a tendency to get lost. "In fact, don't you think it's strange that he looks at me and sees an immediate resemblance? That he also knows that Zio Roberto did drugs and was a bit of a Casanova, yet has no idea that he ended up in jail for murder? A murder that was pretty well publicized, according to our own research."

"Oh yeah," Sofia said, scribbling away on the yellow notes. "He was picking and choosing what he wanted to tell us."

"There were other things, too—something that he said that made me think he was lying, but I lost it. Or something I noticed about him. I don't remember now. It's driving me crazy."

"You'll probably remember at three o'clock in the morning."

"Let's hope." I pointed to a light up ahead. "Is that the turn for the parkway?"

"See the green sign with the pretty yellow state of New Jersey in it? The one that says *Parkway*? That would indicate that this is our turn."

"There's no need for sarcasm, lady. I didn't want to miss it. I'm on the clock here." I accelerated onto the northbound ramp, only to join another long line of drivers—day-trippers heading home. I sighed. "Here we go again."

"That's okay," Sofia said. "Gives us more time to debrief. Let's get back to the tattooed carousel operator."

"Danny thought the guy was an ex-con."

"I wouldn't be so quick to jump to that conclusion," Sofia said. "Anybody without a regulation haircut is suspect to your brother."

"Maybe. But I trust his instincts. If the guy did spend time in jail, couldn't the lion tattoo be connected to a gang or something?"

"I guess," Sofia said doubtfully. "But if the lion does symbolize the Barones, that would mean—"

"That their criminal activity didn't end with Leo's death!" I interrupted. "And that maybe Richard Barone isn't as clean as he'd like everybody to believe. God, I wish I could see him without his shirt."

Sofia let out a laugh. "There you go again, risking death by Iris."

"You know what I mean. I wonder if he's got a lion tattoo. Not that I would *mind* seeing him without his shirt, but that's neither here nor there. But speaking of Iris—if Barone is dirty, does she know it?"

"Never mind Iris," Sofia said. "Did Pete know? That's the big question. If Barone is mobbed up, and Pete somehow got wind of it, that would be reason enough to get him out of the way."

I looked over at her. "Or pay somebody else to do it."

"Probably." She opened the red folder and studied our list of names. "You know, Vic, I think we need to back up the truck here."

"Would you mind translating that highly Jersey-esque phrase for me?"

"You have been in New York waaay too long," Sofia said, rolling her eyes. "You know what I mean—let's re-think this for a minute. All along we've been assuming that Pete drank himself to death at the hand of a person or persons who wanted him out of the way. Given his blood alcohol, it's a likely scenario: He drank himself into unconsciousness and fell facedown in the shallow water in the carousel house. But we still haven't answered the big question of what he was doing there."

"A planned meeting with one or more of the suspects?"

She nodded. "The more I think about it, the more I think it's likely, especially if he was blackmailing any of them."

"So let's review our timeline. Pete showed up as we were serving dinner, somewhere between six and six thirty, before the storm hit." The traffic was breaking up; I picked up speed and my thoughts followed suit. "At some point he interacted with Iris, according to Gale at the library. It was likely after six thirty when I saw him leave, but he was only holding the food bag. Nando saw him after that holding *two* bags, one of which held his food, but another heavier one as well."

"Did Nando tell you a time?"

"No." I shook my head. "We were all so busy. And once the storm was really raging, I don't think many of us were paying attention to the time."

"Okay," Sofia said, "if my memory serves, we all ran inside around seven thirty and Danny got called out at about eight forty. I remember looking at the time when he was leaving."

"That sounds right. And at some point when we were inside, Father Tom came in because he had seen Pete out on the boardwalk."

"So Pete was probably still alive at eight, yes?"

"I think it's likely. But somewhere in that hour between seven thirty and eight thirty, both Jason and Alyssa went missing for a while."

"And you're thinking one or both of them might have met with Pete?" Sofia asked. "But that would mean that either they went out in the storm or Pete came back to the restaurant, right?"

"Right. But now that you spell it out, I can see the difficulty with that theory. If the storm was that bad, and Pete had come by the restaurant, he would have tried to stay and wait out the storm, don't you think?"

"I *do* think. And if either Jason or Alyssa met him somewhere and came back—" she began.

"They'd be soaking wet," I interrupted. "Of course.

You know, I tried to pin down Alyssa about where she'd been, but she was evasive."

"She was probably in a lip lock somewhere with Tattoo Guy," Sofia muttered.

"But remember she also said something about the temps wanting to leave early and splitting tips, but I don't remember exactly when. I'm wondering if Tattoo Guy might have followed Pete at some point. You know what? I think it's time to put in a call to Alyssa," I said. "We need to identify that guy."

"Do you think she'll tell you his name?"

"She will if she thinks we want to hire him."

"That's sneaky, Vic. I like it."

"Would you get my phone out of my purse? It's by your feet."

"How do you find anything in here? Sheesh." After emptying half the contents of my purse, Sofia finally fished out my phone. "Got it. I don't suppose she's in your contacts?"

"No. But if you check the call history, she's the only number with an 848 area code."

"Oh, okay. Yup, it's here. Want me to call?"

"Please. And then put her on speaker." I shot her a grin. "But keep your pretty mouth closed; I don't want her to know anyone is listening in."

Alyssa picked up on the third ring. "Hello?" Her tone was cautious; I guess I wasn't in her contacts, either.

"Hey, Alyssa. It's Victoria Rienzi. How are you?"

"Oh, hi, Victoria. I'm good. Is everything okay?"

"It's fine. I've got you on speaker, okay? I'm driving."

"Sure thing, girlfriend," Alyssa said, her sweet voice carrying in the enclosed car. "What can I do ya for?"

Sofia made a gagging motion with her finger to her

open mouth, and I shook my head at her furiously. "Well, you know how crazy Labor Day weekend is down here, and we're shorthanded at the restaurant without you and Jason. We thought we'd reach out to some of the temps we had on the night of the party." I held up my crossed fingers. "Did you know any of them?" *Of course you did, Alyssa, but will you tell me?*

"Well, I kinda knew Jackson. You might remember him." She giggled. "Actually, you might remember his tats."

Sofia's eyes widened and I put my finger to my lips. "Oh, sure. He helped out a lot when we were packing up to go inside. You think he might want some work?"

"Maybe." I waited, but she didn't offer anything else. "Do you have contact info for him?" I persisted. "A phone number or e-mail?"

"No, sorry," she sang into the phone. "I only met him that night."

Sofia scribbled on her pad and held it up for me to see. *SHE'S LYING!!!* it read.

"Do you know his last time?"

"That I do know. It's Manchester. Jackson Manchester."

I glanced at Sofia, who was frowning as she wrote down the name. "Okay, thanks, Alyssa," I said. "Have a good year."

"You, too, Victoria! Bye now."

Sofia ended the call and held up the pad again. "Jackson Manchester? Anything strike you about that name?"

"Aside from sounding like the name of a British noble, it's about as fake as my mother's eyelashes."

"You bet it is." Sofia zoomed out on the screen of my GPS until it showed the whole of Ocean County, complete with the names of its towns, including *Jackson* and *Manchester*. "This dude took his name from a map."

"So, who is he?" I asked.

"I don't know," Sofia said, "but I'm beginning to think he's the key to this whole thing."

When I got back to the restaurant, things were as hectic and busy as my mother had promised. Lucky for me, my grandmother had gone home before the dinner service, but I was sure she was preparing a tasty lecture to serve me when she got the chance. I put on my apron and grabbed a ticket book, moving automatically around the dining room to check on linens and setups before the dinner rush began. I was setting up the coffee station when the dining room door opened; it was Miss Ferraro, clutching a rusted metal box.

"Hello, miss," she said. "Do you remember me?"

"Of course. But we're not open for dinner yet, and—"

"I'm not here for dinner." She held out the box as though it contained a dangerous animal. "I came to bring you this."

"Uh, okay. What is it?"

She looked around nervously. There were beads of perspiration on her forehead and along her upper lip. "It was his," she whispered. "I found it in an old dresser I had downstairs. It's locked, so I don't know what's in it. I only know I don't want it in my house." She held it out to me, her arms trembling from its weight.

My pulse racing, I took it from her and immediately looked around for somewhere to duck it. "I'm not sure why you brought this to me."

"Well, you wanted to know about him. So I thought maybe you know somebody you can give it to. Somebody who might want his things. I thought about bringing it to Father Tom—"

"Oh no," I said hastily. "I'll take care of it; don't worry. I'll make sure the right person gets this."

"Thank you." She wiped her forehead with the back of her hand. "It's a relief to me to get that off my hands." She left the restaurant, her shoulders sagging.

She looks worried, I thought as I watched her go. *But about what?* Did she have her own suspicions about Pete? Still alone in the dining room, I set the box on a nearby table. Its hinges were rusted, as was the small lock holding the clasp shut. I lifted it, testing its heft, then shook it. Something metal was in there; I could hear the soft *clack* as the object hit the sides of the box. I shook it again and heard the rustle of papers. I *had* to find out what was in there. *Yeah, and so did Pandora,* said a voice in my head, one that sounded a lot like my sister-in-law's.

I grabbed my purse, slipped the box under my apron and crossed my arms over it, and hurried down the hallway toward the kitchen. Tim and Nando were deep in preparations and barely noticed me. I grabbed a pair of vinyl kitchen gloves and slipped them into my apron, then pushed through the back door to the parking lot, where I locked the box in the trunk of my car. With shaking hands, I shot off a text to Cal:

I know it's your day off, but I could use your help with something. Can you meet me at the restaurant? And bring your tools, okay?

A half hour later Cal came into the dining room bearing his toolbox and a puzzled look on his face. "You got somethin' that needs fixin'?"

"Not exactly." I kissed his cheek. "Thanks for getting

here so fast." I guess the kiss must have encouraged him, because he pulled me close.

"I am at your disposal, Victoria." His grin was on the wicked side, as was the look in his eyes. I disentangled myself as gently as possible.

"Glad to hear it, but could you scoot out to the parking lot with me for a minute? Let's go out the dining room door; I don't want to risk Tim seeing us."

"What the heck is this about, *cher*?" Cal asked as he hurried behind me.

"You'll see. It's in my car." We managed to get to the car without anyone seeing us, and I motioned him to come around to the back of it. I opened the trunk and handed him the box. "Can you knock that lock off for me?"

"I can, for sure, but you mind telling me why?"

I looked into his questioning face, tempted to remind him that he had secrets of his own. But he was also concerned, and probably suspicious. I looked around the empty parking lot—no customers yet, so I probably had a little time. "Listen, please don't lecture me, but it belonged to Pete. His landlady left it with me because she didn't know who to give it to."

He cocked his head. "That so? And how'd she know to bring it to you?"

"I, um, paid her a visit. I wanted to see where Pete lived, okay?"

He let out a small breath and looked heavenward, as though to ask for guidance. Or maybe just a little patience. "Why do you feel the need to mess around with this?" He spoke quietly, enunciating every word.

"I'm not exactly sure, Cal, to tell you the truth. But I can't leave it alone, even though I know I should." I looked over at the garden and the statue of Mary in its corner. "I feel like he died on our watch. Do you know what I mean? I feel . . . responsible in some way."

He took my shoulders and shook me gently. "You're not responsible, and neither is your family. And if your suspicions are right—and, girl, I know you think that old man was murdered—there might be somebody out there who'll cover his tracks any way he has to." His face was level with my own and I could see the concern in his eyes. "And I don't want you to get hurt, damn it."

"I won't. I've already decided to go to Prosecutor Sutton with all the information I find. Hand to heart." I slapped my hand over my chest, just to make sure he believed me.

He let me go with a sigh and opened the toolbox. "Give 'er here," he said, holding out his hand. He set the box down on top of the restaurant Dumpster, and with one sharp whack of his hammer, broke the lock. He handed me the box and the lock. "I'm gonna let you open it on your own. Not sure I wanna know what's in it, anyways."

I hugged the box to me, impatient for him to go. "Listen, thanks a lot. And I promise I'll be careful."

"Heard that before," he said as he turned to go.

The minute he was in his truck, I slid into the backseat of my car and opened the box with two very sweaty hands. I wiped them on my jeans, slipped on the gloves, and lifted out a shabby piece of cloth that looked like an old dish towel; I stared at the evidence in front of me. On top was a torn page from the *Cormorant*. The lead article bore the headline "Anonymous Hackers Breach Grading Program," and the story read just as Kelly and Mr. Ainsley had described. *So you knew about Jason.* I shifted the newspaper and pulled out a pamphlet from Richard Barone's foundation. *Another connection to another suspect.* Under that was a scorecard from the Atlantic City Country Club. *Gerry Domenica, fancy meeting you here.* In one corner was a signet ring with the initials AP—for Alphonse Petrocelli? There was also a St. Christopher medal and a church bulletin from St. Rose's, where Father Tom was pastor. *Father Tom?* Tucked into the bulletin was a manila envelope; I opened it with shaking fingers. Inside was a single sheet of paper, signed and notarized: Pietro Petrocelli's last will and testament, leaving his entire bank balance to St. Rose's. Balled up in the corner of the box was another rag. When I picked it up, a purple silk scarf slipped out—one that smelled faintly of patchouli. *And Iris makes five.*

Chapter Twenty-six

*T*im and Nando had helped me close, so I managed to get back to my cottage before eleven. I took the box from my trunk, anxious to get it inside until I could deliver it to Regina Sutton, the county prosecutor. I locked the door behind me and switched on the basement light. Putting it on a high shelf where it would be sure to stay dry, I covered it with an old T-shirt. I trudged back up the basement stairs, every muscle aching. Relieved to be in my own cozy nook after the last couple of days I'd had, I headed to the refrigerator to pour myself a nightcap. I emptied what was left of my chardonnay into a water tumbler and trudged up the stairs with a groan. After driving all day, dealing with the strongbox, and running my tail off tonight, I couldn't wait to dive into my bed.

I saw the light from my computer screen out in the hallway. Had I left it on? I stepped into my darkened room and switched on the light, sending up another small prayer of thanks to the power company. When I looked at my screen, I let out a relieved breath. It was only updating in that mysterious process that allowed computers to turn themselves on and off at will. Setting down my wine, I sat at my desk, and a window opened up with two choices:

Continue updating or postpone?

I clicked CONTINUE, only to see the window close and the screen turn black. Bright gold letters appeared on the screen, scrolling across the page like a news crawl:

This is your last warning this is your last warning this is your last warning this is your last . . .

"Jason strikes again," I said, slamming my palm down on my desk. And tired or no, I was going to get some answers. Clutching my keys, I ran down my stairway on rubbery legs, wishing I'd had water instead of wine. In less than a half hour, I pulled into the entrance of Florence's apartment building, parked hastily, and scrambled out of my car. I strode toward her building, and as luck would have it, there was one light on in her apartment. I had to hope she was in there alone.

She came to the door in her bathrobe, her face tired and devoid of makeup. She opened the door a crack.

"What do you want, Victoria?" she said wearily. "Is this still about that old drunk? Don't you have anything better to do at this hour of the night than drag people out of their beds?"

I held up my phone so she could see the photo on my screen. "Do you know anything about this?"

She leaned forward, squinting at the screen. "I can barely see it—what is it?"

"It's my computer. It has some kind of virus and now

it's scrolling a warning along the bottom of the screen. And the whole computer system at the restaurant is down. I don't suppose your darling son would know anything about that? Is he here, by the way?"

Her eyes shifted away from me. "Jason's at school. He left this morning."

"Is that so? I wonder if he stopped for a spot of breaking and entering at my cottage."

"Please. You have a goddamn computer virus so you come here accusing my son? I should call the police right now."

Not a good idea. I didn't want to have to explain to my brother why I was badgering this woman at eleven thirty at night. I crossed my fingers and went for the bluff. "Yeah, you do that, Florence. And when they get here, we can talk about that empty wine bottle I found in the alley. By the way, did you know that the police can lift prints from that bottle, even though it's been rained on?"

"They won't find any prints on that bottle," she said through her teeth.

"Oh, that's right," I said. "Because one of you wiped it clean."

She dropped her head and to my horror, started to cry. "Why can't you just leave us alone?" She sniffled and swiped the back of her hand across her nose. "And if you're gonna harass somebody, why don't you go find that ex-con that showed up with Alyssa?"

"Are you talking about the guy with the tattoos?"

She sniffed again and nodded. "Who else? I caught him snooping around your father's wine cellar."

If she was telling the truth, this was a valuable piece of information. "How would you know that, Florence?"

I asked. "Unless you were down there yourself? Or was it Jason who was down there?"

Florence's tears dried immediately as her mother instincts took over. She stepped out onto the tiny porch and jabbed a finger at my face. "I don't know what you think you're doing," she said in a low voice. "Or what you think you know, but if you don't leave me alone, I *will* call the police. I told you, damn it—*I* was the one who gave the old man wine that night."

"Maybe so, Florence, but you weren't the one who hacked into the high school's computer system, were you?"

She lifted her head, her eyes wide, her body tensed and alert. "What are you talking about?" she said in a whisper.

"I think you know. And I'm pretty sure Pete knew, too. Was he blackmailing you? And did you and your son find an easy way to get rid of him the night of the party?"

At those words, Florence thrust her face into my own, baring her teeth like a feral dog. "You don't know what you're talking about. But if you think I'm gonna let you— or anybody—stand in the way of my son's success, you're wrong, bitch!" On the last word, her arm shot out, knocking me sideways off the porch and into some dead-looking azalea bushes. I sat up in a daze; there were scratches on my arm and I had a sore bottom, but the bushes had broken the worst of the fall. Any pity I'd felt for Florence evaporated in that moment.

"Hey, you just assaulted me!" I shouted as I got to my feet.

She turned back to me, her eyes glittering darkly. "Yeah, and next time I'll do worse. You come back here again, or you go anywhere near my son, and it will be the last thing you do." And then she went back inside, slamming the door behind her.

The next morning, I woke up feeling muddled and uncertain about my own perceptions. Had I dreamed Miss Ferraro's visit, the computer virus, the trip to see Florence, the malicious shove off her front porch? Well, my butt hurt when I shifted in bed and there were still scratches on my arm. And that strongbox full of evidence was sitting downstairs in my basement. Nothing in it had been a complete surprise, except of course for that will. I couldn't help remembering Sofia's words about Father Tom as a suspect. *Stop it, Vic,* I told myself. That will was only in there because Pete needed a safe place for it. But I couldn't shake my sense of unease.

I got out of bed with reluctance and walked stiffly over to my desk. Last night, my computer had shut itself down, and I started it with trepidation, half expecting to see a scary clown face pop up on the screen. But once I started it, the log-in appeared and all was well. No evidence of a computer virus here, which also meant that except for a fuzzy cell phone picture, there was no evidence *period* of anyone tampering with my computer. *You're a shrewd one, Jason Connors.* Luckily, I was able to access my e-mail, because there was a new one from my brother:

Hey Vic,
   I talked to somebody in the corrections department on Friday and did some digging around the SCIS database.

As my brother was Mr. Acronym, I had to look that

one up. SCIS stood for the state criminal information system. He continued:

I found out that Robert Riese, aka Robert Reese, served time in Trenton State Prison from 1949 until his death in 1978. From what I could put together from my contacts and some old records, the evidence against him for the murder of Mancini was mostly circumstantial. Prosecution couldn't even come up with a clear motive. The whole case hinged on the fact that his car was ID'd fleeing the scene, but there was no weapon ever found.

No motive and no weapon? Yet this guy spent thirty years in jail.

He died in jail from complications of pneumonia. He was only in his early sixties—I guess the drugs took their toll. But apparently he had got clean there and was a model prisoner. He worked in the prison laundry and in the cafeteria.

I had a moment of sadness, thinking about a Rienzi serving food behind bars; it was both fitting and ironic. There wasn't much more to my brother's message:

Records indicate he had no visitors. He came up for parole twice and was denied both times. He's buried in some potter's field in Trenton. And that's all she wrote.

If this guy's our uncle, nobody ever knew it. Sad story, huh?

Danny

Sad story indeed, brother. I opened the library book to the old photo and studied Riese's pleasant, open face. I reread the e-mail, my mind roiling with possibilities. Was Riese framed for the Mancini murder? Or did he take a deliberate fall for someone else, most likely Leo Barone? And as far as the records showed, he'd never had visitors, which made sense if his family knew nothing about his existence, but what about his friends? Wasn't it strange that a party-animal type like Riese would be completely forgotten once he was in jail? Unless . . .

"Someone wanted it that way," I said aloud. Somebody locked up Robert Riese and threw away the key. He was dangerous to somebody, just as Stinky Pete had been. Was it Gerry Domenica? That scorecard from the golf club seemed to suggest that Pete had connected with Domenica at some point. More than ever I was convinced that the secret to Pete's death led back to Atlantic City and Leo Barone.

I was about to go downstairs to make some coffee (as caffeine helps me think) when I noticed a missed call from an unfamiliar number on my phone. When I called it back, a rich baritone voice sounded in my ear. *Why is Richard Barone calling me?*

I listened to the voice mail message, hesitated, and ended the call. I needed time to think. Was Barone calling to give me information or to warn me off? Before I could even theorize about an answer, my phone rang again.

"Victoria," he said. "I noticed you called back, and I'm so glad you did. Do you have some time this afternoon?"

"Well . . ."

"I ask because I was hoping you might meet me at my office for a quick chat."

"It's Sunday," I said, frowning.

He laughed. "I know what day it is. We keep rather irregular hours here at the foundation."

"I see," I said. "I could probably make some time, but could you tell me what this is about?"

"Of course. You had asked me about our shared family history, and I have some information for you if you're still interested."

So Barone had picked Option 1: information. He knew full well I was interested, and he'd just thrown me a pretty tasty piece of bait. But why did he want me to bite?

That afternoon, the strongbox safely locked in my car trunk, I was once again on my way to Richard Barone's plush offices. But this time the corridors were empty and the office doors closed. And there was no sign of his secretary. I hadn't forgotten the Barone Foundation pamphlet among Pete's things, and I was likely alone in a building with a man he might well have been blackmailing. A man who might be a murderer. *No, thank you.* I would find another, safer way to get what I needed. I was halfway back down the hall when I heard his voice.

"Hello, Victoria."

I turned and saw him in the open doorway, wearing jeans and a blue cotton shirt with the sleeves rolled, revealing forearms bare of ink. So no lion tattoo—at least on his arms. There was an amused expression on his handsome face. "My office is this way."

"So it is," I said, hoping I didn't sound as nervous as I felt. "I have a terrible sense of direction." As I followed him through the door, I reached into my purse, now gripped to my side, and closed my hand around my car keys. I could always set off my car alarm if I sensed danger. A lame move, but all I had at the moment.

He motioned for me to sit across from him, laced his hands together, and leaned toward me. Barone had a talent for making a people feel that they had his full attention; it had worked on Iris. And there was no doubt the man was attractive. I sat back in my chair to put a bit of physical distance between us.

"First," he began, "thanks for being such a good sport at the carousel the other night. I thought it would be fun to have a local celebrity take the first ride."

Oh, it was fun, all right, I thought, remembering my queasy stomach and weak knees. But I only smiled.

"Now, when you visited me last," he continued, "you had questions about a man you believed to be a great-uncle of yours—Robert Riese."

"Right. But at the time you said you didn't recognize the name."

He smiled, a slash of white against his dark beard, and I found myself smiling back and momentarily pitying Iris. A girl didn't stand a chance against this guy. "That is so," he said. "But I've done a little detective work since then."

I stiffened at the word *detective*, my smile frozen in place. I felt like a hapless mouse being tossed around by a dark, sleek cat. I had to hope that I could leave without being devoured. "Really?" I managed to squeak out.

He nodded and handed me an accordion-style folder. "It looks as though your hunch was correct. The Robert Riese who was involved with my great-grandfather's organization was born Roberto Rienzi. He was convicted of the murder of Nino Mancini in 1949 and died in prison. It's all there."

I fumbled nervously with the closure on the flap; was it possible I was holding the truth about Zio Roberto in my hands? I pulled out dog-eared papers that included Roberto's prison records, copies of his fingerprints, old pay stubs, and an Italian birth certificate dated 1915 that named my great-grandparents as his mother and father. But the clincher was an Italian passport that carried both names: Roberto Rienzi and Robert Riese. They were one and the same, just as I had guessed. There was also a copy of a death certificate with information that tallied with what Danny had told me. For a moment, I looked at the papers in silence, trying to absorb the information I had in front of me.

I looked up at Barone's expectant face. "Where did you get this?"

"Let's just say I have built up some connections over the years—legitimate ones, of course. But those papers are valid; I've had them verified."

Of course you have, Richard. But you haven't answered my question. "I appreciate this, Richard," I said. "I really do. But I have a question for you."

"Shoot." He sat back easily in his chair with the air of one who has no worries.

"Well, your great-grandfather prided himself on a bloodless organization, yet you've just confirmed that my great-uncle served time in prison for murder. How do you explain that?"

Barone was still smiling and appeared relaxed, but he shifted in his chair. "From what I've been able to piece together, the shooting in the Pine Barrens was not at Leo's behest. It was a private matter between Riese and

Mancini, his victim. Something about a woman. Your great-uncle's car was at the scene. I think the evidence was pretty compelling."

"That doesn't quite line up with what my brother was able to determine about the case."

Barone raised an eyebrow. "Your brother is a police detective on the local force, correct?" The implication was clear: *He's a lowly civil servant. What does he know?*

"Yes, but his law enforcement contacts are widespread. He was able to speak to somebody at the state corrections office. And he has access to criminal databases that the public does not. He learned that the case against Riese—likely our great-uncle—was primarily circumstantial."

"You know as well as I do, Victoria, that plenty of people are convicted on circumstantial evidence. Even now, in the age of DNA."

"That's true. And some of them are innocent." We locked eyes for a moment, but Barone was giving nothing away. I glanced back at the papers in the folder. "According to what you've found here, Riese died in jail. I wonder why he never tried to reach his family in all that time."

Barone shrugged. "He was probably ashamed. Or he was protecting them. As you have pointed out to me, Victoria, we all have family skeletons, do we not?" He pushed away from his desk and stood up. I got the message and followed suit.

I held out my hand. "Thanks for this. My family will be very interested to know what's happened to him after all this time."

I hurried out of the building clutching my keys, questions swirling in my head. How long had Barone been privy to this information? Did he think that giving me what I wanted might stop me from pursuing information about Pete's death? Was that folder merely a bone he was throwing me in the hopes that I would take it and go away? Providing me with the information about my uncle suggested he had nothing to hide, so was that the act of an innocent man—or a guilty one who was taking a big gamble?

Chapter Twenty-seven

I sped away from Barone's offices feeling as though I'd had a narrow escape. The accordion folder on the seat next to me and the strongbox thumping around my car trunk were not only evidence, but physical reminders of what I'd gotten myself into. It was like driving around with two live grenades, either of which might go off at any moment. I was due at the restaurant in an hour; it might be just enough time to take the next step in the case of Pete's death—turn the strongbox over to the right person to be investigating it.

County Prosecutor Regina Sutton lived only a few miles inland, and with the help of my phone, I was able to find her address *and* a map to get there. Once I reached her house, I sat nervously in my car. Sutton was scary, but so was this strongbox I was carrying around. *Just do it, Vic.* I dropped the metal box into a shopping bag and trudged up her front walk, taking a deep breath before I rang the bell. An attractive black man with a close-cropped beard answered the door. Sutton's husband, perhaps?

"Excuse, me," I said. "I'm sorry to disturb you." I held

out my hand. "I'm Victoria Rienzi. I was wondering if Ms. Sutton was available."

He shook my hand and smiled in a disarming away. "Pleased to meet you. I'm Den Sutton. C'mon in."

"Is Den short for Dennis?" I asked as I followed him inside.

He turned back to me with a grin. "Not Dennis. *Denzel*. Mama was a fan."

"Oh, me, too. Hard name to live up to, though."

"You don't have to tell me. Could have been worse—I had a buddy named Shakespeare."

"You did *not*!"

"I certainly did. We called him 'Shakes' for short. Tried to fix him up with a chick named Ophelia one time, but it didn't work out."

Friendly, funny, and warm, Den Sutton seemed the opposite of his brisk, all-business, and rather intimidating wife. I was still laughing when Regina Sutton entered the room, resplendent in a jungle-print maxi dress that set off her golden brown skin. She fixed her amber eyes on me, and my smile froze in place. Not for nothing had I nicknamed her the Tiger Lady.

"Have you brought me a gift, Ms. Rienzi?" she asked, motioning to the department store shopping bag.

"Not . . . exactly. I think it's evidence." I shrank from that cold gold glare. "And I'm so sorry to bother you on a weekend, but I wouldn't have come if it weren't important."

She crossed her arms, her face unsmiling. "Important to whom? To you? Or to that restaurant you and your family live and die for?"

Interesting choice of words there. "I think it will be

important to you, but yes, we do have a stake in this. It has to do with Pete Petrocelli's death."

"Lord, preserve us," she said, rolling her eyes. She looked at her husband, her expression suddenly affectionate. "Baby, would you mind checking on the food?"

He kissed the back of her hand. "I am at your command, my queen." He nodded to me. "Nice meeting you, Victoria."

"Same here." I looked back to Sutton's impassive face. "That's cute how he called you his queen. Because of your name, I mean. You know, Regina . . ." My voice trailed away, silenced by Her Highness's imperious presence. She motioned for me to follow and led me to a small, cozy room lined with books.

"I love your house," I blurted out. "Was it built in the twenties? They did a lot of neo-Tudor stuff then."

She raised an eyebrow. "The late teens, actually. So you have an eye for architecture as well as mysteries. You're just full of surprises. Now, why don't you tell me why you have interrupted my peace on a weekend exactly *one hour* before I am expecting guests?" she asked, tapping the thin gold watch on her arm.

"Again, I'm sorry. But I have reason to believe that Pete's death may not have been an accident."

"I'm listening. But you have ten minutes, Ms. Rienzi. Use them well."

We sat down and I began with Pete's own words to me, went through my family research, recounted the night of the party, my visit to the high school, my conversations with Florence DeCarlo, Richard Barone, and Gerry Domenica, and ended with the computer problems at my cottage and the restaurant.

Regina Sutton listened in silence without interrupting, even when I paused for breath. Her face was expressionless, much in the way my brother's had been when I tried to convince him. When I finally finished, she gestured to the box. "So you think this is evidence, is that it? What you have brought me, Ms. Rienzi, is not evidence, but plot threads. This is a story that your overactive imagination is imposing over a series of unrelated events, some ancient Atlantic City history, an old man's delusions, and a box of junk." She leaned across her desk, her expression almost kind. "It's one big heap of supposition, girl. And because of your family's experience with another dead man, you've convinced yourself there's something here." She shook her head. "I just don't think there is. His death has been ruled an accident. Period."

"But don't you think it's possible somebody plied him with wine deliberately?" I didn't want to mention his blood alcohol levels, because she would know immediately that the information came from my brother.

"It's possible," she said, "but the cause of death was *drowning*, Ms. Rienzi, not alcohol poisoning."

"Couldn't somebody have helped that along, though?" I shuddered at the thought of someone holding the old man's head down on the flooded floor.

"We found no evidence of another person in that carousel house." She was clearly losing patience with me.

"Look," I said, the desperation sounding in my voice, "I understand everything you're saying, but any number of people might have wanted Pete dead. And my gut is telling me there's something wrong here." I pointed to the box on her desk. "I brought that here because I don't want it in my house. I'm actually . . . afraid." I smiled weakly. "Hard as that is to admit to you."

Her eyes searched my face. "I can see that." She sighed.

"All right, then. Leave it with me." She stood up from her chair. "I'll be back in my office on Tuesday. In the meantime, I will give this some thought, but that is *all* I will do. Now if you don't mind, I need to get ready for my company."

I scrambled to my feet. "Of course. I appreciate your seeing me, Ms. Sutton, I really do."

I followed her down the hallway to the front door she was holding open, clearly in a hurry to get rid of me. "This is such a relief," I said. "Thanks again."

"You may not thank me when this is all over. Richard Barone is a very powerful man. You've thought of that, I suppose."

I nodded. "Believe me, I have. You have a very nice husband, by the way," I called as I hurried to my car.

She raised both eyebrows this time, still shaking her head as she watched me drive away.

Tonight would be our last big push before the Labor Day crowds started lining up outside our doors. According to my mom, our computer system was back up and running as efficiently as ever; apparently, Jason worked in mysterious ways. There was no way to prove what he'd been up to here and at my cottage, but that would be Sutton's problem now, not mine. Weekend traffic held me up, so I got to the restaurant a little after four. I parked quickly and hurried through the back door into the kitchen.

"You're late," Tim growled. "And I could use some help. Nando doesn't come in for an hour. I had to wash all this basil myself." He hit the button on the food processor, its loud snarl a fitting background for his mood.

Welcome to my world, dude. "Keep your shirt on there, Chef. I have to wash up." I stood at the sink scrubbing my hands for the requisite two minutes. If Tim was already cranky, I would be sure to get a lecture on cleanliness if I cut corners. I glanced at the menu notes posted on the wall. Tonight's dinner specials included fresh-caught tuna. *Ugh.* "Please tell me I don't have to clean fish!" I yelled over the sound of the machine.

"Please," Tim called over his shoulder. "Do you think I'd trust you to fillet the tuna?" He stopped the processor and turned to me with a scowl.

"Thanks for your vote of confidence. I'll finish the pesto if you want. Is the cheese all grated?"

He slammed his palm on the counter. "No, the cheese is not grated. So you'll have to handle that job yourself, I guess."

"Geez, Tim, would you lose the attitude? What the heck is wrong with you, anyway?" But before he could answer, I had a sudden realization: Lacey Harrison must have made her decision.

He let out a loud sigh and turned to face me. "I'm sorry, Vic. I really am. I didn't mean to be such a jerk. Especially to you. Lacey and I broke up."

"Ah."

He frowned at me. "What's that supposed to mean?"

What it meant was *so my guess was right*, but I didn't want to reveal Lacey's visit to me. His male pride was already battered enough. "Nothing. It's just a sympathetic sound, that's all."

One side of his mouth twitched, but he didn't quite smile. "So now you're feeling sorry for me."

I held up my thumb and forefinger in a *this much* gesture. "To tell you the truth, Tim, you seem more pissed off than heartbroken."

He shook his head. "You know me too well, lass."

You can say that again. "Look, I'm sorry. I really liked Lacey."

"I did, too." He rested his eyes on mine. "But I didn't love her."

I looked into those gray eyes I knew so well, studied his familiar lean form. I knew what he was trying to say, but I wasn't ready to go there. "Well, then," I said, trying to keep it light, "that must mean your heart's in one piece."

"It's not and you know it isn't." He reached out his hand, palm open.

I stared at that outstretched hand, knowing how easy it would be for me to take it. To move into his arms swiftly and easily, as though that would fix what he had broken eight years before. I shook my head in the slightest of movements.

"I don't know what's in your heart, Tim. But I do know this: Your girlfriend breaks up with you, and you expect me to fall into your arms a second later. And why? Because I'm here and we've got a history. It's *convenient.*"

His eyes widened and his hand dropped in slow motion. "That's what you think of me?" he asked in a harsh whisper. "You think I would use you like that?"

"I . . . I don't know what to think, I guess." I felt my face redden and the tears start behind my eyes. I stared down at the checkered pattern on the floor.

"I guess you don't. Listen, I need to get down to the big walk-in for the fish, so if you wouldn't mind finishing the pesto," he said as he strode past me.

I watched him go, blinking furiously to keep the tears from spilling over. *You will not make me cry, Tim Trouvare. Not anymore.*

Chapter Twenty-eight

I woke up on Labor Day with the same sense of relief and sadness I'd felt every year I lived at the shore. By tomorrow, the summer season would be over, and soon the town would retreat into its quiet winter cocoon. While I hated to see summer end, I yearned for the peace that came with September. And now that Sutton had that strongbox, maybe I could find some of that peace myself. I scrambled out of bed and pulled an old bathing suit out from my dresser. Before facing a grueling day at the restaurant, I needed to clear my head.

The beach was still quiet, but within an hour it would be full of vacationers getting those last few hours in before work and school tomorrow. Without letting myself think about it, I ran into the surf and dove under the waves. The water was colder than I expected, and I jumped up shivering and gasping, salt water in my eyes and up my nose. *This is how Pete must have felt,* I thought, and shivered again, but not from the cold. I ran from the water, the waves crashing behind me. Grabbing my towel, I trudged up the beach toward home, where a hot shower and hot coffee would be waiting. I finally felt free of Pete and the obsession with his death; it was someone else's problem now. I would get back to my writing and finish Isabella's story. One more crazy shift at the restaurant to get through tonight, and I'd have all the peace and quiet I needed. When I got to my cottage, I let myself in through the deck—just in time to see a red Dodge Charger cruise past my front door.

That evening at the restaurant, I went through the motions mechanically, barely talking to Lori or the staff. My parents were preoccupied, and my interactions with Tim and my grandmother were limited to them shouting orders and me scurrying to fill them. *Just get through the night,* I told myself, trying to dismiss the image of the red car. I called Sofia on my one five-minute break to fill her in on my visit to Sutton and the appearance of the red Charger near my cottage.

"So 'Jackson Manchester' is still around," she said.

"Apparently. I locked up tight before I left and blocked all the first-floor windows with furniture."

"I don't think you should go back there, Vic. Why don't you come here tonight? Danny's on duty—we can have a girls' night."

"It's tempting, but I've got my bike with me and it's too far to go. The second I'm done here tonight, I'll head over to the boardwalk for the last *zeppole* of the season and then home. If anything looks off, I'll call you to come get me. But you'll be waiting parked out on the street; I don't want you anywhere near the boardwalk if there's trouble."

"You sound just like your brother."

Who is on duty tonight and out of reach if I need him. "Well, we both love you." I took a breath. "I'm sure I'll be fine. If I'm really desperate, I'll bike over to my parents' house."

Sofia snorted. "Let's hope it doesn't come to that. Stay in touch and text me when you get in."

"Will do. Get some rest, okay?"

I shoved my phone into my apron pocket. It was after eight, and already twilight. I was scheduled for another hour and a half, which meant a ride home in the dark. I would stay to the boardwalk side—it would be crowded, well lit, and relatively safe. From there I could go to my parents or wait it out until Danny was off duty.

That seemed like a reasonable plan until I pedaled out of the parking lot in full darkness more than ninety minutes later. My bike light shone a weak beam on the pavement, and I kept looking over my shoulder for a red car. *This is your hometown, Vic. You know every inch of it. Get to the boardwalk and you'll be fine.* I crossed at the next intersection and locked my bike to a lamppost near the corner of Ocean and Tuckerton. I hurried up the nearest ramp, overlooked by the Chowder House, relieved to be among the crowds and the bright lights of the boardwalk. The *zeppole* stand was about two blocks down. I walked on the right side, staying within the lights of the souvenir stores and arcades.

When a call came through from Sofia, I crossed the boardwalk and took a seat on one of the benches along the railing. "Hey, you okay?"

"I'm fine," she answered. "I just remembered something from our interview with Gerry Domenica, and I'm pretty sure it's the thing that's been bugging you. Remember he said that he didn't know Alphonse's last name?"

"Right."

"But later on in the conversation, he used it when he was looking at the picture of your uncle. He told you that you were too pretty to be a Petrocelli."

"Oh my God, you're right. It seems so obvious now. So we've caught Domenica in at least one lie. But we're done with this, Sofe. We shouldn't even be thinking about it."

"Speak for yourself. I'm sitting here and it's all I *can* think about."

"Listen," I said, "I better go. My battery's low."

I ended the call and turned to face the ocean. It was an inky gray under the bright moon, and I sat for a moment, listening to the soft crash of the waves in the distance. Tired and achy from a long day at the restaurant, I leaned my head back. Just as my eyes started to flutter closed, I saw a tall woman standing in front of the arcade across from where I sat. She was on a cell phone, and when she turned her head, I recognized her: Iris Harrington.

She looked from one end of the boardwalk to another, gesturing and talking excitedly. *My God,* I thought. *She's looking for somebody. And I think it might be me.* I slipped off the bench and turned my face away from her. But which way to go? The crowd was thin here and I couldn't risk her seeing me. Slowly, I shifted to face the metal railing, and I knew I had no choice. Without thinking, I gripped the rail, slid down to a squat, and slipped down, feet first, onto the sand. Forget about the *zeppole*; I had no appetite for them now anyway. I would make my way back along the beach until I reached Tuckerton Avenue, and then grab my bike and pedal my butt off to my parents' house.

But the sand was deep under the boardwalk, and it made for slow walking. I could smell the damp on the wooden planks, and above me, footfalls echoed weirdly. The refrain from the old song kept playing over and over in my brain as I trudged through the sand. *Under the boardwalk, down by the sea.* When we were kids, hanging out under here was cool, but now it seemed creepy as I made my slow way in the dark. My sneakers, full of sand, were slowing me down, but I didn't want to stop to take them off. When the roof of the Chowder House came into view, I nearly cried with relief.

Until I heard a swishing sound behind me. I wasn't alone under here, and ankle-deep in damp sand, I was in no position to run. The sound came closer and somebody grabbed my arm. In a panic, I tried to shake it off but was pulled around to face my assailant. Expecting to see Iris, I felt fury rising in me as I looked into the dark, scowling face of Jason Conners.

"Let go of me, Jason," I said breathlessly, "or I will shriek this whole boardwalk down."

"I need to talk to you," he said nervously, but didn't loosen his grip.

"Get *off* me!" I yelled, jerking my arm hard just as he let go. I caught him hard in the ribs with my elbow, sending him tumbling backward into the sand.

"Ow! Will you take it easy?" He stood up, brushing the sand from his hands and arms. "I just wanna talk."

"No way." In a burst of energy born of fear, I kept walking.

"What are you doing skulking around under here, anyway?" he asked, hurrying to keep up with me.

"*Skulking.* That's a big word for you," I called over my shoulder.

"Cut it out, okay? I told you I had to talk to you. I'm supposed to be at school. I'm only sticking around this crappy town because you can't stay out of my business. Damn it, will you just stop?" he yelled from behind me.

My choices were limited—stay alone on this dark beach with Jason or climb back up to the boardwalk and risk being seen by Iris. I stopped and waited for him to catch up. "There's a beach entrance up ahead. You go first."

He shook his head but complied. I waited until he was on the boards before I followed. I gestured to a bench in full view of several concession stands. "We talk here or not at all. Five minutes. And you touch me again and I call my brother and have you arrested for assault *and* breaking and entering."

"I didn't assault you," he said, sneering. "And you can't prove I was anywhere near your house or that restaurant."

"I wouldn't be so sure of that." I pointed to the seat. "You better put at least a couple of feet between us."

He sat at the end of the bench, shaking his head. "Oh, for Chrissakes, I'm not gonna hurt you. I'm here to tell you the truth. My mom's freaking out and it's all your fault."

I slapped my hand against my chest. "My fault? Your mother's crazy. She pushed me off her front steps and probably gave Pete that wine."

He leaned toward me, lowering his voice. "*I* gave it to him, okay? Not her. I wanted him to go away, okay?" he said again, his voice shaking. "I admit I used the napkin so my prints wouldn't be on it. I couldn't risk anybody connecting him to me, but I didn't kill him. That's the truth."

Though I was inclined to believe him, I wasn't quite ready to cross Jason and his mother off the list. "You just said you couldn't be connected with him. Because he knew about the hacking, right?"

He sighed. "Will you just let me finish? Actually, I need to start from the beginning."

I crossed my arms. "You have four minutes." He rolled his eyes dramatically, and I had a moment of pity for Florence having to deal with a surly teenager twenty-four/seven.

He sat forward, his hands dangling over his knees, looking like any number of kids on this boardwalk. I had to remind myself that I shouldn't get too comfortable; I could be sitting on this bench with a murderer.

"Look," he began. "My mother hasn't had it so easy. My father left us when I was little; he lives somewhere out in Ohio and sometimes sends us money when he thinks of it. But *she* raised me, pretty much on her own. I've always been smart, especially with math and science. Computers are my thing. But you know that." He couldn't keep the satisfaction out of his voice.

"Wipe that smirk off your face, Jason. So yeah, I know firsthand you're a computer whiz. Keep going."

"Okay, so I did really good in high school."

Really well, I wanted to scream. *Not really good.* Instead I nodded. "Good enough to get into MIT," I said.

He nodded. "But there was that, uh, trouble last year. And the old guy, Pete, he must have overheard . . . another dude and me talking about it." He pushed his sweaty hair out of his eyes and wiped his forehead. "And then he found my mother at the restaurant one day and told her he knew. He asked her for money. And that's when it started. She'd never know when he'd show up, and she'd give him all her tips. That's when she had the idea I should get a job there."

"That's right," I said. "We hired you a little later. Why didn't she just go to the police? Or to one of us? We could have talked to my brother."

"Right." He shook his head, clearly wondering at my stupidity. "Sure, let's go tell the police I hacked the school computer system. Real smart."

"So instead you gave him enough wine to kill himself. I guess that was real smart, too."

"He didn't die of alcohol poisoning," he hissed. "He drowned." He pulled his phone from his pocket, swiped a finger across the screen, and held it out to me. "I guessed you missed this one, Sherlock."

It was a small item in the *Asbury Park Press*, indicating that's Pete's death was due to accidental drowning. So it was public knowledge now. Which meant Pete's murderer would be feeling pretty safe, unless he or she knew I was pushing to reopen the investigation.

"Big deal." I shrugged. "So maybe you and your mother are looking at a manslaughter charge instead."

"Will you cut the crap, already?" he said through his teeth. "We weren't anywhere near that carousel house the night of the storm. We went straight home from the restaurant. But the thing is, we can't prove it. We only have each other's word on it."

He leaned toward me and I drew back. He let out a loud huff. "I'm not gonna hurt you! How many times do I have to say it? I'm asking you to believe me." He dropped his voice. "My mother worked her whole life for me to have this chance. She didn't hurt that old man and neither did I." He stood up and stuck his hands in his pockets, his hair falling over his scarred face. My heart twisted a little for this genius kid and his waitress mother, who only wanted a better life for themselves. But that didn't necessarily mean I took him at his word.

"Listen, Jason, I'm not a police officer. I'm not even a detective." He let out a snort, which I chose to ignore. "But you'd better be prepared: If this case gets reopened, you might be questioned."

He shrugged, but his eyes were those of a scared kid. "If they get me on the hacking, so be it. But I didn't kill anybody." He pointed. "And I think you know that." He turned to go, and I watched him make his way down the boardwalk to the street ramp.

Was Jason telling me the truth? Was he just a kid who'd made a mistake he was desperate to cover up? Or a very, very shrewd killer?

Chapter Twenty-nine

I sat on the bottom step at the beach entrance to catch
my breath and empty my sneakers of sand. I was only
a couple of blocks from my bike, and I planned to take
the first street ramp down to the sidewalk. But the minute I stood up, I caught the scent of patchouli on the
breeze. I slipped back under the boardwalk and peeked
through a crack in the planks. My vision was limited, but
I could hear a female voice getting closer. The boards
creaked over my head and I froze.

"I saw her; I know I did," the woman said, her voice
muffled by the wooden planking.

A man's voice answered, and there was no mistaking
it: Richard Barone. "Where did she go, Iris?"

"If I knew, I'd tell you!" She sounded exasperated,
impatient.

"Well, how did you lose her?" Barone's tone was calm
and measured; I found that more frightening than Iris's
near hysteria.

"I don't know!" she answered. "It's not like following
people is in my line of work."

"We have to find her before they do," he said, and a

shiver, swift as an electric current, traveled down my spine. Who were *they*? How many people were after me? Much as I wanted to run, I needed to know. I was sure they could hear me breathing right under their feet.

"I know we have to find her, damn it!" Iris said in a harsh whisper. "I warned her to stay out of it, but she can't help herself. Now she's in deeper than she knows." They dropped their voices then, and I strained to hear. Suddenly Iris's voice came through clearly. "I saw that old bike of hers parked over at Tuckerton. Maybe we just wait there."

"That's our only option, then. We'll wait for her on the street." The voices died away, and I sank down into the sand, my heart pounding and their words echoing in my ears: *We have to find her before they do. She's in deeper than she knows.*

I sat in the damp sand, heart pounding. What should I do? Go down to the street and double back to the restaurant? But Barone and Iris were heading in the same direction. Should I climb back up to the boardwalk and head east to my cottage? It was a long walk, out past the rides pier. Even if I had the energy, the memory of that red Dodge doing a slow cruise past my house was enough to give me pause. I needed help. I pulled out my phone, tapping my contacts list with trembling fingers.

"Please be around, Cal," I whispered. "Please." But the call went to voice mail. With my battery power at eleven percent, I tried Tim, who didn't pick up. Why would he, given our earlier conversation? I even called our local cab company, but no driver would be available until eleven. "It's a holiday weekend," they reminded me. I was running out of options. I tried Sofia.

"What's up, Vic? Where are you?"

"I'm, uh, under the boardwalk. And please don't sing. It won't stop playing in my head as it is."

"What are you doing under there?"

"Hiding from Iris and Barone. And I just had a run-in with Jason Connors." I filled her in quickly, mindful of my low battery. "So, listen, can you get here? Just park somewhere along the boards and text me. I'll find you."

She lowered her voice to a whisper. "I can't. My mother showed up."

"Did you say your *mother* is there? What, she dropped in from Florida?"

"Yes," she hissed into the phone. Her voice grew louder. "It's Victoria, Mom. She's doing great. Yes. I'll tell her," she called out. "She sends her love."

"I'd rather she sent me a taxi—I need to get the hell out of here. Can you get through to Danny? I texted him, but he didn't get back to me."

"I think he's out of cell range, but I'll keep trying. He's off duty at eleven."

"I know. I'll just have to hang in there till then."

"Listen, I'll get to you somehow. I'll tell her something. In the meantime, be careful, okay?" she said. "Are you sure you don't want to call your dad?"

"Not just yet, Sofe. I know it's stupid, but I really don't want to worry them. Or drag them into something that might be dangerous. Listen, I have to go; I'm just about out of battery."

I stood up, weak-kneed, and brushed the sand from my jeans. I gripped the rail on the beach entrance and walked slowly up the steps. I was exhausted, covered in sand, and carrying a phone with a dangerously low battery. Before I reached the top step, I heard the rumbling and felt the vibration under my feet, and I knew that rescue was at hand. Waving wildly, I flagged down the red beach trolley and stumbled up the steps, blinking under the bright lights in the car. I paid the driver and flopped into a seat across from the only other riders—a tired-looking couple with two little boys who were very much awake.

"We're goin' on the merry-go-round," the older one announced. His lips and teeth were blue from the snow cone that was dripping over his hand. His mother dabbed at him with a napkin while he twisted away from her.

"Yeah," the little one piped up. "And then the tea-cups." He shoved a handful of popcorn into his mouth, losing several kernels in the process, which his father picked up, one by one.

"I used to love the merry-go-round," I said. "But the teacups made me kind of sick."

"Good to know," their father said. "Maybe we'll skip the teacups this trip."

"Did you puke?" the older boy said, his eyes wide.

"Leave the lady alone," their mother said, and smiled at me a little wearily.

Not for the first time, I wondered if Sofia and my brother knew what lay ahead of them once that baby came. I leaned my head back and closed my eyes, fighting the urge to sleep. *Oh, the hell with all this,* I thought, *I'm going home.* The trolley route ended at the rides pier; from there it would be a relatively short walk to my cottage, and by then Danny would be off duty. The trolley ride would put some distance between me and Barone and Iris, but who else was looking for me? *Or who else is after you?* said a voice in my head.

"We have to find her before they do," Barone had said. So more than one person. But who were *they*? Could it be Florence and Jason? Had Jason told a tall tale just to

keep me off guard? Or ... I sat up, my eyes wide-open now. What if the others who were looking for me meant no harm? What if they were trying to warn me? But any-body attempting to help me — my parents, Danny, Cal, or Tim — would contact me, and my phone showed no mes-sages and no missed calls.

I shook my head, trying to make sense of it all, but in the end, there was only one plausible theory. "They" were looking for me because I had information that was damaging to them. If not Florence and Jason, it would have to be Gerry Domenica or "Jackson Manchester," the ride operator and sometime boyfriend of Alyssa. Both men bore a lion tattoo — was that a coincidence or were they connected somehow? Were they working to-gether? Were they at this moment searching me out somewhere on this boardwalk? I tapped my foot ner-vously, watching out the windows as the trolley chugged past the brightly lit stands and arcades. When it screeched to a stop, I jumped.

"Here we are," the driver called out. "The rides pier. Final destination! Final destination, everybody!"

Final destination. Let's hope not. I stood up, still hold-ing the pole for support, and hung back to let the family go out ahead of me.

"Bye, lady!" the little one said with a wave.

"Bye," I said, "have fun."

And watch out for crazy old gangsters and tattooed ex-cons. And desperate waitresses and lovesick women and rich, powerful men with something to hide. *Hang on to those kids,* I wanted to say as I watched them go, *be-cause suddenly my beloved old boardwalk is a dangerous place.*

I stepped off the trolley, my legs leaden and my head

spinning from exhaustion and fear. I took my phone from my pocket. Almost ten thirty. The rides pier closed at eleven, and once those crowds left, the boardwalk would be deserted. What chance would I have against one or more of them? *You can't think this way, Vic.*

I slipped in among the tourists in line for fresh lemonade. Behind the stand was a small café area with a row of mirrors along its walls. I took a seat in the back; at least I could see them coming. Ditching my straw, I drained the lemonade in a few gulps and stared at my phone screen. I was at seven percent battery power. It would be thirty long minutes before I could reach Danny directly. I turned off the phone to conserve what was left of its power. Meanwhile, there were at least four people, one or more of whom might be a murderer, searching for me at this very moment. I looked around nervously, shaking the ice cubes in the bottom of my cup. *Do I make a run for home? Or do I try to dodge them all until my brother can get here?*

Well, I couldn't do anything until I hit the ladies' room. I stood up cautiously and slipped into the bathroom, used it hurriedly, and washed my hands. I pushed open the door with my elbow, still shaking my hands dry when the smell of patchouli reached my nose. Iris stood blocking the exit, her arms crossed.

"We've been looking all over for you."

I let out a loud sigh. "I know. Where's Richard?"

"He's back at the table where you were sitting. We need to talk to you."

No, I need to get out of here. My mouth went dry and my heart pounded wildly. We were in a public place — what could they do to me in a public place? "How . . . how did you know where to find me?"

"I saw you get on the trolley. And then we drove

down." She frowned. "What does that matter, anyway? It's *imperative* we talk to you."

I took a step backward. "We can talk right here."

"Victoria, you're being ridiculous. Just come back to the table so we can explain."

I shook my head. "I want some answers first."

"Oh, for God's sake! You plan to interrogate me outside the ladies' room?"

"Yes, in fact. Let's start with that missing scarf of yours. How did Pete get it?"

She closed her eyes briefly as though she was considering what to say. "He found it outside Richard's house. Richard is separated, but not divorced. His lawyers had made it clear that I shouldn't visit him there, that it might affect the settlement. And it wouldn't look good for the foundation." She shook her head sadly. "And Richard would do anything to protect the foundation."

Anything? Like murder? "So Pete was blackmailing you?"

"Yes." The word came out as a sigh, both of resignation and relief. "For small amounts, now and then. I'd never know when he might show up at the store." She shuddered. "I couldn't have him hanging around the store, and I couldn't have him bothering Richard, so I paid him to go away." She looked at me directly. "But that's *all* I did. Don't you see that Richard and I are trying to help you?"

So you say, Iris. "I'm not sure I believe that."

"My God, you are exasperating. Just come back to the table and we'll explain."

"Okay. But you go first."

She rolled her eyes but walked past me back into the café area. I followed behind her, looking for a way to make a run for it. I might be able to handle Iris, but there was no way I could get past her *and* Barone. But the table was only steps away now, and I met Barone's dark, angry glare. Without hesitating, without even thinking, I darted past the table, past the startled faces of the other patrons, and tore through the line of people waiting for drinks. While Iris and Barone shouted behind me, I ran for my life, my feet pounding the wooden boards.

Take the sidewalk. Take the sidewalk. But there was only one ramp to the street out here, and it was at the end of the boardwalk. I had reached the Ferris wheel; doubled over from running, I ducked behind it to catch my breath. For a wild moment, I thought about getting on it—they couldn't chase me to the top of the ride. And my fear of heights was nothing compared to my fear of dying. But the line was long, and I'd be waiting out in the open. I shook my head. I had to keep going; I had to hang on another twenty minutes.

I stayed among the crowds near the rides, tired to the point of haziness. Here and there, people were starting to leave the boardwalk, and lights were blinking out in the stores and arcades. I moved into the shadow of the carousel house, studying the clusters of people still milling about its entrance. A broad-shouldered man with cropped hair had his back to me; when he turned, I caught the flash of white of his collar. Father Tom. Now that help was so close, I opened my mouth to call out to him, but shut it abruptly. He had his hands on his hips, a slight frown on his face. Because as I watched him, I realized that Father Tom wasn't out for an evening stroll on the boardwalk; he was looking for somebody. And I knew that somebody was me. Was he trying to help me? I wanted to believe that, I truly did, but Pete's will might be telling a very different story about our old family friend. I had to get out of here.

What have things come to, I thought, *when you can't trust a priest?* I turned cautiously, trying to stay out of his line of vision. Behind the carousel was a grassy lot and an empty stretch of boardwalk that led to the last street ramp. From there it was only a few blocks to my cottage. I would take another minute to rest; if all was clear I'd do a sprint through the lot and down to the sidewalk. The lights of the carousel house partially illuminated the empty lot, but beyond it was dark. *I'll be running blind,* I thought with a shiver. *But I don't have a choice.*

Picking my way around trash and broken bottles, I took one step, then another, looking left, right, and back over my shoulder. I was halfway across the lot when I broke into a run. The end of the boardwalk was just ahead of me; I picked up my pace, my arms pumping, my chest still aching. The street ramp beckoned like an open palm, and I thought, *You got this, Vic. You got this.*

And that was when I saw him. He was walking up the ramp, and in the light from the street I could see the outlines of his shaved head and muscular arms. I pivoted so fast I nearly fell, but pushed back toward the grassy lot. I had nearly reached it when I heard him behind me.

"Hey!" he shouted. "Wait! I have to talk to you!"

You and everybody else. Take a number, brother. I sprinted back across the grass as his voice faded behind me. I rounded the side of the carousel house until I heard his footsteps die away. One or two tourists still lingered. It had to be close to eleven; any minute now Danny would get my text. Just a few more minutes and I'd be safe. But the crowds were thinning. Stands and arcades were closing, leaving me fewer and fewer places to hide.

The lights on the Ferris wheel went black, and I pressed myself against the outside wall of the carousel house, my heart thudding and my breath coming hard. Four of them were looking for me now, and I didn't know which of them I could trust. If any. I stayed against the wall, shifting my feet sideways, thinking if I could get to the door, I'd duck inside. *Not a good idea, Vic. Good old "Jackson Manchester" probably has a key. He might even be in there right now, waiting.*

I bent my head, feeling the tears behind my eyes. I couldn't run anymore. In fact, I could barely walk. And then there was a deep male voice in my ear, saying exactly what I was thinking.

"C'mon, Victoria," Richard Barone said. "Don't you think it's time to give it up?"

Chapter Thirty

*R*ichard took my arm as gently as he had spoken and led me inside the carousel house, where a livid Iris was waiting. The place was empty of tourists, and the carousel horses formed an eerie tableau in the darkened arcade.

"Why do you keep running away from us?" Iris hissed, her angry voice echoing strangely in the empty building.

I jerked my arm from Richard's grip. "Why do you think? I don't know what you might do." I glared at Richard. "And I don't know what you might have *already* done."

Iris let out a loud huff. "Don't you ever get tired of playing detective?"

Richard put his arm around her shoulders. "It's okay, hon. She knows we don't intend to hurt her."

"I don't know any such thing. My brother is on his way, probably with backup, so don't get any ideas." *Please let that be true.* I looked from one to the other of them. "You said you wanted to explain. So answer my questions." I felt like someone in a movie—or in one of my own books. *Keep them talking and help will come. Maybe.*

"Ask me anything you like, Victoria," Barone said.

"Iris has already admitted that Pete was blackmailing her. Was he blackmailing you, too?"

He looked at me steadily. "I was nowhere near this place the night he died."

"That's not an answer," I said. "Pete knew my uncle had probably been set up for a crime he didn't commit. And I suspect he also knew that the real killer was part of Leo Barone's inner circle. So your great-grandfather's organization was not entirely 'bloodless,' was it, Richard?" I raised my chin and looked him straight in the eye, feeling as though I had little to lose at this point. "Keeping that from going public would be motive enough, wouldn't you say?"

He shook his head, a slight smile on his face. "Victoria, think about this for a minute. If I'd wanted to keep Pete quiet, I would have set him up in his own house with a regular pension. I could have given him a hundred times what he asked for. Don't you understand that blackmail was a *game* to him? He felt like it gave him power over people."

"Well, it was a game that got him killed. And you're not immune to that game yourself, Richard," I said. "You can't tell me you don't enjoy having power over people. You knew my uncle was innocent all along. You've probably had those papers for years. You only gave them to me when you thought I was getting close to the answer. Pete may not have been a threat, but *I* was."

Barone shook his head. "I never touched that old man."

"Maybe not," I said, "but you might have hired someone to do it."

"Somebody like me, maybe?" Gerry Domenica stepped from the shadow of the doorway, holding a snub-nosed pistol that looked like something out of an old movie. He looked at each one of us, grinning widely, the gold tooth prominent. *The gold tooth.*

"You were here," I said shakily. "The morning after the storm. You were here with the cleanup guys. I remember now."

"Do you, miss?" he said. "I could tell you were a smart girl. Too smart, maybe." He held the gun out and I shrank back. "Are you smart enough to reck-anize this? Nah, why would ya? It's the gun that killed Nino Mancini."

"The one the police never found all those years ago," I said slowly as a creeping chill settled over me. Because it was all becoming clear now.

"I made my bones with this," Domenica said proudly. "I was only sixteen. Mancini had crossed Mr. Leo, and I couldn't let that go, could I?" He turned to me. "That uncle of yours was always hopped up on somethin'. I made him drive me that night." He gestured with the gun. "Boom, boom. Two shots and it was all over. Then I got outta there like a bat out of hell." He shrugged. "Too bad your uncle got the blame."

"And Pete knew," I said. "Because his brother, Alphonse, had told him. All these years you thought you got away with murder. But Pete knew the truth. He was a threat to you, so you killed him."

He chuckled. "I ain't sayin' I did or I didn't. But if I did, I did it for you, Richie. I did it for you and Mr. Leo."

"You did it for yourself, Domenica," Barone said. "You did it to cover up a crime *you* committed, a crime for which another man took the blame and spent years in prison."

"And that's something you wouldn't want coming out now, would you, Richie? What with your big fancy foundation and all," Domenica said, his voice sly. "Mr. Leo always said he didn't have no blood on his hands. And I know you'd wanna keep people from knowing about poor old Roberto." He twirled the gun around on his index finger and I fought the urge to drop to the floor. "You'd be surprised at how easy it is to get rid of an old drunk. Hypothetically speaking, of course." He grinned widely.

"Shut up, old man!" said a voice sharply. "Don't say anything else."

Four heads turned in unison to look at the tattooed man who stood in the open doorway. *The gang's all here,* I thought. *And which one of them killed Pete?*

"Lorenzo, what are you doing here?" Domenica asked. "I told you to stay out of this."

"I can't stay out of it, Nonno. I'm in it, just like you are." *Nonno?* "He's your grandfather?" I asked.

"You bet he is," Domenica piped up. "He got that tattoo just like mine." He slapped his upper arm. "Leo the lion."

"That's right, Nonno," Lorenzo said. "It's just like yours."

"Yeah," Domenica said. "That's my boy. He got into a little trouble some years back, but he did his time. Right, Renzo?"

"Uh-huh," Lorenzo said, keeping his eyes trained on his grandfather's gun. "I did my time. Hey, why don't you put that down now? Somebody might get hurt."

Thank you, Lorenzo. At least somebody in this room has his wits about him. But that didn't mean he wasn't dangerous. Domenica's grandson had sought out Pete and probably used Alyssa to get close to him. He had access to the carousel house. Was he working *for* his grandfather or against him? Domenica was here the day after the storm, but had he arrived the night before? Had he come to kill Pete or to make sure the job was done?

"Put the gun down," Lorenzo said again.

It was then that Richard stepped forward. "Lorenzo's right, Domenica. We don't want anyone getting hurt here." He looked from grandfather to grandson. "And I'm sure we can all come to some kind of agreement, can't we, gentlemen?"

Lorenzo shook his head and smiled slightly. "He means he'll pay us off. Because Barone thinks that all he has to do is write a check to make things go away."

"I wouldn't put it quite that way, Lorenzo," Barone said smoothly. "But I don't want to see anyone hurt." He turned to Gerry. "Domenica, can't we at least let the women go?"

Yes, please. Let's do let the women go. My heart gave a small flutter of hope, but Domenica shook his head. "Nobody goes anywhere just yet." But he slid his arm down to hold the gun at his side, and I breathed a little easier.

"As I was saying—" Richard began.

"Never mind what you were saying, Barone," Lorenzo said. To my surprise, he turned to me. "Victoria, I was looking for you for a reason. I knew about your great-uncle, and so did he." He pointed to Barone, who raised an eyebrow but said nothing. "I grew up listening to my nonno's stories of the old days in AC, and I'm not gonna lie, I was impressed. He was an old-time gangster, you know. So I got the lion tattoo, thought I was a real badass." He shook his head. "I served time for robbery, and when you're inside, you have a lot of time to think. But also a lot of time to read. I worked in the prison library, and I found a lot of the same stuff you did," he said to me. "And I had my suspicions about the Mancini murder. About . . . who really did it, I mean."

At this, Domenica grinned widely. "He's a smart boy, ain't he?"

My God, I thought, *he's proud of what he did. And he doesn't care that his own grandson knows he's a murderer.* "But why were you looking for me?" I asked.

Lorenzo held up his hand. "I'll explain, but let me go back a bit, okay? I got the job here on the boardwalk, and that's where I stumbled across Pete. I mean, he would just ramble on to anyone who would listen."

"And you connected him to your grandfather and the old days in Atlantic City," I said.

"Yeah. My grandfather used to talk about 'making his bones,' but it was Pete who suggested that it was Nonno who killed Mancini, and not your uncle. But I had to be sure. I asked my grandfather, point-blank, if he'd killed Mancini, and he admitted it." He pointed to Barone. "So I went to see him. I told him what I'd found out and about meeting Pete. I wanted him to set the record straight. But instead he offered me money to make it go away."

I looked at Barone, who stood stone-faced. "I don't know what you're talking about," he said.

"Please," Lorenzo said. He turned to me. "I knew you were wondering about Pete's death, too. I knew you'd gone down to talk to my grandfather; I wanted to warn you."

"*You* wanted to warn me?" I looked at Iris and Barone. "So you two weren't looking for me to protect me. You wanted to make sure you found me before Lorenzo did. What were you going to do, Richard? Offer me money, too?"

Barone shrugged. "Again, I have no idea what you're talking about."

"Yes, you do, Richie," Domenica said. "It was you who told me about Pete. When you came down to the club to play golf. Remember?"

So Barone made sure that Domenica knew Pete was a threat; in a sense, he had signed his death warrant.

"And once that happened," Lorenzo said softly, "it was all over. I tried to warn Pete the night of the party."

"So that's why you were hanging around Alyssa," I said.

He smiled slightly. "Not my best hour. But I had to get to Pete, and I'd seen him around the restaurant. But he was so drunk that night I don't think he understood he was in any danger. So I couldn't save him." He stared at his grandfather. "And I don't want anybody else getting hurt."

"I ain't gonna hurt nobody," Domenica said, but tightened his grip on the gun.

Lorenzo looked at his grandfather, his eyes filling with tears. "I know you did it, Nonno. I tried to stop it, but I couldn't." He swiped the back of his hand across his eyes. "You took my keys to this place and you got him to meet you here the night of the storm. You killed that old man."

"No, he fell, Renzo. I swear! He was drunk and he passed out; he just fell forward on the floor. The water was already coming in."

"And you left him there, right?" Lorenzo asked softly. "You left him there to drown." He paused, his expression weary. "Or maybe you helped him along. One good shove would've been enough."

"I wouldn't put it that way, exactly," Domenica said, gesturing with the gun.

"Will you *please* drop that thing?" Lorenzo said through his teeth.

Domenica's voice hardened and she shook his head. "No can do, son. I got a room full of witnesses here."

I looked from one stubborn face to the other; we were at an impasse. I was just desperate enough—and exhausted enough—to try to break it.

"Mr. Domenica," I said, trying to keep my voice from shaking, "my brother is a police detective and he's on his way with backup. Believe me, it will be much better for you if you don't have a weapon in your hand."

He turned to face me and I instantly regretted calling attention to myself. He tilted his head, studying my face. "You know, miss, I see the resemblance. I always felt bad about Robbie. But what was I gonna do? I was a kid. Had my whole life in front of me."

I seized on his words. "That's true. You *were* only a kid. And if you're saying that Pete's death was an accident—"

"I'll get you the best lawyer there is," Barone interrupted.

Before Domenica could answer, there was a creak and a metallic groan. Then the first slow notes of organ music and the flare of lights as the carousel slowly came to life. As the platform turned, a lone figure jumped from it, and I caught the flash of white against the black collar. Domenica turned in surprise, and never saw the roundhouse punch that caught him in the side and dropped him like a rock. The gun clattered across the cement floor and Lorenzo stopped it with his foot. Doubled over in pain, Domenica looked up in shock at the priest, who was now kneeling next to him.

"I'm sorry if I hurt you," Father Tom said softly, "but this had to end. You know that, don't you?"

Domenica nodded and spoke with effort. "I . . . I know, Father."

Father Tom rested his hand on Domenica's arm. "The police are on their way. It will go better for you if you tell the truth."

Lorenzo set the gun down carefully outside the door of the carousel house and then crossed quickly to his grandfather. "He's right, Nonno."

Father Tom turned to me. "Are you all right, Victoria?"

I nodded. "Thanks to you. That was quite a shot you gave him."

He flexed his fist and grinned at me. "Some things you never forget." He raised his eyes heavenward. "God willing."

In the distance I could hear the sirens, and my knees sagged with relief. For a moment, I met Iris's eye. But she glanced away quickly, turning all her attention on Richard. *Good luck, girlfriend,* I thought. *You're gonna need it.*

At that moment, Sofia rushed in, nearly knocking down Iris and Barone as she barreled toward me. "You okay, Vic?" she said breathlessly. "Father Tom made me wait outside, and it was killing me." She pointed to the still-spinning ride. "But it was my idea to start the carousel to distract everybody. Smart, huh?" As I looked at her broad grin and shining eyes, it occurred to me that even pregnancy didn't cause the glow that surrounded my sister-in-law at this moment. Maybe she had a future in law enforcement after all.

"Not just smart, Sofe, brilliant. Well played." I looked over at Domenica, still on the floor of the arcade, with Lorenzo hovering over him. Barone and Iris were huddled together, talking quietly. Someone had brought the ride to a stop, and I had a sudden yearning for fresh sea air. "Hey, can we blow this joint, sis?"

"Yup," Sofia said. "Danny's on his way. And he gave me strict orders to get you the heck out of here. He said you can answer questions later or tomorrow morning."

"That's a relief."

We headed out onto the deserted boardwalk in silence. We had reached the street ramp when Sofia turned to me. "By the way, did you call me *sis*? What happened to *SIL*?"

"Ah, you were always more of a sister than a SIL to me. Might as well call it what it is, right?"

"Okay, then," she said, "*sis* it is."

I linked my arm through hers as we walked down the ramp together. "And sis it will always be."

Chapter Thirty-one

*I*n the restaurant the next day, I sat at the family table, one parent on either side of me, each with a death grip on my hands.

"Are you sure you're okay, honey?" my mother asked.

I disengaged my hands as gently as possible. "Except for some very sore legs, I'm fine."

"You were so brave, sweetheart," my father said. "Facing down that old wiseguy."

"No, I wasn't, Dad, not really. I was cornered and didn't have a choice. Even Danny knows I didn't want to get involved with this one." I shook my head. "In a way, it was Father Tom who provided the key. Pete had confessed his blackmailing activities, possibly even named Domenica as someone he was afraid of. Father Tom knew Pete was in danger. And me, too," I added. "That's why he came looking for me last night."

"I'll bet you were so relieved to see him," my mom said.

"Uh, *relieved* doesn't begin to describe it, Mom." I thought it better not to share that I'd considered our kindly—and heroic—priest a murder suspect. Some confessions were better kept secret.

My dad grinned. "Sure woulda liked to see Father Tom throw that punch. Once a Golden Glove, always a Golden Glove, I guess. So, what do you think, baby?" he continued. "Did Barone hire Domenica to knock off Pete?"

"That's still unclear. But he bears some responsibility, ethically, if not legally." I sighed. "I'm just glad it's over." I looked out onto the quiet street bathed in sunshine. "Gosh, the storm, the party, the power outage, Pete's murder—it feels like a million years ago."

My mom patted my cheek. "And we got through it all. Oh, that reminds me, hon. Florence called with a message for you." She pursed her lips, clearly trying not to smile. "She says *Thanks for nothing*."

I let out a huff. "Okay, so maybe I harassed her and her sneaky son, but it was for a good reason. He was the one who messed up our computers, by the way."

"I wondered about that," my mom said. "But according to his mother, he's off to MIT, so God bless him." She shook her head. "I still feel responsible for what happened to you, Victoria. I *asked* you to look into Pete's death."

"But it was my own curiosity that set things in motion. Then I got cold feet."

"And I hope you have learned your lesson." My grandmother stood over me, her arms crossed.

"I have, Nonna," I said obediently.

"You better have," boomed my brother's voice from the doorway. At least he was smiling. And Sofia was with him, so I'd have my backup.

My mom jumped up to greet them, ushering them quickly to the table to sit down. "How nice to see you both," she said. "Will you have something to eat?"

Sofia and Danny exchanged a look. "Ah, that's good of you, Ma, but Sofia's mother is with us and she's cooking right now."

"Oh, Lucia's here," my mother said, her smile tight and forced. "How nice."

I glanced at my brother, who merely raised an eyebrow. Now that Sofia's formidable mother, Lucia Delmonico, was in town, there wasn't a room big enough to hold the two prospective grandmothers—not to mention Nonna.

"She sends her best, by the way," Sofia said quickly.

"And give our best back to her," Nonna said. But Nonna's *best* could mean a number things. Time for a change of subject, *subito*.

I turned to my brother. "So, Danny, what can you tell us? Has Domenica talked?"

"Nope," Danny said. "He's lawyered up but good. But that accident story he told won't hold up."

"What do you mean?" I asked.

"Well, Prosecutor Sutton suggested we look at the clothes Pete was wearing that night."

My mom's expression was puzzled. "His clothes? Why?"

"She had a hunch." He glanced at me and frowned. "From looking at some other things of Pete's that had, uh, come into her possession. I don't know if you guys remember, but Pete was wearing a white T-shirt that night."

I wrinkled my nose instinctively. "Yeah, and it was pretty gross."

"It was dirty," Danny agreed. "But not so dirty that you couldn't see a shoe mark on the back of it. A mark that matches Domenica's size shoe." He held up his hand. "And before you ask, Vic, Barone's feet are bigger."

I shuddered. "But that means—"

"That means Domenica either kicked Pete over or used his foot to hold him down in the water," Sofia piped up.

My grandmother pressed her palms together. "Oh *Dio*," she said, and crossed herself.

"How awful," my mother whispered.

"It sure is," my dad said, shaking his head. "And I still wonder whether Barone put him up to it."

"Dan, we all heard Domenica say that Barone had visited him at the country club," I said.

My brother shrugged. "Don't prove a thing, sis. The guy claims he was down there to play golf. He also said that he gave Pete money from time to time because he felt sorry for him. Claimed he had absolutely nothing to hide about his great-grandfather's organization. Unless Domenica gives him up, I don't think we can touch Barone."

"You know what?" I said. "I think Barone is far too smart to explicitly ask Domenica to kill Pete. Just letting him know that Pete was talking about the past would have been enough."

"I don't understand," my mom said. "What do you mean by *talking about the past*?"

"Actually, I have something to show you guys that I think will explain it." I opened the folder and spread out the documents about Zio Roberto. While my parents exclaimed over each one, my grandmother read them in silence.

"Victoria," she asked, "may I see that Atlantic City book again, please?"

"The page is marked," I said, pushing it across the table.

She opened it, stared, and shook her head. "That could be you, Frank," she said, pointing to Robert Riese.

"Or even you, Dan," Sofia said. "In a certain light."

"It's crazy, eh?" my dad said, shaking his head. "And a little creepy, too, when you think about what happened to the guy."

My mom squeezed his hand. "There but for the grace of God, right, honey? But that resemblance *is* remarkable," she said. "Imagine him living only miles away from your father. Maybe it's better he never knew that his brother survived all those years."

Nonna nodded. "I agree, Nicolina. It's better this way." At that, my father and I exchanged an amused look. It was a rare day when Nonna agreed with my mother about anything. She closed the book and passed it back to me. "The question now is: How do we go about giving him a decent burial and putting up a stone with his real name on it?"

"You wanna do that, Ma?" my father asked, a note of surprise in his voice.

Nonna pressed her palms together and rocked them up and down—Italian for *how could you even ask me such a thing?* "*Certo*, Frank. It's our responsibility. He's family. Is he supposed to stay in that place where he doesn't know anybody?"

I didn't feel the need to remind my grandmother that Zio Roberto was dead, and wasn't exactly in the market for friends. But I understood what she meant. She wanted him buried near his brother and parents for a reunion in the afterlife, an existence in which she believed fervently.

"Well," I said, "after spending so many years in a place he didn't belong—for a crime he didn't commit—it seems only right to let him spend eternity with some company."

Nonna shot me a suspicious look, clearly wondering if I was being "smart" with her. I merely smiled and asked Danny how we would go about getting a body moved.

"That's settled, then," Nonna said, "and we will organize a memorial service." Her eyes bored into my own, as if she was daring me to dispute her. But I understood the need for closure, both for Pete and for Zio Roberto. It was time they both rested in peace.

I was in the kitchen, happy to be doing the mundane tasks of lunch prep, when Cal pushed through the back door and dropped his toolbox with a thud. He crossed the kitchen in two quick strides and grabbed my hands.

"You okay, Victoria?"

I nodded. "I'm fine, really." I couldn't help grinning at him. "I don't think I've ever seen you move so fast."

"I felt terrible when I heard what happened. I listened to that message, and it made me feel plain helpless." He bent his head, touching his forehead to mine. "I couldn'ta lived with myself if somethin' had happened to you."

"Well, here I am, in one piece. And glad to be so." I looked into those warm green eyes, so full of concern and tenderness. *This guy cares for you. And you have some feelings for him. But it's time for the truth.* "Hey, Cal," I asked, "that toy I found—it belongs to a child, doesn't it? Your child, by any chance?"

He ran his hand through his hair and sighed, his eyes now sad. "Yes, *cher*. The toy was my daughter's. But I haven't seen her in years." He shook his head. "Her mother took off with her right after Katrina. I've spent years travelin' up and down the East Coast looking for them. And everywhere I go, I get a room ready for her." He shook his head. "I know she ain't a baby anymore, but I hold on to that toy. It's all I got."

"When you take off on those errands of yours—you're looking for her, aren't you?"

He nodded. "They're somewhere in the Northeast. I know that much anyway."

I took his hand. "I'm so sorry, Cal. It must be awful to know she's out there."

"That's why I need to leave town, and for a good long while. 'Cause I plan to find her this time, hell or high water." He put his arms around me and, for a moment, held me close to him. "I know I should have told you, Victoria. It was selfish not to. I couldn't ask you to throw in with a guy like me. And I'm sorry for it."

I *was* sorry. Sorry for so many things. For the loss of his friendship. For a relationship that never quite materialized, and never could, not while Tim was still so much a part of my history. *Face it, Vic. Tim took up occupancy in your heart half a lifetime ago, leaving little room for anybody else.* Even somebody as attractive and decent as Cal Lockhart.

"I know," I said. "Me, too." I cupped Cal's face with my hands. "You're such a *good* guy. That ex-wife of yours must be crazy." I kissed him once, lightly. "And I care about you; I really do. But you and I both know the timing isn't right. And you have a claim on you that goes much deeper than a relationship of a couple of months. But you've been a true friend to me, and I'll miss you." I blinked as the tears rose in my eyes. "I hope you find her, Cal. It's been wonderful knowing you."

"Same here, *cher*." He tightened his arms around me and I rested my head against his chest, a little sad and a little sorry, my heart bruised, but not broken.

Just then the kitchen doors banged open. Tim halted in the doorway, his face reddened in anger and his mouth curled with disgust. "Why don't you two get a room?"

"Don't talk to me that way, Tim!" But the words were barely out before Cal cut across me and faced him. He lifted his chin, clearly not intimidated by the three inches Tim had on him.

"You know, I've just about had it with you. You owe her an apology," Cal said through his teeth.

"Is that so, big man?" Tim said. "You gonna make me?"

They stood chest-to-chest, Cal with his hands already curled into fists. Tim tore off his chef coat, ripping off two buttons in the process.

I looked from one to the other, my mouth gaping wide. "Are you out of your minds? You're acting like idiots. Cut it out!"

"Stay out of this, Vic," Tim growled.

"This is between him and me, *cher*," Cal said.

"Fine," I said. "The testosterone levels are reaching toxicity anyway. You can kill each other for all I care." But those were perhaps the wrong words to use at that moment.

"Outside, Lockhart." Tim swept past me, shoving the back door open, and Cal was instantly on his heels.

"Fine by me, brother," he said.

"What the hell, guys?" I said, scurrying after them. "Please don't do this. You're both crazy. This is ridiculous!" I shouted. But neither guy was listening.

They stood eyeing each other in silence, and for a moment I thought they'd both give it up. Without warning, Cal threw the first punch, a quick cross that caught Tim's jaw. I winced as his head jerked back, his eyes wide with surprise as he hit the ground.

Cal stood over him, his hands on his hips. "Sorry about that, brother. But you had it comin.'"

He took my hand and kissed it. "You're a wonderful woman, Victoria. And I am your friend for life. Remember that, will you?"

"I'll do that. And you take care, okay?"

I watched him drive away, Tim still sitting at my feet moaning and rubbing his jaw. I dropped to the ground next to him and turned his face to mine. The left side of his face was an angry red, with a bruise already forming along the bone.

"You know, this is the second time in twenty-four hours I've seen a guy felled with one punch. The novelty's starting to wear off," I said. "He's right, by the way," I added.

"About what?" he asked, still out of breath. "That you're a catch?"

"That goes without saying." I grinned at him and he smiled back painfully. "No, that you had it coming. You didn't catch us in some big clinch. We were saying good-bye, you idiot." I sighed. "And you acted like an ass."

He leaned back on his elbows and nodded. "I've been acting like an ass for eight years." He turned to face me, and I was startled to see tears in his eyes. "Back then, I walked away from you, Vic. I set you aside like you didn't matter. Like your love was something I could afford to lose. And it was the biggest mistake of my life." He dropped his head and let out a groan.

"Is that your broken heart talking or your broken jaw?" I asked. "We should really get some ice on that."

He sat up again and grabbed both my hands. "In a minute. Just let me get this out, okay? The surfer dude who thought he was God's gift—that's the guy who took you for granted. But I finally grew up. And if you give me the chance, I'll never take you for granted again." He pulled me toward him and briefly pressed both my hands against his lips. "Victoria Rienzi, you are the best woman I've ever known. I've never stopped loving you and I don't deserve you. But will you let me try?"

Our eyes held for a moment, and it was as though our whole history was unfolding in front of us, with all its joys and all its sorrows. "We've loved each other for half our lives," he said softly. "How many people can say that?"

"Not many," I whispered. "And it's something that's too precious to lose a second time. Or to take for granted." I looked at his bruised face and tear-filled eyes, and my heart turned over. But I wasn't going to make this easy for him. "So there are conditions."

"Anything, Vic. Tell me what you want me to do and I'll do it."

"You're going to court me. A good old-fashioned courtship with dates and flowers. You and I are going to get to know each other again. Who we are *now*, not who we were eight years ago. And do not expect me to jump right back into—"

"A relationship?" he asked with a grin.

I patted the good side of his face. "You understand me, then."

"I do," he said, leaning closer. "But is a kiss allowed?"

I pressed my palm against his lips. "Not just yet—there's one more condition."

"Name it."

I took a breath. "You have to teach me to make fresh pasta."

He laughed and then winced, but pulled me to him anyway. And there, sitting on the dusty asphalt of the Casa Lido parking lot, Tim Trouvare and I shared our first kiss in more than eight years. Unlike most things in life, it was as good as I remembered. Heck, it was better. Too bad it was interrupted by the sharp sound of my grandmother's voice.

"You're making a spectacle of yourselves. Get up off that ground right now."

I scrambled to my feet and Tim followed, though more slowly, holding the side of his aching face. As he stood next to me, we linked hands, at which my grandmother gave a snort of disgust. She held out a towel filled with ice and handed it to Tim.

"Put ice on that right now, *Timoteo*, and then hear me well." She gestured to the two of us. "I don't like this between the two of you, but there's nothing I can do about it. There never was." She stepped close, squinted up at him through her glasses, and jabbed her finger in his chest. "But you hurt my granddaughter, and you will have me to reckon with. Understand? Now go clean yourself up. Get that jaw seen to. And then come back here and start the sauces; I don't care how much your face hurts. *Tu capisci*?"

Tim held the ice to his jaw and nodded slowly, clearly too shocked for speech.

"Good," Nonna said. "Now go." After he was dismissed, she turned slowly to me. "And as for you, missy—"

I steeled myself for a lecture, but soon realized that wonders were unceasing today. My grandmother, Giulietta Rienzi, was actually smiling at me. Then she reached out and patted my shoulder.

"You're a good girl, Victoria," she said. "And much too smart to have your head turned by two men fighting over you. You've worked hard here in the restaurant and you've stood up for the family." She nodded to where Tim was making his slow way to his car. "What you see in him, I'll never know. But at least the boy can cook."

I looked at her in shock. She was still smiling, and I smiled back. "Thank you. You have no idea what that means to me, Nonna. I — "

She squared her shoulders, her face back to its usual expression of disapproval. "Now get back inside. Those tomatoes need chopping. And make sure you fold those napkins the right way for dinner. And find out if Lori has the coffee set up. You girls always wait till the last minute . . ."

She was still talking as I followed her back with a grin on my face and a spring in my step. I took a deep breath of the late-summer air and turned my face toward the ocean. I couldn't see it from here, but I knew it was there, bringing familiar comfort with every ebb and flow of its tides. And while I didn't know what the future held for Tim and me, there was one thing I was sure of: Nonna and I had weathered the storm. And though I had taken the long way around, I was finally and truly home.

Author's Note

Except for Enoch "Nucky" Johnson and Paul "Skinny" D'Amato, who were real people, the gangsters appearing in this book exist solely in my imagination. But I was certainly inspired by Atlantic City's colorful history, including that of Ducktown, an Italian immigrant neighborhood in the early half of the twentieth century, so named because a number of residents raised waterfowl there. I thought it would be fun to have Grandpa Rienzi delivering produce to the eateries in that section of the city, and it didn't seem like a stretch to imply that restaurants there may well have been under mob influence. Ducktown is still home to a number of Italian restaurants, many of them family-owned with long histories—just like the fictional Casa Lido.

Recipes from the
Italian Kitchen

My real life sister-in-law, Teresa Genova, serves up this lovely antipasto at family gatherings. It was handed down to her from her mom, Anne Guerriero, affectionately known as "Mrs. G."

Teresa's Antipasto

One can of Italian tuna packed in olive oil (or water if preferred)
Genoa salami and mild provolone rolled together (with cheese inside the salami), approximately a dozen rolls
6 to 8 stuffed mushrooms, homemade or jar type, quartered
6 to 8 stuffed roasted red peppers, homemade or jar type, quartered
6 to 8 celery stalks stuffed with cream cheese
6 to 8 hard-boiled eggs, quartered
8 to 10 pieces of sharp provolone, sliced in strips approximately a dozen whole cooked string beans or asparagus spears
cooked shrimp, if desired
sliced cucumbers
black and green olives for garnish

1. If you are making this for a crowd, you will need to use a large, circular tray.

2. Line the tray with romaine or Boston lettuce pieces. Starting in the center, place the Italian tuna in the middle of the tray in a small bowl.

3. From there, place the ingredients in a pattern, alternating each item so that everyone has access to the variety of foods on the tray. For example, line the edge of the tray with the salami rolls; next, place the stuffed pepper pieces in between the salami rolls. Place the stuffed mushrooms in random areas on the tray. Do this with each food choice until all items are placed on the tray.

4. Take a picture for future reference.

This vinaigrette seems to be a favorite in my family, as I always end up in charge of dressing the salad! This recipe makes more than enough for a large, family-sized salad. Leftover dressing can be refrigerated, but remove the garlic clove if you prefer a milder flavor.

Rosie's Vinaigrette

one garlic clove
good-quality extra-virgin olive oil
white balsamic vinegar, Italian imported
Dijon honey mustard
salt and pepper to taste
glass measuring cup, 8 oz. size (with demarcations)

About an hour before dressing the salad:

1. Peel the garlic clove and bruise it slightly with the side of a knife. Place it in the measuring cup.

2. Pour the extra-virgin olive oil over the garlic until it reaches the ⅓ cup mark.

3. Add enough water to bring the mixture to the ½ cup mark.

4. Pour in the white balsamic vinegar until the mixture reaches the ¾ cup mark.

5. Add several twists of coarsely ground black pepper and salt to taste.

6. Add a generous teaspoon of mustard, and using a

small whisk or a fork, beat it quickly to create an emulsion. Let the garlic steep in the dressing until it's ready to serve. Remove the garlic and emulsify again before dressing the salad.

Like Victoria, I adore a good Bolognese sauce. This recipe is adapted from my favorite cookbook, Italia Cucina *(McRae Books, 2001). When Tim makes this for Vic, he serves it over his homemade tagliatelle, which is flat, ribbon-shaped pasta. However, this hearty sauce works well with many kinds of pasta, including rigatoni and penne.*

Tim's Bolognese Sauce

4 Tbsp. of butter
2 oz. of pancetta (Italian-style bacon) diced
1 small Spanish or Vidalia onion, finely chopped
1 to 2 stalks of celery, finely chopped
1 large or 2 small carrots, finely chopped
4 oz. of ground beef
4 oz. of ground pork
4 oz. of ground veal (Italian sausage may be substituted here)
⅛ tsp. ground cloves
Dash of cinnamon
½ tsp. freshly ground black pepper
28 oz. can of imported tomatoes, chopped
1 cup whole milk
salt to taste

1. Melt the butter in a heavy-bottomed sauce pan and add the pancetta, onion, celery, and carrot. Sauté mixture over medium heat until the onion is light gold in color, about five minutes.

2. Add the beef, pork, and veal or sausage and cook until

all the meat is lightly browned. Add the clove, cinnamon, and black pepper. Stir in the tomatoes and continue to cook them over medium heat for 15 minutes.

3. Add the milk and season with salt. Turn the heat down to low and let it simmer for at least 2½ hours, stirring occasionally.

This recipe comes from my friend Tom Ficarra, who discovered it while traveling in Sicily. Tom is an enthusiastic foodie and Italophile (and has more than a little in common with the character of Father Tom).

Father Tom's Cold Tomato Sauce

10–12 fresh plum tomatoes
5 oz. package of fresh arugula
1 to 2 cloves of garlic, depending on taste
about ¾ cup of olive oil

1. Chop tomatoes, arugula, and garlic well; place these in a large bowl and mix thoroughly.

2. Pour in the olive oil.

3. Let the mixture marinate for at least three hours, taking care to stir it several times.

4. Serve sauce over hot linguine with a generous amount of grated Romano cheese.

OM0140

Also available from
Rosie Genova

The Wedding Soup Murder
An Italian Kitchen Mystery

When Vic asked her nonna for more
responsibility in the kitchen, she didn't mean
forming a thousand tiny meatballs by hand for
the family's famous wedding soup. The dish is to
be served at the reception for a close family friend
at the exclusive Belmont Country Club. And
once there Vic has to deal with a demanding
bridezilla and clashes in the kitchen

The wedding comes off without a hitch—until
the body of the club's president is found on the
beach below a high seawall. Now Vic will need to
use her noodle to find the culprit…before she's
the one who lands in the soup!

**"A vivid and affectionate portrayal of the
Jersey Shore."**
—*New Jersey Monthly*

Available wherever books are sold or at
penguin.com